FIRES OF OBLIVION

SURVIVAL WARS BOOK 4

ANTHONY JAMES

Cover Design by Dan Van Oss www.covermint.design

Follow Anthony James on Facebook at facebook.com/anthonyjamesauthor.

CHAPTER ONE

JOHN NATHAN DUGGAN stared at the steel walls of his cell, finding nothing on their hard, unmarked surfaces that offered any hope of escape. There were no windows, and light came from an unidentifiable source, as if the walls themselves exuded it. The single, oversized door was as impassive as the walls – a thick, unpainted slab of dull metal with a seam so thin it was hard to distinguish unless he peered closely.

Duggan prowled around the room, cursing beneath his breath. In this place, the passing of time become impossible to comprehend until he had no idea if he'd been kept here for weeks or months. With each passing moment, his frustration grew, until it filled him with a futile anger he had no outlet for. He told himself it was the inactivity he hated, when in reality it was the feeling of powerlessness which clawed mercilessly at his resolve.

He sat on the solitary padded bench which doubled as his bed and tried for the hundredth – thousandth -time to think of a way out of this place. He hadn't heard from his crew since they'd been separated shortly after arrival at this Ghast facility. There was no reason to think they'd suffered any harm, yet he couldn't stop worrying about what had befallen them. They'd come here out of loyalty and now they were prisoners. All their previous words about free will meant nothing to Duggan – he was responsible for this. Even worse was the knowledge that each day he remained here, Lieutenant Ortiz and the soldiers he'd been forced to abandon on the planet Kidor came closer to death. Their spacesuits would sustain them for several months – though the drugs would take their toll – but eventually the power would run out and the men and women he'd left behind would starve or suffocate. He wondered if it had happened already and closed his eyes to block out the tormenting thoughts.

A noise caught his attention – a mixture between hissing and gurgling. He crossed over to a horizontal slot in the wall and pulled out a tray. There were several mounds upon it in a variety of greens and browns. A smell rose up from his meal, far from appetising. Duggan stared at the Ghast-sized portions of food with distaste, aware that each different type would taste faintly like warm mushrooms. Even a starving man would lack relish at what the Ghasts served to their prisoners. He picked at the food, using his fingers to lift gobbets of the paste to his mouth. The Ghasts didn't provide razorblades, and it was hard to avoid soiling the beard which had grown during his imprisonment. On the plus side, he had a shower cubicle and a clean toilet in an alcove of his cell. In terms of how his captors treated him he had little to complain about, though this didn't make him feel any better.

In the time he'd been here, he hadn't spoken to a single soul. He'd expected Nil-Far to attempt dialogue, but the Ghast hadn't shown his face since handing Duggan and his crew off to the soldiers on the base. The solitude gave him plenty of time to think about what he'd found on Vempor – there was a pyramid which appeared identical to the ones used by the Dreamers to generate an oxygen atmosphere on otherwise-uninhabitable worlds. Not only that, the scans of the pyramid suggested it had been here for a long time. It raised far more questions than it answered and a small part of Duggan's brain suggested things would have been easier if they'd simply discovered a Dreamer warship parked on a military base. That would have meant war again and unimaginable death, neither of which Duggan seriously wanted to contemplate. The only thing left to him was a fruitless search for reasons and a hope that the signal from the Ghast ship *Ransor-D* had successfully reached Monitoring Station Beta. There was nothing in Duggan that shied away from hard choices, but just this once, he hoped someone else would take charge. *In Admiral Teron we trust,* he thought, laughing quietly and without humour.

He asked himself if he'd placed too much trust in Teron. In some ways, the man was an enigma. He had to deal with people on the Confederation Council and Duggan supposed this meant the Admiral had to handle many conflicting views from powerful people. What it came down to was the certainty that Teron wanted the best for the Space Corps and would do his utmost to ensure the ongoing survival of humanity. This was enough for Duggan to give him the benefit of the doubt. Teron had promised to do his best to support Duggan after the last mission, so that's what he'd do.

With his meal unfinished, Duggan picked up the tray and returned it to the alcove. The tray was sucked away through a slot at the back, leaving splatters of food around the opening. The replicator promptly absorbed them, leaving the opening clean and dry.

When he turned away, Duggan found the cell door was open, having slid aside so quietly his ears hadn't detected any sound. There was a corridor beyond, lit in the same manner as the cells and leading away to the left and right. Two Ghasts stood outside – males as they always were - dressed in their familiar grey, stiff-cloth uniforms. They had heavy gauss rifles pointed forward and aimed directly at Duggan. He looked at them in turn, seeing a combination that was both human and unmistakeably alien. They stared back for a few moments, their expressions utterly inscrutable. Then, one of them made a gesture that was easy to read. He lifted the barrel of his gun, beckoning Duggan to come.

With his heart beating hard, Duggan emerged warily from his cell. He had no idea what was planned for him but he was sure his situation was about to change. Whether that would be for better or worse he had no idea – the only thing which mattered was that something was about to happen which might take him from the interminable existence inside the prison cell.

He stepped into the corridor. One of the Ghasts walked past him, whilst the other made a quick signal to indicate Duggan should follow. Neither of them spoke. There were devices which could provide a live translation of speech – if either of these soldiers were in possession of one, they didn't make use of the facility. The three of them walked at a pace which would have been comfortable to most humans - the Ghasts were strong, without being especially quick. Duggan had only a vague memory of the journey though the facility which brought him here, since he'd been struggling to marshal his thoughts at the time. Now, he forced himself to study the route, uncertain if he'd be able to make use of the knowledge again.

The corridor ran straight for more than one hundred metres. As he walked, Duggan looked to the left and right, noticing the seams of more doors on both sides. The place was eerily quiet and the metal floor absorbed the noise of their passage instead of reflecting it. They saw no others – it was as though the place was deserted except for the three of them. The corridor went to the left and then to the right. Other corridors branched away at intervals, leading to more of the same. Duggan knew the place was big, yet hadn't realised it was quite so expansive. He wasn't surprised – the Space Corps military bases were invariably massive, many with huge underground bunkers that stretched for kilometre after kilometre.

They reached a flight of steps and climbed until Duggan was breathing hard. It was difficult to maintain any sort of fitness in the confines of a prison cell and he discovered he was already out of shape. The steps emerged into a large, square space, at least a hundred metres to each side and with many doorways leading away. There were screens and consoles in abundance, along with many Ghasts to operate them. The occupants didn't once raise their heads to look at the soldiers walking through and Duggan was reminded how single-minded this alien species was. The Space Corps generally only picked the best, but even amongst its employees there'd be evidence of conversation unrelated to Corps business. From the Ghasts, there was nothing more than the occasional utterance in their harsh-sounding tongue.

They exited this room, through one of the doorways in the far wall. Soon after, there was another set of steps, leading up to a closed metal door. The lead Ghast pressed his palm to it. The door slid aside, leading to a short corridor with a second door that opened into a square room, only a few metres to each side. There were nine chairs in the middle of the room. They were in three rows of three, each as functional as every other piece of Ghast furniture Duggan had seen. One of the soldiers motioned with his rifle and Duggan took a seat. Before he realised what was happening, his escorts withdrew from the room and the door closed behind them.

The Ghasts had a reputation for being ruthless warmongers, not for their trickery. Therefore, Duggan was left wondering what was going on. He stood again, looking for a clue as to what this room was for and found nothing. There were no other doors – only chairs and walls, with a single, blank viewscreen.

Movement caught his eye and the door opened again. There were two more Ghasts, along with a third figure. This figure stumbled inside, surprise evident on his face.

"Captain?" he asked, his voice halfway between a mumble and a slur.

"Lieutenant Breeze," said Duggan. "Have a seat."

The door closed once more and Breeze walked across to sit next to Duggan. He looked weary and dishevelled – tired, though not beaten.

"What's going to happen, sir?" asked Breeze. There was fear in his voice and also hope.

"I don't know," said Duggan simply.

The door opened for a third time, once more revealing two Ghast soldiers and a prisoner between them. This time it was Commander Lucy McGlashan. She looked alert and unbowed, as if the period of incarceration hadn't affected her one bit. If she was concerned, she didn't show it and she smiled at Duggan and Breeze.

"Nice to see you," she said. "Looks like we're gathering for a party."

"Only one more to come if I'm any judge," said Duggan.

"I wonder how Frank has taken this," said Breeze.

"He'll be fine," said Duggan.

The wait wasn't a long one. The door opened and Lieutenant Frank Chainer was ushered inside. His hair and beard had grown, but he otherwise appeared to be in good spirits. The man had a melancholy side to him, yet he always got through the toughest situations.

"What a crap place," Chainer said. "I guess we're either going to be executed or set free."

"Hello to you too," said Breeze.

"Who needs a cheerful hello in a situation like this?" asked Chainer.

The Ghast soldiers withdrew and the door slid closed behind them. The four humans remained seated and made only the most unimportant of small talk. They had much to discuss, though none felt the desire to do so while there was so much uncertainty over their future.

"How long have we been in this prison?" asked McGlashan. "I tried to count days and failed."

"A month? Two?" said Breeze. "Feels like forever."

Something made Duggan think it had been longer than two months. He didn't get time to say as much – the single viewscreen flared into light. The image of a Ghast appeared, against a backdrop of bare metal. It could have been anywhere.

"Captain John Duggan," said Nil-Far, his face impassive and the tone of his voice neutral.

"How long are you going to keep us here?" asked Duggan, not bothering to return the greeting.

"You're going to be moved from the prison facility at once."

"Are we being set free?"

"No. Your fate was decided not long after your capture. Your superiors have tried hard to persuade us otherwise, but on this our laws are clear."

Duggan felt himself go cold. Throughout the ordeal of capture and imprisonment, there was a part of him which had remained quietly confident that everything would be resolved. "What is our fate?"

"You will be taken to the area of the base which deals with criminals who have been sentenced to death under our laws. There, you and your crew will be executed. This will happen today."

There was nothing to say, beyond futile protestations of innocence. Duggan held his tongue and looked into the screen. Nil-Far looked neither pleased nor sorrowful at the announcement he'd just made. The viewscreen faded to black, leaving the four of them alone in the room to contemplate the news of their impending deaths.

CHAPTER TWO

THE WAIT WASN'T a long one. The echoes of Nil-Far's words had scarcely faded when the door to the room opened. Two Ghast soldiers entered. They looked belligerent and pointed their rifles at Duggan and the others. There was sound and movement outside - more soldiers were visible, lined up against the walls.

"Come," growled one of the Ghasts. He'd been equipped with a translating device, though he didn't seem inclined to use it for more extensive conversation.

Duggan stood and indicated to the others that they should do likewise. He didn't like the idea of walking meekly to his death, but if there was to be an opportunity to escape, it wasn't now. "Let's see where they're taking us," he said.

The others followed his instruction, their pale faces blank and shocked. It was one thing to be killed by a sudden missile strike, it was another thing entirely to be taken to your death without hope for luck's intervention.

They left the room and walked between the two lines of soldiers. Duggan counted the numbers as he went – there were twelve guards in total, each broad, strong and armed. Throwing a few punches definitely wouldn't lead to success. The prisoners were placed in the middle of the guards - four of the Ghasts went in front, the remaining ones followed behind. They set off, along a series of new corridors Duggan didn't recognize.

"I didn't think it would end like this," muttered Chainer nervously.

"Silence!" barked one of the soldiers, raising his rifle as if to shoot or strike one of the prisoners.

Chainer took the hint and didn't say anything more. Duggan looked across and saw anger in the man's eyes – an emotion that was infinitely better than fear and acceptance. They entered a large foyer, with a high, sloped ceiling. This was the outer edge of the dome-shaped building and there were Ghasts striding purposefully around, almost invariably dressed in the same grey cloth uniforms. There were no desks, though there were screens built into the walls, along with operating consoles. Once again, Duggan was struck by a sense of familiarity between the Ghasts and humans. Another part of his brain identified the many differences and he asked himself if he was actively searching for a commonality between the two races. *Perhaps I want us to be the same,* he thought. *It's easier to know someone if you can find the similarities.*

Their escort didn't pause and walked directly towards the outer wall. Other groups of soldiers went by, most of them carrying rifles. There was no exchange of words when these others walked past – in fact, there was no acknowledgement whatsoever. They either had a strict code of conduct or the Ghasts simply didn't interact in the way humans did.

There were no windows onto the outside, though the exit door was easy enough to recognize. It slid aside at their approach and the group of them walked out into sweltering heat. Duggan squinted as his eyes adjusted to the increased light. It wasn't bright as such and there was a low-lying cloud overhead. After a moment, he realised it wasn't entirely clouds above – there was a thick, greasiness to the air, redolent with the odour of sulphur. He remembered the high levels of pollution they'd detected on Vempor and knew he was breathing in by-products of the Ghasts' industries. The contrast with the coolness of their prison was marked and Duggan could feel himself sweating in the thick and stifling air.

The Ghast soldiers paused for a time and Duggan took advantage of the opportunity to look around in order to see if there was any way he could get them out of this. The military base stretched away in all directions, as far as the eye could see – kilometre upon kilometre of smooth metal landing fields and dome-shaped buildings. There were Ghast warships parked here and there. He saw two Cadaverons in the distance, their outlines fuzzy from the smog. Closer, there were a few light cruisers. Further away, there was a looming, indistinct shape that might have been an Oblivion battleship, or simply a large building. There was nothing flying, though visibility was too poor for him to be certain. They were ushered towards a boxy transport vehicle, which looked like a child's first attempt to build a truck from blocks.

"Inside," said one of the Ghasts. It wasn't clear if it was the same soldier who'd spoken last time.

The four of them climbed up high steps and into the rear of the metal transport. There were hard seats against the side walls and it could have been the same vehicle that brought them here when they'd first been captured for all Duggan knew. Ten of their escort came with them, the remaining two presumably sitting up front to drive. They set off immediately, the transport's engine humming smoothly as it carried them across the base. Duggan looked out through the opening at the rear, watching the building which had been his prison as it receded into the haze. Other buildings came into view, ugly in spite of their curved forms and lines. The base was enormous – at least as big as any on the Confederation planets.

They'd been moving at a steady speed for ten minutes when Duggan thought he saw something in the sky. There was a blurred sense of movement, as if something had disturbed the thick fog. For a tiny moment, his eyes picked out a familiar outline, before his brain dismissed the idea as fanciful. He blinked and wiped at his eyes with the back of his hands. This time, there was nothing to be seen. He looked around at the others – none of the Ghasts looked alarmed and the soldiers continued to stare ahead, their expressions alert, but disinterested. Then, Duggan caught McGlashan's eye and there was something in her face that told him she'd seen something too. With no idea what had happened, he looked out of the transport again, trying his best to be nonchalant. This time, there was no disturbance – everything was exactly as it should be.

Another five minutes passed. It seemed as if the smog had thickened, reducing visibility to little more than a kilometre. There were shapes and forms away to one side – one of them a Cadaveron and the other something Duggan couldn't quite make out. The transport continued onwards. Either the driver was in no hurry or the vehicle's top speed was pitifully low. Then, without warning, the hum of the gravity drive stopped. Duggan was attuned to such things and was therefore able to brace himself when the transport dropped twelve inches to the ground with a heavy thump. Several of the soldiers were caught unawares and were pitched sideways into each other. There was a whining sound and something whipped by Duggan's ear – one of the Ghasts had accidentally discharged his rifle. The transport's momentum carried it along the ground for a short way until it came to a stop.

Four of the soldiers recovered and went towards the rear opening. They jumped the short distance onto the metal landing field and vanished from view around to one side. Duggan couldn't read Ghast expressions well enough to know if the ones who remained to watch over them were alarmed or simply annoyed. A few of them spoke in their own tongue – rasping voices raised louder than usual. There was shouting from outside and four more Ghasts made their way to the back of the transport and climbed onto the metal ground. The two which remained were on the opposite wall to Duggan and the others. These Ghasts raised their rifles and kept them pointed at their prisoners from a distance of eight or nine feet.

Outside, there was more shouting. The two remaining Ghasts glanced towards the rear of the vehicle – none of the other soldiers were visible. If they'd been human, Duggan knew these two would be feeling uncertainty at the moment.

"What's happening?" asked Duggan.

"Shut up," one of the Ghasts responded.

Something ricocheted off the outside of the transport with a metallic ping. The Ghast closest to the exit got to his feet and walked warily towards the steps, his rifle still pointed straight at the prisoners. There was another sound of impact on the exterior and a second later, one of the soldiers who had earlier exited the transport fell into view, collapsing heavily onto the ground. Duggan caught a glimpse of a bullet wound as the Ghast toppled and there was a blossom of deep, red blood on his uniform.

The movement was enough to distract the Ghast soldier who was closest. He turned his head away from the prisoners for a split second. Duggan knew when it was time to act and he launched himself across the interior, wrapping his arms around the soldier's midriff. The Ghast was as heavy as a sack full of sand and Duggan grunted when he made contact. There was movement to his right and he heard the sound of a rifle being discharged close by. The Ghast was much the heavier of the two, but Duggan was a strong man. With his teeth clenched at the effort, he swung his opponent sideways, forcing him to collide with the second soldier.

The next few seconds felt like an eternity. Duggan wrestled with the soldier, trying to twist the rifle away. McGlashan was there and she punched the Ghast in the neck with a lightning-fast jab. The soldier stumbled, yet didn't let go. There was another rifle discharge and Chainer gasped in pain, stumbling away before dropping to his knees.

Close by, Duggan saw Lieutenant Breeze thunder a piledriving blow into the second Ghast's stomach. He was too close for the Ghast to bring his rifle to bear. Instead, the soldier smashed the butt of his gun into Breeze's face, knocking him away. Duggan was unable to assist, since his own opponent was tough and strong. McGlashan struck out with two more blows which would have completely debilitated a human. They clearly hurt the Ghast, but didn't knock him out. With a violent shove, the soldier sent Duggan stumbling a few feet away. It didn't hesitate and swung its rifle towards him. *We're going to lose this one,* thought Duggan with regret. *At least we gave it a go.*

There was movement on the ground outside, which Duggan was only faintly aware of. A voice, unmistakeably human, shouted a command. "Get down!"

There was no chance to react. The familiar hissing fizz of gauss rifles reached Duggan's ears, followed by the clanking sound of slugs on alloy. The two Ghast soldiers were pitched to the floor, blood quickly covering huge patches of their uniforms. The noise stopped and Duggan's brain caught up. There were two human soldiers standing outside, their rifles still raised. Two more joined them, one with a Lieutenant's insignia on his chest.

"Captain Duggan?" said the man. He was broad-chested and grizzled, with the hardened face of a real professional. "I'm Lieutenant Johns. Your guards are dead. Come at once."

Duggan didn't waste time on questions. "My lieutenant here has been injured," he said. "Help me with him."

Two of the human soldiers climbed inside at once. Chainer was on his knees, doubled over and clutching his chest. There was blood – a lot of it – though no sign of where exactly the Ghast bullet had entered his body. The two soldiers slung their rifles and approached Chainer. They hooked their arms under his shoulders.

"Sorry sir," said one. "There's no time to get you a stretcher."

With that, they hauled Chainer to his feet. His face was pale and his eyes unfocused. The patch of blood was high up on his chest, showing as a vivid red against his blue uniform. He grimaced in pain and his jaw tightened. Duggan waved McGlashan and Breeze off the transport and waited for the two soldiers to half-drag Chainer after them. Then, he followed onto the metal ground, the smell of sulphur becoming stronger at once. He looked around and saw bodies, most of them Ghasts, but not all. There were at least a dozen human soldiers dragging the bodies – both the human and the Ghast dead. One woman ran from place to place, spraying a clear fluid from a bottle onto the patches of blood. Duggan recognized this as a make-do clean-up operation.

At first, it wasn't clear where they were taking the bodies – the combat had taken place a long way from anywhere. Then, Duggan's eyes made out a shape. It was almost invisible, as though it somehow warped the light in order that it appear entirely transparent. The effect was imperfect and the longer he stared, the more Duggan's eyes could trace the outline of a spaceship.

"What the hell?" he asked.

"It's the *ES Lightning*, sir," said Lieutenant Johns. "We need to get onboard at once. I doubt we'll have long before the Ghasts realise what's happened."

Johns set off at a run and Duggan followed, with McGlashan and Breeze close behind. They passed the two men carrying Chainer. Duggan paused to see if they needed a hand, but they shook their heads and pressed on, their faces red and beaded in sweat. The closer he came to the *ES Lightning*, the easier it was to make out a few details. He couldn't see how large it was – only enough to know it was there. The boarding ramp was down and whatever cloaking system encompassed the exterior, it didn't extend to the interior. The ramp and airlock were clearly visible when viewed from straight on and Duggan climbed inside. Several Ghost bodies had been dumped here in a careless heap and their blood pooled onto the floor.

He stopped and turned, waiting for the rest of the rescue party to come up the ramp. It wouldn't have seemed right to make his way straight towards the bridge without waiting for the others. It didn't take long. Soon, the last of the Space Corps soldiers were in the airlock, their eyes bright with nervous excitement from the confrontation.

"Shit, we lost Givens," said one of the woman.

"Yeah, Hoster as well," said another.

"Damn."

The boarding ramp came up smoothly and quickly. It slotted home with the comforting sound of heavy-duty solidity and the mechanical clamps thumped into place deep within the hull.

"We need to clear the airlock," said Johns, his voice close to a shout. "Take our dead and leave these bastards here," he said pointing at the Ghost bodies. He turned, his eyes seeking out Duggan. "Captain Julius is on the bridge, sir. You're invited to go and see her. Your crew are bunking with us."

Duggan nodded. "Get the medic to check out Lieutenant Chainer and get me an update as soon as possible."

"Yes sir," said Johns, snapping his arm upwards in a salute.

Duggan moved away from the airlock and into the corridors

beyond. The sights and smells told him at once what sort of vessel this was – he was on a Vincent class or something similar. The engines were running, with the tell-tale signs they were under an enormous amount of stress. He wasn't halfway to the bridge when he detected the subtle changes that indicated they'd taken off.

The bridge confirmed his suspicion that he was on a Gunner. Whatever new technology they'd squeezed into the hull to make the ship invisible to the Ghasts, it hadn't affected the appearance of the control room. There was a woman there, slim and attractive, with jet-black hair and ears pierced in contravention of Space Corps regulations. She saw him and walked across at once, her hand extended. He took the hand and shook it warmly, looking into her eyes as he did so. He thought she was somewhere in her thirties – it was difficult to be sure when it came to guessing someone's age.

"Captain Duggan," she said. "I'm Captain Julius. Fleet Admiral Teron sends his regards."

CHAPTER THREE

LIGHT from the planet's sun glinted and sparkled where it speared through the oxygen-rich atmosphere of the distant planet. Beams of yellow streaked out through space, their raw beauty lost forever amongst the infinity. A spaceship flew amongst the rays, its silvery hull illuminated in an ever-changing patchwork of light and dark. The vessel was considered small by its crew – little more than seven hundred metres in length, with a peculiar shape. The sleek design of the nose and mid-section made an attractive counterpart to the rear third, which was little more than a cube of metal, appearing to have been added as an afterthought. There was a crew of four. They sat or stood on the tiny bridge, breathing heavily from the stifling heat and the pressure of what they were about to attempt.

"They weren't wrong when they said the *ES Lightning* was fast," said Duggan, raising an eyebrow. "We could almost outrun the *ESS Crimson* - on gravity drives, at least."

"Two hours till we reach Kidor," said Chainer.

"Will they have detected our arrival?" asked Duggan. They'd gone through this before their exit from lightspeed and he was seeking reassurance by asking again. He was nervous and wasn't stupid enough to deny the fact.

"There's a chance, sir," said Breeze. "Coming back here was always going to be a risk."

"We should be far enough away that our fission signature wasn't easy to read," said McGlashan. "As ever, it comes down to luck."

"We're going to need plenty of that today," said Duggan. "I'm not leaving until I've got what I came for."

"Nothing on the fars," said Chainer. "I'll let you know as soon as anything changes."

"Can you detect the signal from the emergency beacon?"

"No – it's a very tight beam. I might not pick it up until we're much closer. If it's still broadcasting, of course."

Duggan got out of his seat, trying to hide the outward signs of his agitation. It had been a little over four months since they'd left Kidor in order to escape the Dreamer battleship, and now he'd been given this chance to put things right for the men and women he'd left behind. He no longer felt burdened by guilt and had come to terms with what he'd done. Sometimes there was no right answer and only the strongest could make the hardest choices without being broken by their decisions. Even so, he didn't dare ask himself what would happen if there was no one left alive on Kidor.

"The spacesuits will usually last longer than four months," said McGlashan, reading his mind.

"Unless there's a fault or they're damaged," said Duggan, immediately regretting the words.

"We can't think like that, sir. We'll get Lieutenant Ortiz and the rest away from here. That's what we've come for."

"You're right, Commander. I'll make no more mention of failure."

He returned to his seat and took manual control of the

warship. He looked at his update screens one at a time, to ensure everything was as expected. They were approaching Kidor on the opposite side to the position of the Dreamer pyramid they'd failed to recover on a previous mission. That mission had ended in catastrophe and this was a belated attempt to clean up afterwards. Duggan was gambling that the alien battleship would maintain a stationary orbit over the pyramid, rather than continually circle the planet. If he was right, there was a good chance the *Lightning* would be able to approach undetected. Unfortunately, the troops he was here to rescue were in a valley near to the perimeter of the pyramid's energy shield, so one way or another, they were likely to face significant danger.

"Do you think this stealth stuff is going to work?" asked Chainer.

"It got us away from Vempor," said Duggan.

"I wasn't in any fit state to have a look around," said Chainer. "Something still doesn't feel right in my lungs. Anyway, I know what happened on Vempor, I'm asking if it'll work against the Dreamers. The Ghasts' sensor tech isn't as good as ours. These new alien bastards will be a much harder test."

"We're the guinea pigs," said Duggan. "The data we bring back from this mission will let the research guys know what's working and what isn't. This is a dangerous task that I'm happy to take on."

"And what's this about *Fleet* Admiral Teron, huh?" continued Chainer. "I suppose there were worse officers to promote."

"He came through for us this time," said McGlashan. "He risked starting the war again."

"Well I figure he owes us at least one," said Chainer. "Do you know if anything kicked off after they rescued us, sir?"

"I don't know, Lieutenant. Admiral Teron was tight-lipped when I saw him on the *Juniper*. We were docked for less than four hours before he sent us here, so it's not like I had much time to speak with him."

"And here we are," said Breeze. "Facing an overwhelmingly powerful enemy warship without a single weapon to shoot back with. Softly, softly for this one."

The ES *Lightning* was based on a heavily-modified Vincent class platform. Its weapons had been stripped out to make room for the stealth modules, and the shipyard had added another two hundred metres of engines at the back. They'd also fitted a top-of-the-line AI core to control it all. The result was a vessel that could fly exceptionally fast on its gravity engines, as well as appear invisible to enemy sensors. There was a downside, of course – when it was active, the stealth facility took up nearly the entire output of the sub-light engine. This reduced the spaceship to a low velocity and made it cumbersome to control. The slower it went, the greater the chance an enemy would identify the slight anomalies in their sensor readings. If it was spotted, the ES *Lightning* would be a sitting duck, having only shock drones for defence. Regardless of the limitations, Duggan was glad he'd been given the opportunity to make amends for abandoning his troops.

"When do you want me to activate the stealth modules?" asked Breeze. "If we do it after we've been detected, they're not going to be anything like as effective."

Duggan thought about it. They were still quite a distance away from their destination and he didn't necessarily want to give the new technology an extended stress test if he could avoid it. Given the choice, he wanted to use it as little as possible.

"How long can we maintain stealth?" he asked.

"As long as we can provide enough power for the modules, they should keep running. I've read the guidelines which suggest a maximum running time of no more than twenty-four hours, but as far as I can tell that's just for certainty. The equipment itself should remain stable in extended operation."

"I've never liked the word *experimental*," said Chainer. "Whatever Admiral Teron says, this stuff isn't long off the drawing board."

"These are a little bit beyond experimental," said Breeze. "They're just not ready for widespread use across the fleet. I don't even know how many of our warships are going to be suitable to have the stealth equipment installed."

"It'd be a game-changer if we could make all of our spaceships vanish," said Chainer.

"You have a talent for the understatement, Lieutenant," said Duggan. During the return voyage from Vempor, he'd been impressed beyond measure when Captain Julius had briefly run through the warship's capabilities with him. The Ghasts had their Shatterer missiles, the Dreamers had energy shields and now the Confederation had something of its own – as long as it lived up to the promise. The prototype had been the ES *Lightning* and Teron had offered it to Duggan to get the missing soldiers back and to see how well it worked against the Dreamers.

"Activate the stealth immediately," said Duggan, coming to a conclusion. "I'd rather get blown up by malfunctioning technology than an enemy battleship."

"Here we go," said Breeze.

The effects were instant. The output from their engines dropped to twenty percent and there was a grumbling from within the hull, the sound deep and reverberating.

"That's a whole lot of extra load," said Chainer. "I've never heard anything quite like that before."

"It takes a monumental amount of power to keep us hidden," said Breeze. "Everything's holding steady, though. There's no sign of failure in the equipment so far."

"I'd rather find out here than when it really matters," said Duggan.

The ES *Lightning* continued its course towards Kidor. Duggan only had to make slight adjustments, which was enough to inform him of how unwieldy the warship had become with its stressed engines. Things would get difficult if they had to perform evasive manoeuvres. Even coming into a smooth orbit would be difficult at the speed they were travelling.

"Still no sign of life," said Chainer. "No sign of the beacon either." He frowned. "We're getting to the point where I'd have expected to hear something from it."

The image of the planet on the bulkhead viewscreen became steadily more detailed as the ship's sensors resolved additional details from the surface. Duggan had seen a hundred planets like this one and didn't care if he never saw another. He called up information from the AI and used it to determine when to prepare for the approach to their target area. The plan was to execute a half-orbit at high speed and then land as close to the cave as possible. Ideally, they'd have been able to get a message to the soldiers by responding to the emergency beacon, but it didn't seem like they had the option. The lack of a broadcast was worrying and he tried not to think about it.

When they were only a few thousand kilometres from the surface, Duggan dragged the unwilling nose of the warship until it was pointing where he wanted it. They were travelling much too fast to go through a dense atmosphere without burning up, so he did his best to reduce their velocity. Nevertheless, the hull temperature climbed a fraction. In a few minutes, it would increase rapidly and it would take good judgement to keep their speed high without the outer armour melting to a sludge.

"Beginning the approach," said Duggan. There was no response and he glanced across at the others. Each face was a picture of concentration, their features a mix of focus, determination and fear. Duggan felt pride well up in his chest at the strength of his crew.

At the last possible moment, Duggan turned the headlong plunge of the *ES Lightning* into a steep, banking descent. The nose temperature went up to twenty percent of its design tolerance in seconds. The surface of the planet flashed by far below, barren plains of stone and jagged peaks of high mountains.

"Forty percent on the hull," said Breeze.

"Nothing from the beacon," said Chainer. "If it was still working, I'd have found it by now."

"Sixty percent. Not long till we're too hot."

"I'm detecting another vessel, Captain," said Chainer. "It's big and it's high, difficult to get a lock on."

"The battleship is still here," said Duggan with a grimace.

"Lost them again," said Chainer. "They've gone over the planet's curvature."

"They didn't see us," said McGlashan.

"No, they didn't," said Chainer, realising the significance. He ran through a few quick checks. "With the angles and distance involved, a ship that size would have had a high probability of detecting us. That's assuming a similar level of sensor technology to our own."

"We either got lucky or they didn't see through the stealth," said Breeze.

"I've got my hopes pinned on the latter," muttered Chainer, not taking his eyes from his screens.

"The hull is approaching ninety percent of tolerance," said Breeze. "We need to slow down, sir."

"Understood," said Duggan. He reduced their speed, hoping the additional few seconds of travel time wouldn't prove to be significant. The hull temperature continued to rise, though slower than it had before.

"Five thousand klicks until we reach the target area," said McGlashan.

"The Dreamer battleship is visible again, sir," said Chainer. "They're in a small-diameter circle over the pyramid. We're in full view of them and we'll remain so until the rescue is complete or..." He was wise enough to cut off the sentence before his mouth could finish it.

"Thank you, Lieutenant," said Duggan. "Can you identify any change in their behaviour?"

"They haven't changed course."

"No sign of a weapons launch," said McGlashan.

Chainer wiped his sleeve across his forehead. "The lab guys have come up with the goods this time."

"Let's not congratulate them yet," warned Duggan, wary against tempting fate. "Are we close enough to try direct contact with the spacesuit comms?"

"I'm pretty sure there's too much rock between us and them. I'll give it a try."

The hull reached ninety-five percent of its maximum heat. If it got any higher, the soldiers they were trying to rescue would fry as they ran for the boarding ramp, with or without their space-suits. Duggan swore and reduced their speed even further. The outside temperature remained static, though it felt like eighty degrees inside.

"Twenty seconds till we're at the landing site," said Chainer.

Duggan pulled at the control bars, willing the spaceship's straining engines to overcome the massive inertia. He saw the place – a wide valley strewn with rocks. He guided the ES Lightning between the rough walls, keeping as close to the ground as possible.

"There's our spot," said Chainer. "I count three big missile craters and plasma burns in the surrounding area. There's metal alloy amongst it – that's the landing shuttle. I'll bet the beacon got taken out at the same time."

Duggan saw a good place and went for it. He ignored the AI's recommendation to engage the auto-landing systems and instead dumped the *ES Lightning* hard onto the rocky ground. The ship scraped along the surface for a distance, ripping deep grooves into the rock and smashing several huge boulders away.

"Get on the comms!" said Duggan. "I'm damned if we're going outside to look for them."

For the briefest of moments, he felt a panic when he realised the cave might have collapsed from the missile strikes. He checked the external sensor feed and to his relief, the cave mouth was still there, tall and narrow in the face of an overhanging cliff.

"Anything?"

"Not a peep, sir," said Chainer.

Duggan thumped his fist against his console in anger and frustration.

CHAPTER FOUR

"WANT ME TO SUIT UP?" asked McGlashan.

Duggan wasn't sure what he wanted. The last transmission from the troops had mentioned Ghasts. He wondered if they'd had an engagement with the enemy and come off worst. If they went to explore the cave there might be nothing more than dead bodies to be found. Duggan wasn't sure he wanted to see the dead, though another part of him knew he would never rest until he was certain. Above, the Dreamer warship continued to circle, each passing moment increasing the chance it would detect an unusual visual reading or the heat pouring away from the ES *Lightning*'s hull. Duggan had recently learned there are times when choice can be nothing more than an illusion and now was one of those times.

"I'll go," he said, pushing himself from his chair. "Give me ten minutes after I leave and then take off if there's no sign of my return."

"We're going nowhere while you're still alive," said McGlashan, her face resolute. "Don't think you can throw yourself after the others to repent for your own feelings of guilt."

Duggan stopped mid-stride, wondering if McGlashan had spoken the truth. He shook his head. "That wasn't the plan, Commander," he said softly. "Truly it wasn't."

She stared back, not knowing if she believed him. "If they're gone, they're gone, sir."

"I know and I have no intention of losing myself as well. I've come to terms with it. This is just how I am – I can't let others do my duty for me."

Chainer laughed. "No kidding?"

Duggan smiled in return, though his face remained grim. "I've been told I'll never change."

Chainer's mouth opened to say something in response. Whatever he'd planned to say didn't come out. Instead, he jerked as if in shock. "I've got a voice on the comms," he said.

"One of ours?" asked Duggan before his brain told him it could be none other.

"Shhh...it's faint," Chainer replied, holding his hand in the air. "This is *ES Lightning*, please respond."

The bridge speakers came to life, with words that sounded as if they were spoken from an infinite distance. "This is Lieutenant Ortiz, do you copy?"

"This is Captain Duggan. We've landed outside. How many of you are left?"

Ortiz didn't waste time on greetings. "We lost four in a fire-fight, sir. The rest of us are coming to you."

"Four? Shit. Don't hang around. The Dreamer battleship hasn't gone anywhere."

"Roger that." The connection went quiet for a few seconds. "We're coming now. A few of the boys are pretty weak."

"We've brought a couple of med bots with us. Get them aboard and fast. We're packing some stealth technology. Don't be surprised if you need to look hard to find us."

"I gotcha," she said. Her breathing sounded laboured and her voice lacked its usual strength – four months in a suit would take its toll on even the fittest person.

"How long till you get here?" asked Duggan, anxious to complete the pickup and be away from the planet.

"Minutes," said Ortiz tersely. "Not many minutes."

The bulkhead screen showed the mouth of the cave. Darkness wasn't a significant impediment to the ship's sensors, but the cave sloped steeply downwards, limiting their view within.

"What a shitty place," said Chainer to himself.

"Keep an eye on the battleship," warned Duggan.

"I am, sir."

"Come on," said McGlashan. "Look! Movement in the cave!"

"You're right," said Duggan, stepping closer to the screen. There was something within. The details were indistinct but it looked like a figure in a spacesuit.

"Uh, we've got movement above as well, sir," said Chainer.

Duggan turned sharply. "What sort of movement?"

"There's been a deviation in their course."

"No sign of a weapons launch," said McGlashan.

Duggan didn't like it and he became even more jumpy. "Lieutenant Ortiz, you need to move faster."

"We can't go faster than this – not without leaving someone behind."

"Very well," said Duggan. "Things might get hot soon."

There was more movement in the cave and the crew squinted, as if this would somehow make the details clearer.

"I count four," said McGlashan. "There's number five."

"And six," said Breeze. He panted as if he'd been holding his breath.

"Four missing, Lieutenant Ortiz said. Six is all that's left."

Chainer delivered the bad news. "I'm fairly sure the crew on the battleship are suspicious, sir," he said. "They're coming in lower and they're no longer circling."

"Do you think they've spotted us?"

"I think they know there's *something* not quite right," said Chainer.

"How high are they?"

"Eighty thousand klicks, give or take."

"They're going to see our troops as soon as they leave the cave, aren't they?"

"There's a decent chance – it might take them a few seconds if they aren't looking for something as small as a bunch of soldiers."

Duggan did some quick working. If the enemy launched missiles, it would take slightly under twenty seconds for them to reach the surface. The *ES Lightning* was close to the cave mouth so there wasn't far to run. Duggan estimated a soldier at his or her peak could cover the distance in fifteen seconds whilst wearing a spacesuit. He snarled angrily at the numbers – as much as he wanted to, there was no way he could predict how this would play out.

Owing to the perspective, it wasn't easy to be sure if the troops had left the cave. In the shadow of the overhang they gathered into a group and then as one they broke into a clumsy run towards the *ES Lightning*. At least two of the figures struggled and they leaned against the others for support.

"Come on Lieutenant, you're nearly home," said Duggan.

"I'll believe it when we're at lightspeed, sir," she replied, the words sounding as if they'd taken a great effort.

"Don't speak, just run."

"The first pair have passed beneath our hull," said Chainer. "They're going to make it!"

Duggan didn't want to greet success prematurely. "Like Lieutenant Ortiz said. When we're at lightspeed."

"Crap, there's a launch from the battleship," said McGlashan. "Fifty missiles."

"Have they targeted us or the soldiers?" asked Duggan. It didn't make much difference – the splash from so many missiles would kill everyone and destroy the ship.

"The missiles are dropping in a grid pattern, sir," said McGlashan. "With a few hundred metres between each one."

"They don't know exactly where we are!" said Duggan. "There's still a chance."

"The lead two soldiers have come onboard," said Chainer. "Now four...six." He was silent for another moment. "That's the lot! Got them! Closing the boarding ramp. Done!"

As soon as he heard those words, Duggan pulled at the control bars. The *Lightning* surged away from the surface. Once they'd reached two hundred metres, Duggan gave the engines full power and the warship gathered speed, howling under the stress of maintaining the stealth shroud. He closed his eyes for the briefest of times, hoping against hope they would escape unscathed from the incoming missiles.

The external feeds blazed white. Enemy missiles detonated against the surface in many places nearby, spilling plasma for hundreds of metres in all directions. Each blast overlapped with the others, making several square kilometres of the planet brighter and hotter than its sun. The *ES Lightning* didn't sustain a direct hit, but was caught by the ferocious heat. The warship was rocked and buffeted. Its armour, already blisteringly hot from the approach to Kidor, became molten. Several thousand tonnes of white-hot alloy were pulled away from the hull, leaving a trail of white streaks in the air behind, visible through the fading light of the Dreamer missile blasts. On the bridge, damage alerts flew across a half-dozen screens.

"We're too hot," shouted Breeze.

"The battleship has descended to thirty thousand klicks," said Chainer.

"They've launched another fifty," said McGlashan, steely

and calm. "Same grid pattern. There's another fifty coming right after. You need to change course, sir."

There was hardly a moment to react before the second wave of missiles exploded. This time, the *Lightning* was at the periphery of the inferno. Heat licked across wounded metal, yet without inflicting the same damage as the first wave. Duggan increased their altitude as quickly as he could and soon they were dozens of kilometres above the bombardment.

"We need to get out of here," said Chainer, letting everyone know what they'd already realised.

"We can't go to lightspeed with the stealth modules active," said Breeze. "There's a cooldown period after they're deactivated before we can use the fission drive."

"I know, I know," muttered Chainer. "The battleship is following us. If they knew exactly where we were they'd have destroyed us by now. Since they must only have a general idea of our location, they might follow us until they manage to get a proper lock on."

"We haven't got much choice," said Duggan. "We've done well to get as far as we have." He watched the tactical display. The Dreamer warship was less than twenty thousand kilometres away from them – a monstrous construction of alloys and weapons, with spindly outcrops and curved edges. "It's still directly behind us. We can't go any faster while cloaked."

"And we'll be blown to pieces the moment we disengage the stealth," said Breeze. "At least the modules are robust. They could have easily been knocked out by those near-misses."

"Missile launch. Six hundred!" said McGlashan.

Duggan saw them on his screen just as McGlashan spoke. Wave upon wave of missiles, flooded through space in their direction. The distance between the two ships was such that the barrage had skated past the *ES Lightning* almost before they'd detected the launch.

"They've not got much chance of scoring a hit like that," said Chainer, the worry clearly etched on his features.

"We'd better hope they can't alter their missiles to detect heat," said McGlashan.

"Yeah," said Chainer. "Thanks for the thought."

The planet receded into the distance and still the pursuing warship kept after them. It was as though the enemy could detect the *Lightning* to within a few hundred kilometres of its location, without knowing exactly where it was. It made their beam weapons and missiles almost useless and Duggan felt a harsh satisfaction – too often he'd found himself in a position where the Space Corps weaponry had been rendered powerless by enemy technology.

The battleship followed them for more than an hour, during which it launched more than three thousand missiles at the *ES Lightning*. Several came close, though none scored a hit. The enemy vessel came near and then circled around, as though it was attempting to triangulate their exact position. Duggan did his best to foil their efforts by changing course and speed at regular intervals. The tactics worked, though he was aware his luck would inevitably run out and he cursed the captain of the other vessel for not ending the chase.

"Whoever they are, they're as stubborn as you, sir," said Breeze.

The comment cut through the tension and Duggan laughed, feeling his death grip on the control bars loosen and relax. "I'll bet they're *really* pissed off that they can't target us. They'll be desperate to salvage our wreckage and see what equipment we're carrying." With that, he settled in for a long pursuit, content to keep heading away until the enemy either gave up or destroyed the smaller *ES Lightning*.

Eventually, the battleship broke off. One minute it was thirty thousand kilometres to starboard, the next it was on its way back towards Kidor.

"Over two thousand klicks per second," said Chainer. "I don't think we could have outrun it. There's something else, too. Our primary comms are functioning properly. Whatever they use to jam our equipment must need a direct fix our location."

"That *is* interesting," said Duggan.

"Want me to prepare for the jump to lightspeed, sir?" asked Breeze.

"Not yet, Lieutenant. I'm wary of tricks."

With that, Duggan altered their course and kept them pointing directly away from Kidor. He maintained the new course for more than four hours. When it seemed certain the enemy weren't going to reappear on their sensors, he ordered them to decloak and get ready to depart. A short while later, the damaged and scarred *ES Lightning* rocketed away into the darkness.

CHAPTER FIVE

"HOW DID SHE FARE?" asked Fleet Admiral Teron. He'd been filled in on the details from Duggan's advance report, but was clearly eager to learn more.

"I'm impressed, sir," said Duggan. "Whatever the guys in the tech labs did, they've earned my gratitude. The stealth modules fooled a Dreamer battleship long enough for us to rescue our troops from right under their nose."

Teron clapped his hands together in delight. It was the most overt display of excitement Duggan could recall seeing from the man. "I told you we were on the brink of some new discoveries and this was the one I had pinned fewest hopes on. I'm happy to be wrong – our scientists have overcome some enormous hurdles in mere weeks. Just a shame it's not ready to install on every ship in the fleet, eh?" Teron said.

They'd gone over this briefly prior to Duggan's departure on the rescue mission. "How long till they can control the power draw sufficiently?"

Teron shrugged. "Not long – a few months or a couple of years. Whether that'll be soon enough, I don't know. They're going to patch the modules into a couple more warships, but as yet we aren't able to cloak anything much bigger than a Vincent class. They'll be able to get up close to the enemy, without packing enough of a punch to do much harm – especially to a Dreamer energy shield."

"And there's no way around the limitations?"

"If you're asking whether or not we've found a way to maintain the cloaking on a spaceship that's packed with weapons, then no we haven't. Not yet, anyway. Once we've cracked the problem with the energy draw, that's when we'll be able to run rings around the Dreamers." He lowered his brows. "And the Ghasts too, if needed."

"A shame we can't copy the Shatterers, even with the missiles and launch tubes in our possession."

"We'll get there. The problem we're facing is the targeting systems are completely different to the way we've been doing it up until now, rather than being an extension of existing technology. We're having to take several steps backwards in order to walk forwards. I've been told they're quite crude, which made me ask the gentlemen who told me this fact why they're taking so long to copy them."

"Have things started to settle down?" asked Duggan, referring to the diplomatic fallout from his recent mission to Vempor and the subsequent rescue.

Admiral Teron sighed and slumped into his seat. He seemed diminished by the question and didn't have an immediate response. His chair creaked as he shifted his weight and then he threw his hands up in exasperation. "Damnit, why can't anything be easy when it comes to you, Captain Duggan? Why couldn't you have simply located a Dreamer warship sitting happily on one of their landing pads? At least that way we'd have answers, albeit unpalatable ones. And I wouldn't have to spend eighteen hours of every day trying to answer difficult questions about your disappearance from the Ghast military base."

It was a familiar line. Teron wasn't blaming Duggan as such, it was simply that Duggan invariably raised more questions than he brought answers.

"Are we returning to war, sir?"

"It might yet be the result. Believe me when I say I don't want it to happen. We're not ready to take on their battleships or heavy cruisers, so our only response would be to destroy their planets, one-by-one. I would order it in a heartbeat if I had to, but I hope I'm not pushed to it."

"What do the stats teams say about the possible outcomes?"

"The same as they always say. A percentage chance of this, that and the other with no way to corroborate any of it." Teron realised he was letting the uncertainties get the better of him. "I've dealt personally with a few of the Ghasts and while I don't exactly like them, they seem a lot more trustworthy than most humans I have to deal with."

"That's what I've noticed. The truth is important to them, rather than something to be manipulated. I've never caught Nil-Far lying. If there's something he doesn't want to tell you, he comes right out and says that it's none of your business."

"Exactly!" said Teron. "Their chief negotiators are the same. I can't believe it's nothing more than an act."

"The evidence is there, sir. I found what looked like a Ghast on Trasgor. Lieutenant Ortiz lost four of her soldiers to what she believed were Ghasts in the cave system on Kidor."

"Did Lieutenant Ortiz give a reason why these *Ghasts* were in the caves beneath Kidor?"

"She only had guesses, sir. Lieutenant Ortiz is one of the best, so I'd give credence even where she's speculating. There were extensive caves and they led under the energy shield. They encountered the enemy in a cavern only a few hundred metres from the cave entrance. She believes five of the enemy were killed, except she didn't want to go looking – she judged the risks too great. They spent the rest of the time hiding, though it eventually became obvious there were no search parties out looking for these dead *Ghasts*."

"You didn't find much evidence of large-scale personnel deployment in the first pyramid on Trasgor, did you?" said Teron. "Once more, it's a great shame you were unable to obtain samples of the dead. However, there's nothing we can do to change that now, so we'll move on from it. From what we know, the facts suggest these artefacts do not need a large crew – only a small number for monitoring purposes."

"In that case I wonder why the battleship didn't send down a contingent of troops to investigate further," said Duggan.

"It would make sense, wouldn't it?" asked Teron. "Nevertheless, they chose not to do so and we should be grateful for what seems to be incompetence. Maybe they assumed their missing crew got lost and perished somewhere. Who knows?"

Duggan nodded. He'd seen the Dreamers make a few tactical errors so far. Behind their technology, there was little sign of skilled military minds. There was ruthlessness certainly, but little more. "We can beat these bastards. As soon as we learn how to reliably counter their shields, we'll chase them out of Confederation space."

"Brave words and ones I agree with," said Teron. "For now, we must wait for our technology to catch up with our aspirations. It gives us a chance to find answers. The Dreamers are our enemies – this we know without a shadow of doubt. We need to find out more about the Ghasts. The pyramid you found on Vempor was definitely created by the makers of the other two – the sensor data is clear on that. It's a few hundred years older but otherwise identical."

Duggan felt continued relief that the sensor streams from

Vempor had reached Monitoring Station Beta. The raw information was undeniable proof. If the Space Corps had been asked to rely on Duggan's word alone, there was a chance a few important people would choose not to believe him. "Perhaps the Ghasts are early settlers from their race. It's only recently the Dreamers have managed to come through the Helius Blackstar, so they may have previously sent their spaceships vast distances to find new planets. The Ghasts might have lost touch with the others of their species."

"It would go some way to explaining why they were so irrational when they saw this new pyramid on Trasgor," said Teron. "Anyway, we believe the Ghasts are unaware we've unearthed their secret. They were most displeased by your appearance as you're aware, but I don't think you were specifically singled out for brutal treatment. Their laws appear to be strict and implemented without prejudice."

"The Confederation Council didn't think it wise that we simply ask what the pyramid is doing on Vempor?" asked Duggan mildly. He had a good idea of the answer already.

"You'll never make Admiral if you're truly so naïve," said Teron without irritation. "We're looking after many billions of people and we shouldn't give up our secrets so easily. There's an opportunity for us to find out what the hell is happening – on our own terms. And if that fails, we can still ask the Ghasts outright."

Duggan chuckled. "I assume there are plans afoot?"

"There are always plans. You'd be surprised at how many plans we're juggling at any one time. Ninety percent of them never go beyond discussion. It just happens you manage to get involved more regularly than most of our senior officers."

"What do you need me to do?"

"My first thought was to send you back to Vempor or Kidor on the *ES Lightning*, in order to do some more investigation on the pyramids."

"To bring back a dead alien?"

"More or less. I would dearly like to examine the genetic makeup of this new alien species and compare it to the samples we've taken from the Ghasts over the course of the war. While this is important, I've recently been handed a report that has changed our priorities."

Duggan saw from the change in Teron's face that the news wasn't good. "What is it, sir?"

Teron nudged a brown folder across the desk and nodded to indicate Duggan should take a look. "I know it sounds as if I hold the Projections Team in less than high regard. In truth, I study everything they send me with the utmost care. They are the ones who assign solid numbers to the ephemeral and that appeals to me. They are also the people who will – every so often - pluck a completely unforeseen possibility from nowhere and let me know if it's significant or not. There's more than one occasion where I've been able to forestall our enemy by giving credence to what's in these little brown folders."

Duggan skimmed over the text on the pages. It was classified as top secret and contained a number of scenarios distilled from the unknown, each provided with a likelihood of the scenario coming to pass. Much of it was easily guessed, but one item had been highlighted in red pen. There was something in the words which would have jumped out at Duggan regardless.

"Destruction of Atlantis within the coming twelve months – forty-eight percent?"

"Makes for unpleasant reading, doesn't it? The previous report was only a week ago and at the time, the stats guys judged the likelihood at somewhat less than one percent."

"Why the change?" asked Duggan. He read the highlighted text once more and felt a shiver run through his body.

"We don't know. They have some exceptionally intelligent

people in that department and their simulators are designed to second-guess chaos, if you will."

"Have there been any more reports of the Dreamer mothership?" asked Duggan. "Our last discussion put Atlantis at the greatest risk of discovery, which is presumably where this figure of forty-eight percent was derived from."

"Quite right and at the time, that risk of Atlantis being found was judged to be less than one percent. The Garon sector is huge and almost empty. There should be close to a zero chance of our enemies accidentally stumbling across our only habited planet in the zone. Now that's changed. The worst part of it is, the Projections Team judge there to be a nineteen percent chance of the Ghasts being party to the annihilation."

"Damn," said Duggan.

"There are other sections of the report, which I have withheld from you owing to the nature of their contents. However, I can tell you that the planets Overtide and Freedom have now been given chances of six and four percent to suffer the same destruction as Atlantis. If we believe these figures, the situation for humanity is as bad as it ever was at the height of the Ghast war."

"What is the new priority?"

"We need to find our enemy. Your encounters with these lesser Dreamer warships have given us invaluable information about their strengths and weaknesses. However, we know little about their mothership, aside from its ability to devastate many of our own spacecraft with its plasma beams."

"We don't know where it is, do we?" asked Duggan.

"The only thing we have to go on is this report predicting the likely destruction of Atlantis," said Teron, lifting the brown folder and pointing it at Duggan. "If we believe the details, that allows us to predict the likely course of our enemy."

Duggan's head swum when he heard these words. He respected Admiral Teron, but there was something which sounded entirely wrong about the idea of anchoring a plan on the foundations of a statistical projection that could be no more than an anomaly. Duggan wasn't a man to keep his opinions to himself. "Something about this doesn't sit comfortably with me, sir."

"It doesn't have to sit comfortably – I'm making this decision for you. The *ES Lightning* will take eight days to patch up here on the *Juniper*. We don't have the facilities of a proper shipyard, so it won't look pretty. The stealth units will still function and that's all you're going to need. Your destination is a solar system mid-way between Kidor and Atlantis. One of our Anderlechts on routine patrol detected three, fast-moving vessels travelling in formation between two of the planets."

"Three?" asked Duggan sharply.

"That's correct. It's the first time we've seen this many of their warships in a single location. We think it might indicate the presence of something more significant. The captain of the *ES Viking* followed orders and got out of there immediately, to ensure the safety of his vessel and crew."

"Is there any way they could have been Ghasts?"

"If they were, they were travelling faster than any known Ghast vessel."

"You're sure these were Dreamer spaceships and you think they indicate the presence of the mothership?"

"That's what we hope. At the very least, this is something worth checking out. Your visit to Kidor has shown me that the stealth modules are viable and this time you'll be testing them against several foes."

"Assuming they've not moved elsewhere."

"There's always a chance there won't be any sign of the enemy," admitted Teron. "Which is why we'll provide you with a series of additional destinations to explore if you don't find anything."

Duggan grunted. "Keep looking till we find something that starts shooting at us," he said.

"I thought you liked it that way, Captain."

There were several responses Duggan could have made. He knew it wasn't wise to speak any of them, since he didn't know what he felt anymore. "What about the Ghasts and the power sources for the pyramids?" he asked.

"You're like me," said Teron. "You need to be everywhere at once, doing everything for everybody. The Space Corps is a vast, sprawling organisation, John. We'll try our best to explore every avenue using other personnel. For the moment, you've got your mission and it's an extremely high priority. There's only a single ship in the whole fleet like the *ES Lightning* and you're the one in charge of it."

"I wasn't looking for motivation, sir."

"Indeed not – that doesn't mean I can't offer it."

Duggan got to his feet in preparation to leave, when a sudden thought came to him. "Have you asked the stats team to plug details of our new stealth technology into their simulators? Might that have a significant effect on these projections?"

Teron frowned. "I'm not sure," he said. "Thank you, Captain – I'll check to see if that's been overlooked." Duggan headed for the door, but Teron wasn't quite finished. "Terrible thing for Lieutenant Nichols, getting killed like that. He put up a good fight, I'm told."

"That's what I heard as well, sir. Saved one of the men at the cost of his own life."

"There's always a chance for redemption."

"So I've been told."

With those words, Duggan left Admiral Teron's office.

CHAPTER SIX

THE REFITTING of the *ES Lightning* was completed in five days instead of the eight days Teron had stated. The warship was parked in Hangar Bay Two and Duggan visited from time to time, watching with interest as a swarm of automated repair robots busied themselves with replacing the sheets of armour plating which had been melted away by the Dreamer plasma missiles. The robots themselves were dozens of metres tall - functional slab-sided units of grey alloy, with many-jointed limbs that could weld or squirt molten metal over the damaged areas and mould it into shape. Other repairs were completed from the overhead gantries in the hangar bay. Cranes and other machines whizzed along the length of the vessel, trailing sparks behind them.

Internally, the damage had been slight. Still, nothing was left to chance and a thorough testing process was performed on the vital systems which kept the ship running. On one occasion, Duggan watched through a viewing window as the stealth modules were tested. When they were activated, the *ES Lightning* simply disappeared, leaving the repair bots motionless in apparent confusion. At their most basic level, the stealth systems pulled and twisted light to make an object appear transparent. There was more to it than this and Duggan was aware they could nearly eliminate heat and noise output. It wasn't perfect as he'd already discovered on Kidor. When he stared closely into the Hangar Bay, he could just about see a distortion in the air. Whatever the rough edges, the results were incredible.

When the call came through to let him know the *ES Lightning* was ready, Duggan hurriedly threw a few items into his pack and made his way to the hangar bay. The work was complete, but the signs of hastily-repaired damage were easy to see. The hull was a patchwork mixture of shiny and dull, with uneven joins and areas where the molten injections had dripped without being adequately smoothed off. Commander McGlashan was a little way ahead, her neck craned to examine the work.

"It looks like it'll fall apart as soon as we take off," she said, her eyes betraying a hint of excitement at the thought.

"It'll hold together," said Duggan. "If I was young and it was my first ship to command I might be offended by the appearance. As it stands, I can appreciate what we have onboard."

"Four days ago, I asked myself if it'd be easier to move the stealth modules to another ship," said McGlashan. "I spoke to one or two people and apparently it's not so easy."

"There's all those extra engines at the back to think about as well," said Duggan. "And the new AI."

"I know, I know," she laughed. "I was badly mistaken - don't rub it in."

"I wouldn't dream of it," he said. "We should get inside and run some pre-flight checks."

"You're not as confident as you sound," she said, looking at him from the corner of her eye. She didn't follow up on her statement and changed the subject. "I wonder if Frank has found something to complain about yet."

"I think it keeps him sane," said Duggan, heading towards the spaceship.

Flores and Dorsey were at the bottom of the boarding ramp, watching the activity around the hangar bay with suspicion and interest. They snapped to attention when they saw Duggan and McGlashan approach through the crowds of maintenance personnel.

"Sir!" said Dorsey, bringing her hand to her forehead.

Duggan returned the salute. "Are we waiting for many?"

"I'm not sure, sir. Some of the troops aren't here yet. Lieutenant Ortiz is inside."

Duggan shook his head in wonderment. His office was a considerable distance from the hangar bay, but he'd not hung about. Somehow Ortiz always seemed to arrive before him, as if she sweet-talked the administrative staff until she was assigned a room within fifty metres of wherever she needed to be. He couldn't recall seeing a more enthusiastic member of the Space Corps this side of Commander McGlashan.

The bridge was as he'd left it a few days earlier, the lighting and smells the same as any one of a hundred other Gunners. Lieutenant Chainer was at his console, his face reflecting patterns of green light from his console.

"Hello, sir," he said, giving a salute as an afterthought. "They've ignored my request to upgrade the food replicators. I told them we had more than enough power for one of the latest models, but they didn't listen."

Duggan exchanged a glance with McGlashan and watched her smother a smile at Chainer's words. "We can't have everything, Lieutenant. This is a fleet warship, not a hotel."

Chainer pulled his eyes away from his screen. "The better I eat, the better I fight," he said. He pressed a hand onto his chest as if he felt a momentary pain. "I think poor quality food will slow down the healing process."

"The medic cleared you for duty," said Duggan. "Perhaps you've grown soft eating from the replicators on the *Terminus* and *Rampage*."

He took his chair and scrolled through the repair logs for the *ES Lightning*. Everything was in order as he'd expected it to be. He accessed each major and minor subsystem, checking carefully for alerts.

"They've done a good job," he said. "We'll leave as soon as we've got a full complement."

"Want me to let the *Juniper* know?" asked Chainer.

"Please do so, Lieutenant. It'll take them a good while to empty the bay and I'd rather they got started early."

Chainer sent his request for clearance to depart. The external sensor feeds showed deep red warning lights cycling from dark to medium, accompanied by an orderly procession of people and many of the smaller machines following their predetermined routes to clear the area.

"That's going to make it tough for Bill, since he'll be coming the opposite direction to everyone else," said McGlashan.

"He can handle himself," said Chainer.

It took longer than Duggan hoped and an hour passed before the bay doors slid open. He didn't delay and took the warship straight out through the opening. The pattern of stars about the *Juniper* was familiar to him given the amount of time he'd spent on the orbital, and he watched the distant pinpricks of white light, wondering what lay out there.

"Everything's ready when you are, sir," said Breeze.

Duggan checked they were sufficiently distant from the *Juniper* for them to enter lightspeed. "Get us ready. We'll go as soon as the AI's got the course and engines prepared."

"Aye, Captain."

Less than a minute later and they were away. Duggan thought he heard a peculiar noise from the engines that might indicate a fault. There were no alarms on his console so he put it down to being jumpy.

"Only five days to the Dastin system," said Breeze. "I've read the mission briefing, but it seemed to be somewhat light on details."

"As usual," said Chainer. "We're on a need to know basis."

"Don't worry, Lieutenant, you'll find out," said Duggan.

"Want me to arrange a meeting with the guys below?"

"Not just yet, Lieutenant. In due course, perhaps."

"This *must* be top secret," said Breeze.

"Not necessarily," said Duggan. "There isn't always a requirement to let everyone know the details of what the Space Corps has planned."

"You're talking like an Admiral, sir," joked Breeze.

Duggan had never once thought of himself as a rebel or a maverick but the light-hearted comment made him feel uncomfortable for some reason. There were times his loyalty brought him too close to the men and women who served under him. It was a fine line to walk and he felt a sudden concern that he might have ventured too far across.

With five days to fill, Duggan spent much of his spare time in the gym. In the nine weeks of incarceration he'd neither gained nor lost weight, but felt the edge of his strength and fitness had gone. He'd tried to get back to his peak in recent days – it hadn't been enough and he was keen to resume his efforts.

He met with Lieutenant Ortiz once or twice. She'd come away from Kidor with fewer scars than the others – her mental strength was second to none. Even so, Duggan had been uncertain about letting her come along so soon after the ordeal. She'd produced several medical reports that proved she was in excellent physical shape, leaving Duggan wondering how she'd managed to recover so quickly. He knew she'd only recently turned thirty years old, so she had youth on her side. Whatever the reports said, she looked slightly gaunter than he remembered, though her eyes remained as sharp as ever.

"Do you think we're going end up facing the Ghasts and Dreamers at once, sir?" she asked one morning when they were sitting in the mess room.

"I can't give you a good answer," he said. "There are things we don't know. We don't know what to do with the Ghasts. There's no proof they've entered an alliance."

"It was Ghasts shooting at us on Kidor, sir," she said.

Duggan wasn't sure he wanted her to know about the possibility the Ghasts and Dreamers were the same species. She wasn't a one to spread rumour, but there were some things it was better to keep to himself. "Any chance they were different and only looked similar?" he asked.

"No chance. They were Ghasts, sir."

"What weapons did they have?"

"Gauss."

"With the same design as what the Ghasts normally carry?"

She wrinkled her nose, which made her look like the girl she'd been years before. "It's a bit hard to say. You know how it is when someone's shooting at you. You don't always look to see what colour shoes they're wearing."

Duggan smiled. "Anyway, to answer your initial question, we might end up fighting the Ghasts or we might not. I don't think anyone wants to – if it starts up again it's going to be devastating for both sides."

"They won't get another chance, will they?" she asked quietly. "Not with us having the Planet Breaker."

"I wouldn't pin your hopes on it being the answer to everything," he said. "We've only got one weapon and as far as I'm aware, only one warship we can fit it onto. All it would take is for the *Crimson* to get shot down early and then we'd have to face the Ghast fleet which is still superior to our own. Even if we destroyed their worlds, the warships they have in space might eventually find one of our planets. War isn't a favourable outcome for any of us."

"A few of those two gigaton nukes would do the job if we lost the *Crimson*."

"What if they have sufficient planetside defences to take those out before they could detonate?" said Duggan. "If we lose the Planet Breaker, everything becomes a gamble – a gamble we can't afford to take. If it comes to it, this time we won't sit back and see what comes at us. We'll fight with everything we've got and we'll be as ruthless and savage as our opponents. If we lose, it won't be because we had our heads so far in the sand we couldn't see what was kicking our backsides."

"I'm glad," she said. "I was becoming accustomed to the idea we might end up the victors. I'd hate to have that snatched away."

"Weren't thinking of settling down were you, Lieutenant?"

She looked at him, her dark eyes like bottomless pits. "One day, sir." She had a thin silver chain around her neck, which she'd worn for as long as Duggan had known her. She pulled it clear of her uniform and there was a ring attached – a plain silver band of metal. "A promise ring," she said. "It's been almost ten years now and I've not spoken to the man who gave me it in five years. I don't even know why I still wear it." Her eyes glistened.

"You wear it because it's the only link you have to a life outside war," said Duggan. "A memory of the past and a path to your future, no matter who gave you it. Keep it safe – it's the most precious thing you own."

She nodded her head once and tucked the ring away. Duggan finished his breakfast, hardly remembering what it was he'd just eaten. He took his leave and left Ortiz with her thoughts.

CHAPTER SEVEN

THE *ES LIGHTNING* exited lightspeed several hours away from the destination solar system Dastin-16. This was a far greater distance than usual and was intended to reduce the chance any enemy craft in the area would notice the fission signature of their arrival. After initial scans found no sign of activity, Duggan pushed the *Lightning* to full speed, aiming straight for the planet. He was feeling more confident in the ability of the stealth modules to withstand extended periods of use, so he ordered them to be activated as soon as they'd reached maximum velocity. The plan was to coast in and only use the reduced-output gravity drives for manoeuvring when they came closer.

"We're looking for three Dreamer warships and a gargantuan mothership?" asked Chainer. "If we can evade that many spaceships, I'll do a happy dance for you all."

"What about your chest injury?" asked McGlashan, smiling sweetly.

"I didn't say there'd be any handstands in the happy dance, did I?"

Duggan waved them to silence. He was busy running

through the known data in order to refresh his memory on what was out here. "We've got a big, dying sun, with six unremarkable planets in orbit. The ES *Viking* recorded the enemy warships travelling between the fourth and fifth planets – Corai and Diopsis. Both planets are too cold to support life even if there were sufficient oxygen."

"The far scans have just come back to confirm no significant atmosphere exists on either planet, sir," said Chainer. "I've tallied our data with that gathered by the ES *Viking* and there's a perfect match. If the enemy have deployed a pyramid anywhere around here, it's not generating oxygen."

"What about the third planet - Kiyro?" asked Duggan. "I'm certain it's too hot for life, but perhaps they have technology to overcome such obstacles."

"Negative on the third planet as well, sir. There's been no change since the *Viking* came here."

Duggan drummed his fingers on the arm of his chair. "What would bring them out here, I wonder?" He looked at the others. "Suggestions?"

"It seems unlikely they know where they're going," said McGlashan. "If they had to come through a wormhole, they won't have any charts for this sector. Maybe they're just picking whatever solar system interests them and jumping towards it to see what they can find there."

Duggan took another look at the chart which showed the confirmed sightings of the aliens. There was no clear pattern that he could use to join the dots and predict where they might be heading. It was certain the Space Corps had dozens of people analysing the data, so anything obvious would have been picked up already. What was most puzzling was the fact the Dreamers appeared to be taking a course that would bring them closer to Atlantis, yet without actually intersecting it. This conflicted with the report from the Projections Team which predicted a high chance of the planet's destruction.

"Commander McGlashan might be correct," said Breeze. "What does the Confederation need? We need places for our people to live and we need planets with resources. Perhaps the enemy is here seeking both."

"It seems a bit haphazard," said Chainer doubtfully. "I mean, the idea is sound, but their execution is random."

"If they can transform an inhospitable world to one with a breathable atmosphere, who knows what other methods they could have to find what they're looking for?" said Breeze.

"We should hopefully have a better idea soon," said Duggan. "Two hours until we're close enough. I'll take us past Corai and come back for a loop around Diopsis. It's been a few days since the sighting and I won't be surprised if the enemy are no longer in this system."

"Bad things have a habit of turning up anyway," said Chainer, a cynic to the last. "There are two small moons orbiting Corai and one orbiting Diopsis. I'll need more than a single pass to make a thorough scan of everything, assuming you want full surface data."

Duggan pondered the matter. "Surface data is secondary, Lieutenant. Get what you can but prioritise the search for enemy warships."

Chainer acknowledged the order. "Will do, sir. We might still need more than a single circuit."

"Fine, we'll keep going until you're satisfied," said Duggan.

For the next two hours, Duggan did his best to keep his mind clear. He wasn't sure what to expect from this mission and it was difficult to keep from turning over the possibilities. He distracted himself by watching the approaching planet on the main viewscreen. Corai had a dusty orange appearance, streaked with large bands of a rich, brown colour. Its two moons were currently visible, showing as dark-rimmed spheres off to one side. The orange hue was a welcome change from the interminable greys of every other planet they'd visited in the last couple of years since they'd located the ESS *Crimson*. Duggan chuckled at the inner workings of his brain and wondered if he were developing a romantic streak as the years progressed. He was shocked to find the idea was appealing.

"I'm going to bring us in high and wide," he said. "There's a lot of carbon dioxide in the atmosphere and I don't want to come in too close. The ship handles like crap when the stealth units are active so it's easier this way."

"Not too high and wide," said Chainer.

"I'm aware of what you need, Lieutenant," said Duggan. "I want to be away from here as soon as we can – we'll do this as quickly as we're able."

The ES *Lightning* hurtled onwards, skimming across the extreme edges of the planet's upper atmosphere. There was a tiny amount of drag and the hull temperature fluttered upwards, remaining well within its operating range. The warship wasn't nimble at this speed, given how much of its engine output was taken up maintaining their stealth cloak, and Duggan had to reduce their velocity in order to keep to his preferred trajectory. He looked across and saw Chainer and McGlashan hunched over the sensor feeds, trying to pull sense from the reams of raw data. With the *Lightning* stripped of its weapons, there was little for McGlashan to do, so it seemed best that she help Chainer out.

"The planet's surface is inhospitable," she said. "Sandstorms and high winds. I wouldn't like to be down there unless I was in a something more substantial than a spacesuit. Other than that, it's a blank so far."

"I can't see anything to suggest there's a single enemy ship here, let alone three," added Chainer.

"Keep looking," said Duggan. "As soon as we're certain, we'll make our way to the next solar system on the list we've been given."

They completed a three-quarter circuit of Corai and Duggan adjusted their course in order to loop around each of the two moons. Neither had an atmosphere and they were little more than bleak spheres of stone. As Chainer and McGlashan completed their scans, a brief summary of the results was fed through to the captain's console. There was little of interest here, with plenty of ores which could be found in abundance almost anywhere. Duggan was readying a new course towards Diopsis, when he was given the news.

"I've detected an enemy warship, sir," said Chainer, his voice eerily calm. "They must have been orbiting Corai and we've simply missed them up until now."

"What sort of warship?" asked Duggan. He also felt strangely calm – the reassurance offered by the stealth modules had given him a feeling of confidence.

"Slightly over two klicks in length. It's one of their mid-sized warships like we destroyed near Trasgor."

"A cruiser," said Breeze.

"A significant resource to leave out in the back-end of nowhere," said Duggan. "There must be something here."

"There's a second one a few thousand klicks behind it," said McGlashan. "It's not following the first – its course will take it on a separate orbit. That's two significant resources out in the back-end of nowhere. There's no indication they're aware of our presence."

"How many damn warships did they pack onto that mother-ship?" asked Chainer.

"They won't have room for many battleships, but I reckon there'd be plenty of space for a few more of these cruisers in their hangars. Along with a couple of dozen pyramids for good measure," said Breeze.

"I wonder how many motherships they have back where they come from," said Chainer.

"That may not even be their biggest ship," said Breeze.

"Great," muttered Chainer.

"If there are two warships here, there's a good chance the third one is somewhere near," said Duggan. "Don't let up with your search."

"Try and keep your distance, sir," said Chainer. "The battleship on Kidor would have been equipped with a lot more detection equipment than these smaller vessels, but we can't get complacent."

"I hear you," said Duggan. "If these two are orbiting the planet, I think we've found our destination."

"What do you mean?" asked McGlashan.

"The fact that they came here and have stayed put tells me they're likely to be watching out for something."

"Something on the surface?"

"Exactly. Keep an eye on the enemy but switch focus to what's on the surface of the planet and the moons."

"Both enemy vessels are in a high, fast orbit, sir. You might have to be careful they don't catch us unawares."

Duggan nodded. "The battleship came close enough without being able to pinpoint us. Still, you're right – we don't want to push our luck."

With that, he took advice from the ship's AI on what it considered to be the best speed and trajectory to maximise their distance from the enemy at all times. When it fed through its recommendations, he changed their course in order to enter a slightly higher orbit than he'd initially intended.

"We might need one more loop at this height," said Chainer.

"The AI has taken that into account," said Duggan. "Get scanning and tell me what you can see."

The first orbit was comparatively slow. The two enemy

warships were on divergent orbits and they were soon lost from sensor sight. The turbulence on the surface was more violent than they'd first thought and it made the surface scan slower than it otherwise would have been. On more than one occasion, Chainer cursed as he tried to draw a clear picture through the interference. There was no sign of a third enemy warship. Nevertheless, Duggan was certain it was somewhere in the area and he became progressively more worried when it continued to evade detection. Halfway through their second orbit of Corai, Chainer found it.

"I've got a third vessel pulling away from Corai's surface," he said. "Eighteen thousand klicks to starboard."

"The same as the others?" asked Duggan. "And has it detected us?"

"Negative on both questions, sir. It's lifting off vertically and at a fairly low speed. I'm not sure what it is. It's three klicks to a side and shaped like a cube."

"What the hell are they up to?" asked Breeze.

"It's nothing like a warship in shape," said McGlashan. "There again, the mothership isn't either and we know what that can do."

"See if the scanners can pick up anything else," said Duggan. "Send me the coordinates of its take off site – we're going to see if it's left anything behind."

"You've got the location now, sir," said Chainer. "If there's anything there, we should see it when you come closer."

"It's just a plain old cube," said McGlashan, sounding disappointed that she'd discovered nothing more interesting about the enemy vessel. "Built for a specific purpose, do you think?"

"No doubt," Duggan replied. He was gripped by the certainty that there was something significant going on here and he was desperate to find out more.

"It's picked up a bit of speed," said Chainer. "Not what you'd call fast compared to their other ships, but it would keep up with an unmodified Gunner. Still heading straight up and away."

"Where will its course take it?"

"Nowhere, unless it goes to lightspeed."

"There's no sign it's preparing to do so," said Breeze.

"Odd," said Duggan.

"It's left something behind on the planet," said Chainer. "I don't know what it is – it's a hard alloy object, a few meters in diameter and maybe twenty metres long. It's cylindrical in shape."

"Is it doing anything?"

"Nope. There is nothing coming to or from it."

Without knowing quite why, Duggan felt gripped by a coldness. Nothing the Dreamers had done so far had any positive outcome for the Confederation. Whatever this object was, he doubted it served a benign purpose. With every part of him wanting to be away from here, Duggan breathed deeply and then spoke.

"We're going in for a closer look," he said.

CHAPTER EIGHT

THE *ES LIGHTNING* descended steadily towards the surface. The cube-shaped spacecraft had accelerated away until it was nothing more than a pinpoint on the fars. There was no sign of the two enemy warships and Duggan kept his fingers crossed it would stay that way. A short distance above the surface, they entered the upper reaches of a ferocious sand storm, which raged across a thousand kilometres. Particles of grit scoured the *Lightning*'s armour and high winds buffeted the spaceship. Inside, the crew felt nothing – the *Lightning* was much too heavy to be affected by atmospheric conditions, no matter how harsh.

"How'd you manage to see the object through all of this?" asked Duggan.

"That's what they pay me for, sir," Chainer replied.

Duggan had always known Chainer to be a skilled officer and it was times like this he was grateful to be accompanied by some of the best men and women from the Space Corps.

"I'm impressed," he said, not shy to admit it.

"Thank you, sir."

They sank lower through the storm, until they were only a few hundred metres above the alien object. The surface was uneven, though there were few substantial variations in the elevation. This was about as flat as it got in places like this. While they descended, Chainer continued gathering data about their target. Unfortunately, there wasn't much more to say.

"It's definitely a cylinder, with a four-metre diameter and a total length of seventeen metres. It's standing perfectly upright, so it must have a way of self-levelling. The sighting we've had of the two warships strongly suggests they will fly directly overhead on each orbit. They're keeping an eye on it. I guess they're orbiting to maximise their chances of detecting any unwanted arrivals in the area."

"Could it be a weapon?" asked Duggan. This had been his first thought and he'd kept the *ES Lightning* purposefully off to one side, in case the cylinder could fire at objects directly above it. If it was anything sophisticated Duggan knew his method was unlikely to keep them safe. He'd decided to investigate and these were the risks.

"It looks a bit like a missile tube," said Chainer. "There's no place for the ammo to go, so it's single-use if that's what it is."

"A beam weapon or disruptor? Or a simple high-explosive?"

"It doesn't seem likely," said Chainer, picking up on Duggan's worry. "There are no readings that suggest it's any of those things. It could be something we've not encountered before, I suppose."

Duggan furrowed his brow in thought. "They took away the *Lightning*'s four armoured vehicles when they fitted the stealth modules, but there's still part of the cargo bay that hasn't been filled with engines. Would there be room to fit the object in there?"

"It should squeeze in, assuming it's not too heavy for the gravity clamp to pull it up," said McGlashan. "We're designed to deploy only and leave the collection to someone else, so I'm not sure it would be a good idea to try."

"The cylinder isn't noticeably heavier than you'd expect, given its size," said Chainer. "There shouldn't be a problem picking it up. It's getting it inside that will cause problems. We have no way to rotate it into place."

"We could hold it in one of the tank launch tubes," said Duggan.

"It might break the clamp under hard acceleration," said Breeze. "I wouldn't want it crashing into the underside of the launch hatch at high speed."

"Damnit, we need to see what it is," said Duggan.

"Won't the enemy notice it's gone?" asked Chainer.

"I should imagine so," said Duggan. "How long are their orbits taking to complete and do we have enough data to pick a decent window where we can land, steal their cylinder and be on our way?"

"Assuming they're maintaining the same speed as when we first saw them, they're taking about fifteen minutes per orbit. In fact, one of them has just come into sensor sight. It hasn't deviated from its course, so we're safe for the moment."

"How long a window can we expect?" repeated Duggan.

"Anywhere from eight to twelve minutes," said Chainer. "With no way to be certain exactly where in that range."

"We'll need to land with the launch hatch directly over the cylinder, get someone out there to attach the clamp, get that person back onboard and then fly to safety before the enemy realises what we've done and start searching. Does that about sum things up?" asked Duggan.

"Yes, sir."

"Send a message to Lieutenant Ortiz. Tell her what the plan is. I want her suited up and ready to go as soon as she gets the nod. She'll need a second person with her for backup."

The message was relayed. It would take about ten minutes for Ortiz to get into her spacesuit and then make her way to the boarding ramp. Duggan kept the ES *Lightning* hovering, a hundred metres above the ground and a few hundred metres to one side of the target.

"The enemy ship will be out of sensor sight shortly," reported Chainer. "I'm expecting to see the second one arrive two or three minutes after."

Duggan checked the timings. It was going to be a close-run thing for Ortiz to get ready for this coming window. Several minutes went by and the second ship didn't appear.

"It's running late," said Chainer nervously. "I don't like it when the enemy starts behaving erratically. The first ship is due back in eleven minutes."

Duggan didn't enjoy having his plans thrown into disarray. He was a man who believed robust planning could eliminate much of war's uncertainty. He was the first to admit he liked having to adapt to changing circumstances, but only when this fell within the bounds of his wider strategy.

The voice of Lieutenant Ortiz came through the bridge speakers. "Sir, I've got Dorsey with me. We're suited up in the forward airlock and ready to go."

Duggan was frozen by uncertainty. There was no sign of the second enemy warship, whilst the first was still eleven minutes away. In theory, there was no specific need to rush, since the stealth modules were operating far above the level Duggan would have expected. Still, he didn't like the idea of waiting in a single place for longer than necessary. The sand storm would provide a degree of additional cover, but he knew the enemy would be focusing a great deal of attention on this area when they flew overhead. Duggan felt pushed into taking a gamble he might have otherwise avoided.

"We're landing immediately. I want you to run out, attach the targeting box for the clamps and then get straight back onboard. We'll be leaving in a hurry."

"Understood," said Ortiz. "There're two hundred metres between the ramp and the tank launch hatch. It'll feel good to stretch my legs."

Duggan grunted an acknowledgement. His focus had already shifted to getting them onto the ground as quickly as possible. The positioning had to be so exact that he'd have preferred to utilise the autopilot for it. Unfortunately, there were so many in-built safety systems, the autopilot was painfully slow. This was fine if you were docking with an orbital or landing at a base. When you needed to act fast, manual control was a better option.

"Give me the underside sensor feeds," he said. Images appeared on one of his screens, showing swirling clouds of sand. They billowed in eddying winds, before being whisked away by the powerful gusts. The ground was lost amongst it and it was hard to distinguish what lay below. Suddenly, the image sharpened and the sands cleared. The ground became visible – with a peculiar undulating appearance, as though it was viewed through a covering of water.

"That's the best I can give you, sir," said Chainer. "The AI's working overtime to filter out the sand, one grain at a time."

Duggan was sure there was a technological miracle happening in order to see through the maelstrom, and he was grateful for it. He was also unable to spend time thinking about it. Instead, he looked carefully for the target object.

"Got it," he said. The cylinder was below the front of the ship, not too far from the underside hatches.

"Eight minutes left for the first enemy ship, sir," said Chainer.

"No sign of the second," said McGlashan. "The third vessel is a long way out now – still running at the same speed." She was silent for another few seconds, then she gave a half-shout of surprise. "I've located the second enemy ship, sir! It's three hundred thousand klicks away from Corai and travelling in a straight line away from the surface – just like the cube-shaped spacecraft!"

"What does that mean?" asked Duggan, unable to divert his brain to the task of thinking about it.

"I'm not sure," said McGlashan. "It gets them out of our hair."

"Where's the last ship?" muttered Chainer. "Is it still in orbit?"

Duggan couldn't engage in conversation. He struggled to fine-tune the position of the warship – he wanted to get it right first time. If the cylinder was too much offset from the hatch, there was a chance they'd have to take off again and they might have to abort the whole recovery attempt if the last enemy ship detected something amiss. The landing feet descended from ten metres to five metres, then two. With a soul-destroying slowness they touched down, making hardly a bump.

"Forward ramp opening," said Duggan.

"I see it," said Ortiz. "Shit, it looks nasty out here."

"Don't get lost," said Duggan. In reality, the suits would be fine outside and the sensors would be able to pierce the shrouds of sand well enough for the soldiers to find the target and get back.

"I've located the final ship," said Chainer, the tone of his voice telling Duggan he wasn't going to like what he was about to hear. "It's almost a quarter of a million klicks away and still going. The angle between us and the planet means I've only noticed it now."

"Any suggestion they are preparing for lightspeed travel?" asked Duggan. The coldness he'd felt earlier had become dread and he couldn't put his finger on why.

"None whatsoever."

"I'm getting something from the cylinder sir!" said McGlashan. "It's sending out a series of short signals – there's less than a second between each one and they're all identical."

"Is it something we've done?" he asked.

"I doubt it, sir," said Chainer. "We've not interacted with the object in any way, unless it's designed to respond to proximity."

Duggan's mind churned through the uncertainties. With a flash of realisation, he came to a logical conclusion that explained everything which was happening.

"Lieutenant Ortiz, return to the *Lightning*. Drop what you're carrying and do it *now*. As fast as you can."

"Roger that, sir," said Ortiz at once. "We were almost at the cylinder, it's going to take a few seconds to run through this wind."

"What's wrong, sir?" asked McGlashan.

"The cylinder isn't a weapon," said Duggan with certainty. "It's a beacon of some sort and it's just started signalling."

"You think something's going to come in response?" asked Chainer.

"Yes, Lieutenant, something very bad. Those three Dreamer ships aren't going anywhere – they're simply keeping their distance."

Chainer's face went pale as he figured out what Duggan was getting at. "Crap," he said.

Breeze still didn't get it. "What's going to happen?"

"If I'm right, they're using the beacon as a target and they're going to destroy this planet in the very near future."

Breeze's mouth fell open and he swore loudly.

"We're in the airlock, sir," said Ortiz. "I'm bringing the ramp up as we speak."

"Get to quarters and pray I'm wrong about what I think is about to happen," said Duggan.

Ortiz wasn't the type to ask questions and the comms channel went dead at once. Duggan dragged the control bars back along their runners. Engines howled and the warship burst upwards into the sky. On the ground below, the alien beacon sent out a steady stream of pings. When the *ES Lightning* was a thousand kilometres away, the beacon received a reply.

CHAPTER NINE

"SOMETHING'S JUST ANSWERED," said Chainer with alarm. "It looked like a standard handshake response."

"Want me to prepare lightspeed?" asked Breeze.

"There's no point, Lieutenant. We won't have time – we'll need to get far enough away on the gravity drive."

The ES *Lightning* felt pitifully slow with its engines emasculated by the power draw of the stealth modules and the distance counter didn't increase with anything like the speed required to escape the debris of an exploding planet. Making a snap decision, Duggan disengaged the stealth systems. The power gauges of the engines rocketed upwards to indicate the availability of far greater reserves. He tapped into these immediately, utilising everything available. The distance counter became a blur of numbers as the spaceship tore away from Corai. Duggan's mind and hands worked in harmony, plotting courses and possibilities. His crew spoke suggestions and ideas, letting him know the positions of the enemy warships, in order that he could head on a trajectory as far from them as possible. Then, a beam of pure, total darkness came from the depths of space and struck Corai at the exact location of the beacon.

"Here it comes," said Chainer, his voice flat and distant.

The planet Corai exploded. The surface fractured, a myriad of tiny lines appearing everywhere. The cracks appeared small on the bulkhead viewscreen, when in reality they were kilometres wide. The cracks separated and huge chunks of the planet broke away. From this distance, the destruction appeared ponderous and lazy, as if it were happening in slow motion. The larger chunks splintered again, each smaller piece continuing to do the same, until the viewscreen was filled with a hundred billion shards, each one travelling at a tremendous speed. At the centre of it, the comparatively small part of Corai's core which remained hot lit up the vacuum with a series of reds and dull oranges.

"Some of those pieces are travelling quicker than we are," said Chainer.

Duggan wrenched his eyes away from the spectacle of an ancient planet's demise. He'd seen it twice before and there was something sad about it, even when it didn't result in a billion deaths. His tactical display was zoomed out as far as it would go and it was filled with a crowd of objects, varying in size and speed. Some of these objects collided with each other and became smaller objects. Others raced outwards from the centre towards the ES Lightning. The ship's AI highlighted at least a hundred items on the display which it calculated as threats. Some of them were travelling substantially faster than the warship and Duggan tried to figure out which course would avoid them. If they'd been equipped with Lambdas it would have been a simple matter to destroy these chunks of rock. With the weapons stripped out, the only option was evasion.

"Recommend we go to lightspeed or activate stealth," said McGlashan.

"There's little chance of the enemy detecting us amongst this mess," Duggan replied. "I want to see what they're up to. They've just destroyed a planet and I want to know why."

The tactical screen showed the first piece of the planet go flying past them at a distance of three hundred kilometres – a tiny margin in the circumstances.

"Look at the size of that!" said Breeze.

"Three trillion tonnes, I make it," said McGlashan.

"There's another one at twelve hundred klicks distance," said Chainer. "Fifty klicks across at its widest point."

More shards went by and twice Duggan had to change course to ensure the safety of the ship. None would have hit them directly, but one was projected to come within fifty metres. It was best to have a good margin and fifty metres was definitely closer than he wanted, especially when this particular object was thirty kilometres wide and showed signs it was fragmenting. This was the reason he hadn't activated the stealth modules – he didn't want a sluggish response from the ship if he needed to take rapid evasive action.

"I don't like this," said McGlashan, her face unusually pale in the bridge's blue-tinged light. None of them did and there was tension in the air. More pieces of the broken planet went past, until, after a few minutes, the tactical screen showed only green. The ship's AI continued to track over a million individual targets, yet deemed none of them were on an intercept course with the warship.

"Bring the stealth systems online," said Duggan.

"Done," said Breeze.

The available power plummeted into the red zone all across an array of instrument panels and gauges. Duggan was conscious that if he slowed down or made a change in their course, he might bring them into the path of additional shards of the planet. He interrogated the AI and had it run through a series of simulated paths which would allow them to avoid the inbound pieces.

"This thing's quick," he said, marvelling at the speed with which the AI spat out his options. "The mainframe on a standard Gunner would have frozen for minutes doing what this one's doing in seconds."

Cautiously, he swung the ship around, intending to head towards the last-known position of the cube-shaped Dreamer spacecraft. He had no idea what its purpose was, but he was certain it had placed the beacon on the surface and he was very interested in seeing what it would do next.

"I'm still trying to get a fix on it, sir," said Chainer. "The distances are extreme and those bastards are difficult enough to find when they're close in. And there's quite a lot of rock between us and them."

"Keep trying," said Duggan. "We've relied on stealth up until now and we'll continue to do so while we investigate what they're up to."

"We should let the *Juniper* know what's happened," advised McGlashan.

"Agreed. Lieutenant Chainer, please send a message."

"Well, our main comms are still operational," said Chainer. "It doesn't look as though they've spotted us yet."

With the spacecraft unable to perform sharp turns, Duggan kept things steady. The surrounding area was crowded with Corai's remains as they dispersed into the infinity of space. After a few minutes of careful flight, something came up on the sensors.

"The debris has cleared enough that I can see what's happened to the two moons," said Chainer. "One is completely gone. The other has been broken into three pieces and knocked away from its orbit. The largest piece is five thousand klicks across. It's moving comparatively slowly and I think it's going to clip Diopsis on the way past."

"Crap," said Breeze.

"Can anyone run me a simulation on what that'll do?" asked Duggan.

"Might take a while to set up," said McGlashan.

"Now's not the time, then. Curiosity got the better of me," Duggan replied.

"It'll be catastrophic, whatever happens," said Chainer. "This solar system is already doomed with all this rock floating around. The final effects might not be known for years. The largest pieces are moving the slowest. They could get sucked into the sun or drawn in by another planet."

"Why the need for such destruction?" asked Breeze, shaking his head. "These are nothing but empty planets and I shouldn't care about them, but for some reason I do."

"I know how you feel," said Duggan.

The fastest pieces of debris were long gone. The vast bulk of the planet had separated away from the centre much more slowly and the tactical display remained a sea of potential hazards. Duggan couldn't remember a time when he'd had to take such prolonged evasive action and his eyes began to ache from the concentration. After another fraught ten minutes, he succumbed to the inevitable and handed control to the AI. As soon as the control bars became unresponsive to his inputs, he slumped back, feeling the tension in his wrists and shoulders. Ever since he'd recovered the ESS *Crimson* and been forced to pilot it manually, he'd become reluctant to use the automated systems. He was glad his stubborn insistence on being in control hadn't stopped him doing what was right.

"I've always celebrated technology and the benefits it can bring. I'm damned if I know why I'm reluctant to let it take over."

"Nobody likes to feel redundant," said Chainer simply.

Duggan wasn't sure if there was more to it than that. The time to think about it was when they were at lightspeed heading away from this place.

"Where's that cube-shaped craft?" he asked.

"We're coming close to where I think it could be," said Chainer. "The debris is spread out far enough that I should have detected it a while back, but it could have moved away from where it was. It's also conceivable that it's remained hidden behind some of these larger pieces of rubble."

"If it had continued flying outwards from Corai, we'd have seen it, right?" said Duggan. "From what you're saying, the enemy vessel either reached a certain distance and then stopped, or it possibly even flew back towards the centre."

Chainer blinked. "I've not been scanning for it towards the middle. I kind of expected it to be where we last saw it."

"You should expand your search, Lieutenant," said Duggan.

"Will do, Captain. It's crowded with rocks, so anything amongst them could be easily missed."

While Chainer and McGlashan worked on the sensors, Duggan's eyes drifted onto the bulkhead screen again. A jagged slab of rock drifted by, rotating sedately as it did so. The distance made it look like no more than a pebble, when in fact it was many thousands of times heavier than the ES Lightning. While he watched, he pondered on what the enemy spaceships were doing here. His suggestion that the cube-shaped craft might have flown towards the centre had come from nowhere and he wasn't sure why he'd thought it. There was no obvious reason why they'd fly into the debris. There again, there was no apparent reason for them to blow the planet up in the first place.

"I want a composition report for these rocks," he said.

"I can do that, sir," said Breeze. "It'll let Commander McGlashan and Lieutenant Chainer continue what they're doing."

"Please," agreed Duggan.

It didn't take long. "Well I'll be," said Breeze. "The crust holds nothing of interest – a Space Corps prospector scanned it ten years ago and found common ores. However, Corai's an old, old world and its core was well on the way to cooling down. Some of these pieces here are still hot, and guess what? They hold significant reserves of molten Gallenium."

"That's what they're here for?"

"It gets better than that, sir. Or worse, depending on how you want to view the matter. Where the heat of the core is exposed to the cold of space, there's a reaction taking place between the Gallenium and the rocks which hold it. I've detected a thin crusting of the substance we discovered in the Dreamer pyramid."

"The power core?" asked Duggan, his voice louder than he'd intended.

"My geology is a bit rusty, but I'm fairly certain that's what it is – the same stuff."

"Sir, I've located the target spaceship," said Chainer. "You were right – it's gone inwards instead of outwards."

"Can you tell me what it's doing?"

"Dodging rocks, from the looks of it."

"Anything else?"

"There's too much of this debris in the way."

"I think we've found out what they're looking for," said Duggan. "I've got to be sure, though."

With those words, he instructed the AI to take them towards the enemy spacecraft. The AI chimed a warning to let him know the danger level was too high and denied his request. With a snarl, Duggan switched back to manual and turned the *Lightning* so that it pointed directly towards the expanding wreckage of Corai.

CHAPTER TEN

THE EXPERIENCE for Duggan was not a pleasurable one. Even if the *Lightning* had been operating with full gravity engines, it would have been a testing time. With it as sluggish as it was, he had to think far ahead and rely on alerts from the tactical screen to let him know when he'd crossed into the path of something that would hit them. The trouble was, each evasive manoeuvre brought him into the path of additional threats, which in turn brought more. With each passing moment he worried that he'd get it wrong and the spaceship would be struck by an object too big for the hull armour to deflect. On top of this, they'd entered an area which was thick with dust and smaller rocks. They were impossible to avoid and were travelling fast enough that they would eventually scour away the surface of the alloy plates. Deep within the body of the spacecraft, the crew heard and felt nothing of the bombardment against the exterior. The only way they could tell it was happening was the series of warnings that appeared on the status update screens.

"There's a chance we'll lose some of our sensor arrays if this keeps up, sir," said Chainer. He had a sheen of sweat over his face and his cheeks were red from the heat.

"We almost there," said Duggan. "A little more."

A cluster of hundred-metre rocks skated past the *Lightning* and Duggan was only just quick enough to guide the spaceship around a pair of larger pieces. These two shards collided with each other moments after they'd gone by. The contact sent one of them into a fast spin, while the other shattered into a hundred thousand parts. If the collision had happened even ten seconds earlier, the result would have destroyed the *ES Lightning*.

"The enemy must have evasion routines programmed in for this," said McGlashan. "They're ungainly but still managing to dance around without taking any damage."

"We'd be fine if the AI hadn't objected," said Duggan through gritted teeth. "Sometimes I ask myself who's in charge."

"It'll override, won't it?"

"Yes, after a great deal of pissing about. There wasn't time."

"I'm finding more and more of the power source material, sir," said Breeze. "The metal is fusing into the molten rock or maybe it was already joined by the pressure in the planet's core."

"It had them stumped in the lab, last I'd heard," Duggan replied, hauling at the control bars. A hundred fist-sized rocks cascaded against the spaceship's nose, punching the thick alloy plates into a mess of deep indentations.

"One of the forward sensor arrays has failed," said McGlashan, her voice strained.

"Plenty left we can use," said Chainer.

The bulkhead viewscreen changed to show a pin-sharp image of the alien spacecraft, centred upon the display. It was a dull grey, with flat sides and no deviation from the basic shape. Tiny specks of light flared up across a hundred different places along the two sides of the cube which were visible. Traces of white sped away into space.

"They've got an offensive countermeasures shield," said Chainer. "Mini-gauss weapons to break up the pieces coming towards them. They also have an energy shield in case something gets through. It's flickering on and off to let the gauss projectiles out and staying on for the bigger pieces. The synchronisation is something to behold."

"Looks like they're waiting for something," said Breeze.

"They're going to collect whatever pieces of the Gallenium-fused rock fit their requirements," said Duggan. "I'm convinced that's a mining vessel of some type – designed to do exactly this."

"You mean these Dreamers destroy planets everywhere they go in order to obtain material for their power sources?" asked Chainer.

"I'm sure of it, Lieutenant. They've come through the Helius Blackstar in order to conquer and settle. It's as if the mothership is preparing the way for a massive invasion." As soon as he spoke, Duggan knew he was right. The alien species had sent through one of their capital ships to pave the way for whatever else they might decide to send to this sector of the universe. There was no way they'd have committed such a powerful warship as a gamble – they'd sent the mothership because they knew they'd conquered the technological hurdles required to traverse the wormhole.

"Why haven't they sent dozens more ships?" asked Breeze.

"The mothership and its escort are enough," said McGlashan.

"There was no sign of the additional spacecraft when the Dreamers destroyed the human and Ghost fleets at the Black-star," said Duggan. "I wonder if they could only survive the trip if they stayed within the hold of the mothership."

"If they're not capable of coming through on a whim, that gives me some hope at least," said Breeze.

"I'd like a bit more hope than that," Chainer replied. "Anyway, do we need to stick around for this?"

"The Space Corps isn't usually willing to accept supposition in the place of proof," said Duggan. "Otherwise, I'd turn us around and go straight to the *Juniper*."

"Whoa!" said Chainer. "Their energy output just went up twelve hundred percent and they're maintaining it!"

"They must have colossal reserves of power," said Breeze. "The *Archimedes* could generate less than half of that and even then, it would only be for a split second."

"They've stopped moving," said Chainer.

"I wish I could do the same," said Duggan, wrestling with the controls. The *Lightning* was caught in a thousand-kilometre cloud of hard grit. It washed over the spacecraft, raking a million furrows across its armour. The Dreamer ship was twenty thousand kilometres away and completely stationary. Any debris which came towards it either deflected from the energy shield or was smashed into tiny pieces by the storm of gauss-fired slugs.

"I think I've located their target," said Chainer. "There's a block heading straight towards them, approximately one cubic kilometre in size."

"Pure black rock with Gallenium," said Breeze. "Enough to power a few more of their pyramids."

"I'm not sure how they're doing it, but the rock is slowing down, sir. Its rotation has stopped and its deviating fractionally from its original course."

"Power output up to sixteen hundred percent above their normal," said McGlashan.

"They're dragging it in," said Duggan.

"Another technology we haven't mastered," said Breeze.

"Add it to the list."

Duggan didn't want to stay any longer, but he was determined to capture a sensor recording of what was happening. The data they were gathering showed that the target object had slowed from three hundred kilometres per second down to a hundred, then twenty and then ten. It appeared as if the Dreamers had miscalculated and the rock would crash into their spaceship. In the end, they brought it to a crawl and it vanished into the hold of the enemy vessel.

"Shame that face of the cube was hidden from us," said Breeze. "I'd have liked to see what was inside."

"If I know mining vessels, there wouldn't have been much worth seeing," said Duggan. "I've witnessed enough - we're getting out of here."

"Happy to hear it," said Chainer.

Duggan brought the *ES Lightning* around in as tight a circle as he could manage. He accelerated to the maximum speed the engines would allow, breathing a sigh of relief as he did so. It would be much easier to avoid the inbound debris when they were flying away from it.

"One of their two warships has come into sensor sight," said Chainer.

"Do they know we're here?" Duggan asked at once.

"I'd guess not, sir. We'll pass pretty close to them if you stay on this course."

Duggan swore under his breath. "It'll slow us down since we have to drop the cloak in order to go to lightspeed. We'll have to stay hidden until they're out of range." He watched the new red dot on his tactical readout and altered the *Lightning's* course in order to give the enemy craft a wide berth.

"It's going to be hours until we get far enough on the gravity drives," said McGlashan.

"We might as well get used to the idea," said Duggan, taking a deep breath to calm his frustration.

"Their mining craft is following us out, sir," said Chainer.

"Following?"

"Sorry, bad turn of phrase. They're heading in the same direction as we are, on a more or less parallel course."

"They must have got what they came for."

"An entire planet gone, just for one cubic klick worth of rock," said Breeze. "What a waste."

"They might not be as sentimental as we are," said Duggan.

"There's a priority message coming through on the comms, sir. It's Fleet Admiral Teron."

"Patch him through."

"Captain Duggan?" Teron's voice had the peculiar echo which spoke of the vast distances between them.

"Sir. We found the enemy."

"You need to get out of there right now and return to the *Juniper*."

The alarm in Teron's voice made Duggan sit up. "What's the matter?"

"It's the Ghasts. They've declared war on us again."

"What? Why?" asked Duggan. "What do they have to gain?"

"Everything's gone to crap here, John. We don't know what the hell they're playing at. I need you to get back as quickly as you can. We should know more by then."

"Understood, sir. We're in close proximity to the enemy – it'll be a few hours until we can go to lightspeed."

"As quickly as you can. I'll see you here soon – don't be surprised if your visit is a short one."

The connection went dead.

"He's gone sir."

Duggan turned to look at the others. They each met his gaze, faces displaying a dozen emotions, with fear and uncertainty prevalent amongst them. There was no point in speaking since they were thinking the same thoughts. None of them wanted a return to the war they'd fought in for so long.

"You get used to the fighting and then when it stops, you

suddenly realise how much you hated it," said Chainer. "It feels like someone's offered to shake my hand and then kicked me in the balls instead."

"Yeah."

"We can't do anything about it ladies and gentlemen," said Duggan. "Except do what we've always done, whether we like it or not." He swung towards his console again and closed his eyes tightly for a moment, wishing he'd not heard from Teron. However, the day was not done with giving bad news.

"Sir, there's a fission signature at three hundred thousand klicks. It's one I've seen before."

Duggan felt the walls of the bridge close in on him and he closed his eyes again. "The mothership?"

"Yes sir. It's just appeared in local space."

Anger overcame inertia and Duggan shouted once – a harsh sound of rage and defiance which sounded like it had come from the mouth of an animal instead of a human being.

CHAPTER ELEVEN

THE DREAMER MOTHERSHIP appeared on the *ES Lightning*'s sensors. Duggan had seen it briefly before, but the memory had a hazy, ethereal quality to it, like it had happened long ago and been brought up in a dream where the reality and his imagination clashed to produce an imperfect facsimile of the truth. Here it was again, in all its menace and glory – a cube of alloy with rounded edges and corners. In his mind, Duggan remembered it to be featureless. Now he saw that was not the case. The surfaces of the spaceship were covered in a mixture of dimples and bumps, their purposes unknown. There were other, more complex, structures protruding from the surface. These came in dozens of shapes and sizes, made from curved and straight alloy beams which bristled with antennae and sensor nodes. The crew stared in awe at the sight, while Duggan kept the *ES Lightning* heading in the opposite direction. The die was effectively cast – if the enemy ship was able to penetrate their stealth cloak, their deaths were assured. The only option was to run and hope.

"Are those domes for the beam weapons?" asked Chainer.

"I reckon," said Breeze. "There must be dozens of them. Those ones in the centre are over a kilometre across. It's no wonder they could destroy a Hadron or Oblivion so quickly."

"And is that what I think it is?" Chainer got up and pointed at a triangular emplacement mounted on one corner. There was a short barrel, clearly visible, and with an unthinkably large bore.

"They could shatter a small moon with that," said McGlashan.

"A few rounds would see off our largest warships."

"In my head, I'd convinced myself that the mothership was just a cargo-carrier. It's nothing of the sort, is it?" said Chainer. "It's densely-armed like a warship, only it's vastly bigger than anything we've got."

"And much, much bigger than that Ghast capital ship we glimpsed during the attack on the *Archimedes* a couple of years ago," said McGlashan.

"We've not got a hope in hell against it, have we?" asked Chainer.

"Not yet," said Duggan. "That single ship could wipe out the entire Space Corps fleet and have plenty in reserve to face the Ghasts."

"That's assuming they're not working together," added McGlashan.

"It's academic," said Duggan. "We lose either way. The only hope is that we can stay hidden for long enough and they travel elsewhere." He sighed. "It's beginning to look inevitable." He didn't need to spell out what he meant by those words.

"Our main comms have just gone offline. Switching to back-up," said Chainer.

"Was there something directed at us?"

"Your guess is as good as mine, sir. The other Dreamer warships didn't knock out our comms while the stealth modules were running. The mothership isn't moving, so I don't know what happened."

"It must have enough power to produce an undirected pulse through the space around it," said McGlashan.

"Could be," said Chainer. "Most importantly, we're not dead." He paused as if he'd just realised something of great significance. "We're not dead," he repeated.

Duggan felt a giddiness and he laughed. It wasn't that Chainer had said anything amusing, rather it was relief and excitement that the Dreamer mothership hadn't immediately detected their presence. "When this is over, I'm going to personally buy a drink for each and every one of the people who worked on these stealth modules."

"That might be over five thousand people, sir," said Breeze. He also laughed.

"Well shit, I'm going to buy them a drink anyway."

"I'm quite partial to whiskey if you're going to the bar," said Chainer, joining in the laughter. "No ice in mine."

McGlashan shook her head at the conversation. "This is what a brush with death does for you men, huh?"

"It's the discovery of something significant, Commander," said Duggan, sobering up at once. "A tiny speck of optimism when everything else has gone badly wrong."

Chainer brought the mood crashing down. "They've started moving - fast."

"Towards us?"

"In our general direction. Just shy of two thousand klicks per second, so they're not exactly slow." Chainer grimaced. "They did a jump."

"Where to?" asked Duggan.

"They're one hundred thousand klicks above and behind, sir."

"Still moving?"

83

"Yes, sir. Same speed as before."

"Do you think they're looking for us?"

"I'm not certain," said Chainer. Then, he made up his mind. "Yes, sir. I think they know we're here."

"That's not good news, is it?" said Duggan, not expecting anyone to provide him with the obvious answer.

"Another jump. They're seventy thousand klicks ahead of us."

"There's a big power spike each time," said Breeze. "I'm sure you're aware that when I say *big,* I actually mean *indescribably enormous.*"

"I get the idea, Lieutenant," said Duggan. This was one of those moments where the only plan of action came to him without the need for conscious thought. If the Dreamer mothership was hunting for an anomaly on its sensors, it would eventually track them down. It was faster and infinitely more powerful than the *ES Lightning.* There was no chance they'd be able to decloak for long enough to warm up the deep fission engines, which left only one thing. "We're going to try and lose them amongst this rubble."

The crew responded admirably. "Let's get on it!" said McGlashan.

"I'll build up a picture of the larger pieces of rock," said Chainer. "It might help you plot a trajectory."

Duggan wasn't thinking about specifics yet. He picked a course towards the densest area of Corai's debris and aimed the *Lightning* towards it. The fastest moving objects were long gone, but the majority of the pieces moved far more slowly as they drifted from the centre. Far away, the remains of the two moons had interspersed amongst the pieces and they clashed and deflected, creating a maelstrom of spiralling stone.

"They discharged one of their particle beams," said

McGlashan. "It missed us by three klicks. A second one followed the first, again three klicks away."

"Like pissing in a pot with your eyes closed," said Chainer. "They might hit the target eventually and we have to hope it doesn't happen soon."

"Very descriptive," said Breeze wryly.

It didn't take long for the *ES Lightning* to reach its maximum sub-light velocity, stunted as it was by the stealth power draw. A hundred thousand tiny particles rattled off the hull as the vessel forged a way towards the densely-packed pieces of Corai. A few larger rocks smashed into the armour plates, leaving a series of dents across the nose section. Duggan would have preferred to avoid these, but this wasn't the time for taking extra care. Soon, they were amongst the larger debris – thousands upon thousands of rocks, each large enough to destroy the spaceship if they collided.

Chainer scrutinised the area ahead and around, his mop of sandy hair plastered across his forehead by sweat. "I never want to see another asteroid belt again," he said.

"This isn't an asteroid belt," said Breeze.

"Yeah, whatever. I just don't want to be here, okay?"

"Where's the mothership?" asked Duggan.

"High and wide. They've not made another jump – they must know we're close."

A huge fragment of splintering rock, fifty kilometres across, drifted into their path. On the viewscreen, it showed as half-molten, half-grey and it left a trail of luminous specks behind it, like a trillion fireflies pursued it through space. When Duggan pulled at the control bars to adjust their course around it, the rock suddenly exploded, disintegrating into countless pieces. Greys, oranges and reds filled the viewscreen, as the remains spread out in an unavoidable wave.

"Shit," said Duggan, putting the *Lightning* into a sharp dive. "What was that?"

"Particle beams," said McGlashan. "The mothership fired six at once. Took out the rock."

It was too late to avoid the incoming objects. The best Duggan could manage was to keep clear of the largest pieces and keep his fingers crossed. The hull took a series of punishing blows. The warship was too dense for these lesser impacts to alter its course, but the sounds reached the bridge – distant, dull thumps. Just when it looked as if they might be through, two of the larger pieces smashed into each other, deflecting at an unexpected angle. Duggan tried his best to evade the incoming rock by dragging the warship's nose upwards at the last moment. He was too late and the sharp edges of a five-hundred-metre rock struck them at an angle. This time, they were knocked off course and Duggan struggled to correct matters. The emergency lighting came on and a siren warned of danger. More rocks crunched against the hull, in a never-ending cascade.

"Someone shut off that damned siren!" shouted Duggan. "I can't hear myself think!"

"There's a hole right through our armour," said Breeze.

"Any breach into critical areas?"

"Negative, sir. There's about three inches of alloy covering one area of the engines, but the damage is minimal. If there'd been an engine breach, the trail of positrons would be easy to read."

"Three inches between us and death," said Duggan. "That's a little closer than I like it."

The warship passed through the last of the rocks and into an area that was comparatively clear for a few thousand kilometres. Such had been his focus that Duggan hadn't been able to keep an eye on the pursuing mothership.

"Where are those bastards?" he growled. "Was their destruction of that fragment intentional to cause us trouble?"

"They're keeping pace with us, sir," said Chainer. "Ten thousand klicks to starboard."

"I'm sure that was planned," said McGlashan. "If they can't see us, they stand a better chance of killing us by blowing up anything that comes close. They're not in the clear themselves – take a look at this."

McGlashan brought up a view of the mothership in one corner of the bulkhead screen. A thousand lines of white streaked away from it in an ever-changing pattern across the sky. The incoming fragments of rock were chewed up by gauss rounds into particles of dust which were too small to trouble the mothership's energy shield.

"They're probably not using half of their weaponry," said Breeze with grudging admiration.

Duggan gave the image only passing attention. His mind was elsewhere, doing its best to pilot the *ES Lightning* into a position from which they could escape the pursuing aliens. He was convinced there'd been no alternative than to head towards the centre of Corai's shattered remains. Unfortunately, the mothership was much better equipped to follow the same path and showed no indication it was willing to break off the chase. Wiping away beads of sweat from his face, Duggan got on with his task.

CHAPTER TWELVE

THE NEXT FEW minutes were the most stressful Duggan could recall enduring over the many years he'd spent in the Space Corps. Someone had managed to stop the bridge siren from wailing, but the red warning lights continued to cycle. More rock fragments bounced away from the *Lightning*, each strike leaving a deep indentation in the armour plating. Duggan tried his best to ignore the accumulating damage, but he knew the constant assault would eventually get through. Once that happened, it wouldn't be long until one of the ship's vital systems was knocked out of action.

As they went deeper towards the place Corai had once existed, the fragments of the planet became bigger and more densely clustered. Although these pieces weren't moving quickly, they crashed against each other and it seemed as if their courses were constantly changing. The *Lightning*'s AI was using up a huge percentage of its available resources trying to predict collisions in advance and the new trajectories the boulders would follow afterwards. The computer had enormous reserves of processing grunt, but there were far too many variables for it to provide the exactness Duggan required. All the while, particle beams stabbed into the void, some coming within a few hundred metres of the *Lightning*'s position.

"Something's gotta give," said Chainer.

Duggan nodded his head without turning to look. The man was right – if nothing changed, the *Lightning* would be destroyed in the next few minutes. Duggan wasn't ready to die yet – he felt as if he'd been through too much to be killed by a piece of rock or an unlucky particle beam hit. "I'll think of something," he said.

"It'll need to be soon, sir," said Chainer. "There are two big fragments inbound. One's seventy klicks across and the other more than one hundred. They might collide or they might not."

"I think they're going to shatter those two pieces with their particle beams," said Duggan, knowing that would be game over for the ship and its crew.

"Absolutely," said McGlashan. "And then they'll have us."

"Maybe," said Duggan, that moment spotting something which might give them a chance.

"What is it?" asked McGlashan, picking up on the tone of his voice.

"If we keep on our current course, the enemy vessel is going to come up against some trouble of its own," said Duggan, trying his best to make sense of the crowded tactical display.

"Nothing that's going to destroy them," said Chainer.

"I just need a distraction," said Duggan. "If they lose track of us for a few seconds, it might give us time to get away from here."

No one asked where exactly he thought they would get away to. His words offered a tiny amount of hope and that was enough. The *ES Lightning* ploughed on through a sea of smaller particles, heading towards the two huge chunks of rock ahead. The Dreamer mothership kept the same approximate distance and continued to fire its particle beams in their general direction.

"They've got something *really* big heading their way," said

Chainer. "A thousand klicks of red-hot planetary core spinning towards them."

"Keep your fingers crossed they're too proud to take evasive action," said Duggan. The mothership hadn't deviated significantly from its course so far and he hoped the aliens would choose to destroy the fragment instead of avoid it.

"Thirty seconds until we'll have our own problems to contend with," said Chainer.

"They'll have to act soon," said McGlashan.

The alien warship did exactly as Duggan wanted. The huge cannon they'd seen earlier – one of two on the mothership – rotated with blinding speed, until it pointed at the incoming wall of rock. The cannon fired, its short barrel becoming a blur of recoil and repositioning. All across the centre of the thousand-kilometre length of spiralling rock, huge holes appeared, each more than a hundred metres in diameter. The Dreamer cannon didn't stop and its projectiles continued to pummel the object, knocking away vast pieces of the whole. Within fifteen seconds, an unthinkable quantity of stone had been split, ruptured and broken. Particle beams and smaller gauss fire raked through the fragments, breaking them down into smaller and smaller pieces. Like the waters of a great sea parting, the section of Corai split around the alien mothership, allowing them to fly through the middle.

The moment the enemy vessel vanished amongst the rubble, Duggan acted. He turned the nose of the *ES Lightning* away until they were heading in almost the complete opposite direction. With the enemy lost amongst the obscuring rock, Duggan hoped they had a few seconds to put some distance between them.

There were several large rocks ahead. Duggan skimmed over the top of one and dropped the spaceship behind it. He reduced their speed and kept pace with the tumbling stone. "I need help," he said through gritted teeth. "We've got to keep as much stone between us and that mothership as we can. The moment they have a clear sight of our location, they'll be onto us."

"Understood," said Chainer. "I'm trying to work out a new course."

"Can't we just stay where we are?" asked Breeze.

"Negative, Lieutenant. We're too close for comfort. We need to get further away."

"I'm overlaying a course onto your display, sir," said Chainer. "We should be able to hide behind that five-klick piece below and to the left."

"The enemy should be clear of the debris by now," said McGlashan.

"Yeah, we're going to be making some best-guesses as to where they'll go, Commander," said Chainer. "There's no room to get it wrong."

"Statistics and chance," said Duggan without bitterness. "We should learn to worship them."

"I do, sir," said Chainer. "In my head I'm their most fervent acolyte."

Under Duggan's control, the ES *Lightning* plunged away from the shielding rock and onwards to the next. The greater the distance they managed to travel, the more obstacles they'd put between themselves and the mothership. Without the stealth modules, this tactic would be useless – any modern warship would detect them immediately. Once again, Duggan found himself relying on technology. It was comforting and he mentally celebrated humanity's ingenuity for producing something which none of their enemies possessed.

"Don't let them see us," said Breeze quietly to himself, as if his words could stave off discovery.

"If I can't see them, they can't see us," said Chainer. "At least that *should* be the case in theory. Who knows what these bastards can do?" He cleared his throat. "Anyway, I haven't picked up on their new position yet."

Duggan completed the manoeuvre and tucked the *Lightning* behind the target rock, once more keeping pace with it. The strain of relying on manual control was building within his muscles. His heart beat fast and his hands were clammy. "Where next, Lieutenant?"

"In twelve seconds, a new course will become available, sir. The overlay is on your screen."

"Got it," said Duggan, preparing to follow the new flight path.

After exactly twelve seconds, he hauled the *ES Lightning* away from the cover of stone and pointed the warship's nose towards the new target. This next fragment was almost a thousand kilometres in diameter. It was peculiarly spherical and burned bright with heat from the cataclysm. Duggan took them as near as he dared – several hundred kilometres away. The ferocious heat lapped around the hull and the temperature climbed rapidly.

"Got to get in close, sir," said Chainer. "Otherwise they'll see us."

"It's too hot to get closer," snapped Duggan.

"Never stopped you before," said McGlashan.

"Damn right it hasn't," he replied, swinging another two hundred kilometres nearer to the burning surface.

"Closer," said Chainer.

"We'll burn up!"

"It's that or be destroyed by the mothership, sir."

I've never been scared to take a chance before, thought Duggan, berating himself for his hesitation. *And I'm not about to start.* With a deep breath, he flew within a hundred kilometres of the furnace. The temperature of the already-damaged hull went far beyond its design maximum and the metal softened and shifted. "How long?" he asked. "If the armour gets much softer, even the smallest particles will go through it at this speed."

"Not long...now!" yelled Chainer.

A new course appeared on his screen and Duggan immediately directed the warship along it. This time, there was a large gap to the next suitable object and it was more than thirty seconds until they were back in cover. Whatever information Chainer was squeezing out of the AI it hadn't let them down yet. The area behind them was cluttered with debris of all sizes – the alien mothership was going to find it progressively harder to spot them.

In his head, Duggan thought of it as a game – a high stakes contest between Space Corps technology and an alien behemoth. The longer the game progressed, the more important it became for him to win, as though he and his crew were representatives of the whole Confederation. He was desperate to show the Dreamers that their most powerful warship could be outwitted by something as small as a Gunner, albeit a heavily-modified example. They made three more hops, each one taking them further from the last known location of the enemy.

"Is it fifty-two seconds for lightspeed?" asked Duggan, holding the *Lightning* a steady five kilometres from a vast chunk of Gallenium-laden rock.

"Plus a couple of minutes for the switchover from stealth to deep fission. They'll detect our signature as soon as we warm the engines up for the final fifty-two," said Breeze. "It won't matter if we're hidden behind the largest piece of Gallenium-rich ore that Corai has thrown out here."

"They've got another three ships that we know about, sir," said McGlashan. "We're at the periphery of the debris and the longer we stay here, the greater the chance one of their warships will detect us once we deactivate the stealth modules."

"We're going," said Duggan. "The *Juniper* is where we need to be. Prepare a course for us."

"Yes sir," said Breeze. "Cloaks disengaged. In two minutes we can prepare for lightspeed. Expect all hell to break loose when we light them up."

"Two minutes," said Chainer to himself.

The enemy didn't appear on their sensors and Duggan had to force himself to breathe evenly. After what seemed like a lifetime, Breeze spoke again.

"Fifty seconds and counting down before we can jump." He grinned. "Approximately five days until we arrive."

"Any movement on the sensors?"

"I'll let you know as soon as I see something, sir," Chainer replied.

"Forty seconds."

"Still clear."

"Thirty seconds."

"Still clear."

Before Breeze was able to announce twenty seconds, the *ES Lightning*'s sensors identified a series of detonations amongst the tumbling rocks further towards the periphery of Corai's debris. White plasma was visible at the extremes of range, spilling around dozens of different fragments of the planet.

"They're coming," said McGlashan.

"Twenty seconds."

"It's not the mothership, at least," said Breeze. "The smaller ships can't knock out our engines."

"Small mercies," said Chainer with a shake of his head.

"I'll take mercies no matter how small," said McGlashan.

"More missile impacts," said Chainer. "At least two hundred. They're trying to blast their way through to us."

"How far?" asked Duggan.

"Can't tell."

"Ten seconds."

"We're going to make it."

Just then, something punched clean through the sheltering chunk of Gallenium ore, sending a huge shower of stone into violent collision with the battered hull of the *ES Lightning*. Another impact struck the shield of rock and then another. *They've turned their cannon on us,* thought Duggan. *There's no way in hell we'll get away.*

The onslaught continued and dozens of enormous-calibre slugs pummelled their way through the rock. Each strike tore away a vast chunk of their defence and ejected a fountain of shards thousands of kilometres away from the surface. From the other direction, the Dreamer cruiser had cleared a path through the barricade of spiralling pieces and it came towards them at a speed of two thousand kilometres per second. A flood of red dots on the tactical screen indicated the launch of several waves of missiles. Something cracked into the *Lightning*'s hull and the lights on the bridge flickered and dimmed. The warship rocked under another impact and Duggan stumbled, catching hold of his chair to steady himself. He felt sickness rise in his stomach and wondered if it heralded his death.

Then, everything went quiet and the lights stopped flickering. The urgent red of the alarm continued to cycle and Duggan's ears made out the humming of the engines. He looked at the other members of the crew and saw the still expressions of people who had expected death and had made peace with themselves. Today wasn't their day.

"We made it," said Duggan.

CHAPTER THIRTEEN

IN MOST CIRCUMSTANCES, achieving lightspeed was a guarantee of escape. On this occasion, Duggan was concerned in case the Dreamer mothership had managed to direct its engine scrambling weapon against them just before the *Lightning* departed. It soon became apparent this hadn't happened and the only reason he could think of was because the sheltering rock had given them enough cover to prevent the weapon's use. Their situation remained far from ideal.

"I've got plenty of red alerts across several major onboard systems," said Breeze.

"Will we hold together until we reach the *Juniper?*" asked Duggan.

"Probably."

There were times when it was best to summarise the possibilities with a single word and this was one of those times. "*Probably* is better than we had a few minutes ago," Duggan replied. He opened an internal comms channel. "Lieutenant Ortiz, please report."

"It got a bit bumpy down below, sir," she said with her

customary level of understatement. "We've been watching that big bastard of an alien warship on the screens down here. Witnessing things as they happen beats going to the movies, that's for sure."

Duggan had worked with Ortiz long enough to know she'd have given him news of casualties before anything else and her silence on the matter gave him an enormous feeling of relief. "We're going to the *Juniper*. ETA five days, as long as we don't break up first."

"It's that bad is it?"

"Yes, Lieutenant. When you see what the hull looks like, you're going to wonder how it held together."

"I never waste time thinking about how close to death I came, sir," she said. "It'll happen when it happens and there's nothing I can do to change it."

"That's a good philosophy."

"It's served me up until now."

"We'll catch up later."

"Right you are. The guys here reckon you did a good job. You and your crew."

Duggan smiled. "Thanks. I'll let everyone know."

As soon as he'd finished speaking to Ortiz, Lieutenant Breeze announced that things weren't going to plan.

"Sir, one of these alerts is on the life support system. It began as amber and now it's turned red."

It didn't seem likely that Breeze had mentioned it without specific reason. "How serious?" asked Duggan.

"I can't be sure – I've not seen this happen before. I've read enough about similar incidents to realise we're in a proper mess."

Duggan had a look and McGlashan also came over. They trawled through the failure warning logs for a time. Between them, they couldn't understand what the underlying cause was.

"The life support is degrading," said McGlashan.

"It might stabilise," said Breeze, scratching his head in thought.

"Want to take that gamble?"

"Nope."

"Nor me," said McGlashan.

That was enough for Duggan. "Where's the closest space port that can handle a fleet warship? Atlantis?"

"Yes, sir. If we change course, we'll be there in three days."

"Will that be soon enough?" asked McGlashan.

"It'll have to be. Please set us on a new course to Atlantis, Lieutenant."

"Atlantis it is."

The three days passed slowly. The life support system modules went offline one by one. The crew did their best to identify the problem and resolve it, to no avail. A warship had so much redundancy it was usually possible to re-route or simply use one of the many backup systems. Rarely – very rarely – a multiple hardware failure meant the only option was to dock and undergo a full programme of repairs. This was one of those times and it put the crew under stress while they waited to see if they would live or die. Duggan became impatient and irritable, whilst the others sank into themselves and made little attempt at conversation.

It wasn't only the failing life support system that they had to contend with – the warship had been badly damaged in numerous places and the last fusillade from the Dreamer mothership had opened two small breaches into the engines and damaged the *Lightning*'s structural integrity enough that it was in danger of breaking up. Hour-by-hour, one of the penetrations through the hull became wider and longer, exposing more of the engine mass beneath.

Oddly enough, the thing Duggan found most annoying was

the alarm light on the bridge - it refused to shut down and bathed the crew in depressing, red illumination. It was no danger, but its persistence was galling. Eventually, McGlashan stuck a metal tray from the food replicator over it. The red light remained visible, but it was less irritating than it had been.

"Where are we going to on Atlantis?" asked Breeze when the third day was almost over. It was like he had a superstition that forbade him from asking about a precise final destination when there was a danger they weren't going to make it.

"There's only one space port with the ability to refit us."

"Tillos?"

"That's the one. I'm sure Admiral Teron will want us on our way again as soon as we've been debriefed. There'll be a ship for us either on Atlantis or one they can get to us in a day or two."

"War on two fronts," said Chainer gloomily. "One front was bad enough."

"I'm itching to hear what's gone wrong with the peace negotiations," said Duggan. "We had it in the palm of our hands and it's gone."

"You sound like you're blaming the Confederation, sir," said McGlashan.

"I'm really not, Commander," he replied. "There's too much that's up in the air with what's happening between the Ghasts and the Dreamers. Too many unknowns for us to commit to peace without certain reassurances. I suppose I'm not too surprised. I'm disappointed, that's for sure."

"It probably didn't help when they shot all those Ghast soldiers during the mission to rescue us," said Breeze.

"This may be a stupid idea," began Chainer.

"It usually is when you start a sentence with those words," said McGlashan.

Chainer lifted his hand to indicate she should give him a

chance to speak. "If it were me at the negotiating table, I'd have told the Ghasts that we had doubts about them because we found their pyramid on Vempor and because we found creatures that looked exactly like Ghasts on Trasgor and Kidor when they had no reason to be there. Then I'd sit back in my chair and ask them to explain what the hell is going on." As if to demonstrate, Chainer leaned backwards in his seat and reached out for his cup of coffee.

"It's not that easy, Lieutenant," said Duggan. "If only it was. We've had to keep things in reserve, in case we gave up an advantage. We don't trust them and it seemed better to play our cards close to our chest. In the end, the Ghasts have resumed hostilities. In my mind that goes a long way towards justifying the way we've handled it."

"But we're at war again," said Breeze. "Whether or not it was justified, we're back to the fighting."

"I don't want it that way," said Duggan. "Sometimes all roads lead to the same place and you've got to try and reach the end in the best condition you can. We're at war, yet we retain the advantages we had when the truce started. We know where their planets are and they don't know the location of ours."

"If they're allied with the Dreamers. Hell, if they are the *same* species, it's not looking good for us," said Chainer.

"Same as it ever was," said Breeze, shrugging his broad shoulders. "We had a little break and off we go again."

"What do you think, sir?" asked McGlashan. "Are the Ghasts and the Dreamers the same thing?"

Duggan realised he hadn't taken the time to speak to the crew about it in any great detail. He had guesses, the same as they must have their own ideas. "We have no way to be sure," he said. "Assuming there is no alliance between the two species, which I think there is not, then there are only two possibilities. The first is that the Ghasts and Dreamers have somehow developed in ways that makes them physically identical. I can't see that being the case, which leaves the second possibility - that they are in fact one and the same species."

"With vastly different levels of technology and also a determination to kill each other," said Chainer.

"The Dreamers could have launched expedition forces hundreds or thousands of years ago. It's entirely possible one of these groups came so far that they lost touch with their home planet and set themselves up as an independent civilization. Their technology would have been the same as it was when they originally left their home world. Cut off from the resources of the others, they might have developed at a much slower rate and along different paths, leading to the situation we find today."

"Why are they trying to kill each other?" asked Breeze. "Instead of greeting each other with open arms, like long-lost family?"

"Maybe they have no idea who the other side is," said McGlashan. "They are both well-known for shooting first and asking questions later."

"I suppose it partially fits together," said Chainer. "It still doesn't answer the question about why the Ghasts got so jumpy when we found that pyramid on Trasgor."

"I don't have a fraction of the answers, let alone all of them," said Duggan. "If I see Nil-Far again, I'm going to put my foot on his neck and press down until I squeeze some answers out of him."

"Good luck with that, sir," said Chainer. "You might have to shoot him in the arms and legs before he'll give you the chance."

"If that's what it takes, Lieutenant."

They broke out of lightspeed three minutes earlier than expected. Atlantis came up on the screen – a tropical paradise of lush forests, deep blue oceans and a single military space port located on the Tillos salt flats.

"I don't think I've been here before," said McGlashan.

"It's a lovely place to come for a vacation," said Chainer. "I came a couple of times when I was a kid. I bet it's been spoiled now."

Duggan was sure it would be just as nice as Chainer remembered it. The Confederation had too many regulations to allow a planet to be ruined by industrial pollution. These rules and regulations had been introduced far too late to save a number of the earliest Confederation planets, but even the original Earth had been cleaned up and the air made safe to breathe.

With a building feeling of excitement, Duggan set a course towards the space port. The *ES Lightning* was down on power, even without the stealth modules activated. The sub-lights had taken only moderate damage, yet there was a persistent fault which drained off twelve percent of their output. Three days hadn't been enough to track down the cause and Duggan was sure the ship was going to be out of action for a considerable time.

"We've got someone from the ground on our comms," said Chainer. "A real person and he wants to speak to you, sir."

"Bring him through," said Duggan.

"*ES Lightning*, this is Tillos. We've been tracking you since you emerged from lightspeed travel. You're leaving a ten-thousand-klick trail of positrons behind you."

"We'll land vertically from fifty thousand klicks," said Duggan. "There'll only be a limited amount reaches the atmosphere."

"I can't permit you to land," said the man. He didn't refer to Duggan as *sir,* suggesting he was someone senior on the base.

"Who is this?"

"Colonel Jabran. I'm in charge of running the Tillos installation."

Colonel was a land-based rank and one of broadly equivalent

seniority to that held by Duggan. "I thought you were equipped to handle engine leaks, Colonel?"

"We are. I'm just not allowed to accept a warship outputting as much antimatter as yours at such short notice. The local Confederation Council members will shut us down."

"Damnit, we need to land!" said Duggan.

"Sorry, Captain. I can't give you clearance. And don't try giving us any surprises."

"I won't," said Duggan. He closed the channel. "We've come all this way and we're not permitted to land?"

"The *Juniper* is three days flight," said Breeze.

"Even if I thought the ship would hold together for that long, I don't think they have the facilities to fix us up," said Duggan angrily. "I have to speak to Admiral Teron as soon as possible about what we've found!" He shook his head in sudden realisation that he didn't need to wait until he reached the *Juniper* for that. "Get me the Admiral."

It only took a few seconds. "I've got him, sir. Does the man ever sleep?" asked Chainer.

"Don't ask me," said Duggan, before beckoning Chainer to bring Teron through.

"Captain Duggan?" asked Teron, his voice carrying an impatient edge.

"Sir, we've got news and a badly damaged warship. We need to land at Tillos."

"They've denied you permission?"

"We're leaking positrons, sir."

"Leave it with me," said Teron.

"He's gone," said Chainer.

"Doesn't hang around, does he?"

"Let us hope not," Duggan replied.

They weren't left waiting for long. Hardly five minutes had

passed when Colonel Jabran came onto the comms once more. "You have permission to land," he said stiffly.

"Thank you," said Duggan. He engaged the auto-pilot and leaned back while the ship's AI took them in towards the landing field.

CHAPTER FOURTEEN

THE TILLOS military base was larger than some and smaller than most. Atlantis was one of the more recently discovered worlds and though its population had boomed for a variety of reasons, the planet had never been assigned any great strategic importance. The salt flats were expansive and not in high demand for civilian purposes, therefore the Space Corps had been able to expand the base inefficiently. The main landing field covered twenty-five square kilometres and could only just accommodate a Hadron, though it was doubtful one had ever needed to spend significant time here.

"We've been given dock number one," said Chainer. "Look at the activity below."

He showed them the sensor feeds of dock one – it was a long, deep trench, the same as could be found at any other Space Corps base. The area around it writhed with activity as automated machines sped from their hangars, ready to commence repairs at once. Duggan had sent a damage report to the base mainframe and had received a response which asked he and the crew to remain aboard for the two hours it would take to squirt a temporary sealant into the hull breaches and thereby stop any antimatter pollution until a permanent fix could be implemented.

The ES *Lightning* thumped into place and the army of unmanned robots got to the task at once. Breeze watched, fascinated, but the rest of the crew kept themselves busy with other activities.

"They'll be done in ten minutes," said Breeze.

"Fine, let's get ready to disembark," Duggan replied. He stood and indicated to the others that they should follow. Chainer sent a message to the troops below and soon they were gathered in the airlock at the top of the front boarding ramp. The air smelled stale and impure.

"We're getting off just in time," said Ortiz.

"Looks like," said Duggan. "They nearly sent us away."

Ortiz rolled her eyes. "Wouldn't that have been just great?"

Duggan had given the Tillos mainframe control of the ES *Lightning*. The base computer was evidently satisfied that repairs had progressed sufficiently to permit the crew to exit, and the boarding ramp shuddered open with a screech of warped metal. Bright white light and stifling heat roiled inside.

"Just like being back on Vempor," muttered Chainer. "It'll be good to have a proper bath again."

"Maybe treat yourself to a shave," said someone in the crowd. There were a few chuckles at that – Chainer constantly broke Space Corps rules by sporting plenty of stubble on his face, which he occasionally let sprout into a full beard. He'd been reprimanded a few times without any appreciable change in his behaviour.

When the ramp had locked into its down position, they left the vessel. Duggan was forced to wait a few minutes in order to sign over the ES *Lightning* and then he made his way to the nearest lift. The interior of the lift was mercifully cold and it whirred as it carried him the three hundred metres to the top of the trench. He stepped out onto the reinforced concrete ground, blinking in the bright sunlight. The heat intensified the smells and his nose picked up the cloying scent of melted rubber, along with the tang of molten alloys. Ten or twelve repair bots hovered at various places along the length of the ES *Lightning*, sparks crackling from their welders. McGlashan, Chainer and Breeze waited here, looking over the damaged warship.

"I'm surprised it lasted long enough to get us here," said Breeze.

"I don't want to think about it too much," said Chainer. "I've seen enough to realise we shouldn't have come out of that alive."

"I thought you'd had a good view of the hull through the sensors?"

"That's right, Commander. Sometimes you need to see it in the flesh, so to speak."

Duggan ran his gaze over the part of the vessel which was visible. It didn't look too much like a warship anymore - it looked like a vaguely wedge-shaped piece of metal which had been picked up and smashed off a hard surface many times. There were dents and splits in the exterior. In other areas, the armour had melted and reformed imperfectly. There was nothing left of the original, sleek lines.

"Will it return to service?" asked Breeze.

"Maybe. I doubt it," answered Duggan truthfully.

"Think they can get the stealth modules out intact?" asked McGlashan.

"They should have the expertise, if not the experience," said Breeze.

"I'm sure the hardware on the *Lightning* isn't unique," said Duggan. "We were the ones doing the testing, but they'll have several more pre-built examples ready to install as soon as the decision is made to do so."

"I don't want to look at it. I'll catch up with you later," said

Chainer, heading towards a row of cars. Moments later, he was on his way towards the main building on the base, located a few minutes' drive away.

"It's not like him to be upset," said McGlashan.

"I'll have a word with him later," said Duggan, also worried at this shift in Chainer's mood. "Do you know where you're going?"

"I'm hitching a ride with you, sir," said McGlashan.

"Me too."

"Come on, then."

Duggan climbed into one of the vehicles. It was the same as the thousands of others used by the Space Corps – a cheap, rugged and reliable mode of transport that could seat eight people and ferry them slowly to their destination. At least the air conditioning in this one had been recently serviced and it blew out such a powerful, icy draught that Duggan had to turn it down after a couple of minutes.

"What happens next?" asked Breeze.

"I'm not sure of the specifics. One thing I'm certain of is that there'll be no time to get comfortable. We'll be assigned something new as soon as they can get a warship out here."

"There's an Anderlecht in trench three," said Breeze.

"It's been given to another officer," said Duggan. "It's due to depart in less than twelve hours. If we're onboard, we'll be passengers rather than crew."

They arrived at the base headquarters. This particular building showed more artistic flair than most other Space Corps structures, with its arched windows and pillars flanking the main doorway. It looked uncomfortable with itself, as though it had been designed by several different people at odds with each other. Once the fripperies were removed, it was nothing more than a square, five-storey building designed to hold several thousand members of the Space Corps administrative staff.

The lobby area was large and welcoming, with a tiled floor,

furniture and even a few artificial trees. People hurried about, showing just the right amount of activity for the place to appear purposeful without being overcrowded.

"See you soon," Duggan promised, as the three parted ways.

He presented himself at the main greeting desk. A smartly-dressed lady smiled at him with veiled disinterest. Duggan's arrival hadn't been scheduled, so there was a short delay while a suitable office was located for him. The Space Corps had increased its personnel numbers faster than it had built new places to contain them, so Duggan ended up in a small office on the top floor which looked as though it hadn't seen a decorator's brush for at least twenty years. He wasn't a man who demanded a status office, so he accepted what he'd been given without complaint.

His seat was given no chance to become warm from his sitting. With a squawking buzz, Duggan's desk communicator let him know there was someone who wanted to speak to him. He answered and a gentleman from reception spoke.

"Captain Duggan, you're required in Meeting Room 73 for a video conference. I was told to let you know you must go there immediately." The man sounded nervous when he delivered this instruction. "It's on the third floor, quadrant E."

"Who will I be speaking to?"

The receptionist cleared his throat. "I don't know, sir. The message came through a reserved channel, so it must be someone important."

"Very well," said Duggan. "Thank you."

"No problem, sir."

Duggan left immediately. The meeting room wasn't difficult to locate, owing to the fact that it was clearly marked. The signage was usually excellent within Space Corps buildings, since the corridors were otherwise completely indistinguishable from one another. There were terminals located here and there, but you could never find one on the rare occasions you became lost.

When Duggan arrived, the former occupants were filing out. They were smartly dressed, though their level of seniority was unclear. He overheard one or two complaining loudly about the interruption to their meeting which they'd arranged more than a week prior, and from this Duggan deduced that they'd been told to leave by a very senior officer at very short notice. One or two looked at Duggan askance, as if they considered him to blame for this minor inconvenience.

Duggan entered the room and found a woman shuffling some papers into a semblance of order. He stared at her until she got the hint. She scooped up the papers and left at once. When the door had slid shut behind her, Duggan took one of the seats. He didn't even register the fact that this meeting room could have existed on any Space Corps base throughout the entire Confederation and it would have looked identical.

There was a video screen, covering most of one magnolia-painted wall. The receiver unit pinged to let Duggan know there was someone waiting at the other end. He pressed the button to accept the video stream and sat upright, waiting for the image of Fleet Admiral Teron to appear.

To his surprise, it wasn't Teron's face he saw. The view through the screen showed him a dimly-lit office. It was well-appointed in dark woods and leather. Three men sat at a round table, positioned so they could face the screen. They were dressed in identical grey suits and were of approximately the same age – early fifties, Duggan guessed. There was nothing remarkable about their physical appearance – they were three normal-looking men sitting in the office of someone important. Duggan checked to see if the video stream included information about their location. It did not.

"Captain John Duggan," said the man to the left. His eyes gleamed with a calculating intelligence.

"Who are you?" asked Duggan. He didn't see the need to be polite since the other party had chosen not to introduce himself.

The man smiled thinly. "I am Director Russell. You may not have heard of me. I work for Military Asset Management. These with me are Director Jordan and Deputy Director Lane."

Duggan knew at once which way the conversation would go. He experienced a cold anger, which came from nowhere and it was all he could do to keep his expression neutral. These were powerful men and they would have powerful friends. "What do you want?" he asked.

"An associate of ours – Director Nichols - served under you recently. He was assigned the rank of Lieutenant."

Duggan's mind raced. It looked as if Nichols had been a senior man indeed. And now here were his friends, come looking for answers. He didn't see a need to speak and waited for the man to proceed. He was duly obliged.

"We would like to ask you some questions, regarding the circumstances surrounding the death of Director Nichols."

"I'm not at liberty to speak about matters which occurred during Space Corps business," said Duggan. "I have filed my report and it is with my superiors. It is they you will need to speak with."

"You have nothing to say?" asked the second man, leaning forward intently. "This may well become a criminal matter, Captain Duggan. You would do well to talk to us."

Duggan couldn't help but laugh. "Criminal matter? The Space Corps deals internally with its own affairs. The civil courts hold no sway. If there were a case to answer, my superiors would have told me." He shook his head in disbelief. "What exactly did you hope to achieve with this? I'm not a man to be bullied, nor frightened by a suggestion of threats! Please, do not waste any more of my time. Lieutenant Nichols lost his life on active duty - he was one of a number to do so. That is the risk every one of the Corps' soldiers takes when he or she signs up."

The three men exchanged looks, though no obvious communication took place between them. The first man spoke again. "Thank you for your time, Captain Duggan. Rest assured this won't go away. We will follow every available avenue to get the answers we seek."

"It sounds to me as if you're searching for the answers you want, not the truth."

"As you will, Captain Duggan." The man nodded his head slightly and there was the faintest hint of a smile on his face. The screen went blank, leaving Duggan alone in the room.

CHAPTER FIFTEEN

DUGGAN WASN'T ENTIRELY sure what to make of the events which had just taken place. He was bemused, rather than cowed by his conversation with the directors from Military Asset Management. He wasn't sure if they'd attempted to strong-arm him or if they'd thought they were being subtle. Since he was left without a clear idea of their intent, he assumed they weren't very good at making threats. A second inner voice suggested these men were likely to be seriously competent if they'd got to the positions they were in, therefore it might be Duggan himself who lacked the capacity to understand the significance. He gave a mental shrug – he knew he'd done nothing wrong and his report to Admiral Teron contained everything necessary to prove as much.

He arrived at his office to find the desk communicator buzzing. With a sigh, he answered the call. This time, the familiar voice of Admiral Teron came through.

"Captain Duggan? Apologies it's taken so long - you can appreciate I'm busy. Time is short and I have less than an hour for a debriefing. Someone at the Tillos reception desk has squeezed in a booking at Meeting Room 73. I'll speak to you there in five minutes."

"Is it imperative we have a video stream, sir? Can't we speak now, while I'm in my office?"

"I can't stand doing business by voice only. I need to see who it is I'm speaking to."

Duggan left his office again, retracing his steps towards the meeting room. He got there in time to find a cluster of junior officers outside the door, milling in confusion.

"Cancelled, you say?" said one.

"Some idiot's overridden the system and booked the room out from under us," said another.

"What a waste of our time! I'm going to put in a complaint – I'm sick of this shit happening."

Duggan chuckled to himself as he walked through the middle of the pack. They recognized his uniform and fell into a distinctly uncomfortable silence. The incident hadn't remotely bothered Duggan but it did serve as a reminder of how little he enjoyed working in an office. There were too many petty rivalries and politics for him to put up with. Moments later, he was in the same chair, looking at the same screen. On this occasion, it was Admiral Teron to whom he spoke. The Admiral was in his office on the *Juniper*, which was clearly his favoured place from which to operate.

"Let's get your debriefing out of the way quickly. Afterwards, I have bad news to tell you – exceptionally bad," said Teron. He cleared his throat. "So, the stealth modules continue to outperform expectations?"

Duggan didn't like the sound of what Teron was going to tell him. He didn't think about it for the moment – the Admiral liked his meetings to be conducted in a controlled, pre-ordered fashion and Duggan wasn't about to try and disrupt things. "I don't know what expectations you had personally, sir, however they *substan-*

tially outperformed mine. The Dreamer mothership is packing enough advanced weaponry to knock out our whole fleet, yet they couldn't pinpoint our location. How go the plans to install the technology on some of our more potent warships?"

"We'll get onto that in due course. I'm pleased at the results of your testing – very pleased, as it happens. I've ramped up the funding five-fold. There are still a number of technical hurdles which we can't buy our way over. Money doesn't solve everything, but it's better to have it than not."

"From what I've witnessed of our enemy's behaviour, I've concluded they are an expeditionary force to gather materials as well as to prepare a number of worlds for their longer-term plans to populate this area of space."

"It's interesting to discover how much destruction is necessary to obtain their obsidian power sources," said Teron.

"Perhaps they have less overt methods available to them elsewhere," said Duggan. "The mothership likely has a series of goals to accomplish and the enemy are completing them in the most practical way available to them."

"Very diplomatic," said Teron wryly. "I don't care how they do it back home, it's what they're doing here that worries me."

"And me, sir."

"The negative side is that it illustrates how this potential power source is unobtainable to us. We could crack open a few planets, but we lack the dedicated spacecraft to gather the material. Aside from that, we lack the knowledge on which planets are suitable to destroy. Finally, we are currently unable to harness the power source itself. We know its potential, without being capable of putting it to use."

"How long until we can overcome these obstacles?"

"Five years? Ten? I guess it depends on where we focus our efforts. I don't need to tell you that our efforts are presently directed towards the mess with the Ghasts."

"What's happened?"

Teron meshed his fingers together and appeared to be gathering himself. "They've accused us of destroying Vempor."

The news was every bit as bad as promised. Duggan had no immediate and coherent response, though his mouth insisted on speaking. "What?" he asked.

"They've accused us of wiping out their home world," repeated Teron grimly.

"We haven't, have we?"

"We've done nothing of the sort, John."

"Has it definitely been destroyed?"

"That's what we're trying to verify. Vempor is a long, long way from Confederation space and it's proving difficult to corroborate. I have no idea why the hell they'd lie about it. If they wanted war, they just needed to start shooting at us."

Duggan had to ask the question. "Could it have happened without you knowing, sir?"

Teron didn't take it as an insult. "No, it could not. The Space Corps is surprisingly united, though you might think otherwise if you were to read the news reports. We have no loose cannons with the authority to accomplish this as well as keep it hidden. Besides, I've run a thorough audit of all resources which would be required to perform such a feat. The Planet Breaker hasn't moved from the research lab and the *Crimson* is...elsewhere."

"How did it happen? Could a rogue captain have launched a surprise nuclear attack?"

"We've not had a ship anywhere near Vempor since we sent you in the *Ransor-D*. I have assured myself that the alleged destruction of their planet has not come from us. Anyway, they accuse us of *shattering* the planet. Ten thousand of our largest nuclear warheads wouldn't accomplish that. Our conventional weapons would leave them with an irradiated wasteland, but they couldn't break the planet apart."

"If we didn't do it and the Ghasts aren't lying to us, there's only one realistic option remaining," said Duggan.

Teron pushed a brown folder across his desk, as if Duggan could somehow read the contents through the video screen. "It's all in there."

"It surely didn't take a statistical analysis of probabilities to conclude the Dreamers are the culprits?" said Duggan.

"If we accept it as fact, we're left in a position where we're at war with the Ghasts because of their suspected alliance with the Dreamers. Only their supposed allies have now allegedly destroyed Vempor."

"There are a lot of maybes to contend with."

"We need confirmation that Vempor is destroyed. Then we can act decisively without risk of burning our bridges."

"How long until we know?"

"We have Monitoring Station Beta scrutinising that area of space. The distance involved means their mainframe has its work cut out to analyse the data."

"Couldn't we just fly another ship there?"

"We have one on its way. We anticipate a quicker response from Monitoring Station Beta."

Duggan wasn't a man who always followed his hunches. On this occasion he was sure the Dreamers were responsible for destroying Vempor. "How did the mothership manage to fire from such a range?" he asked. "How did they know to aim?"

"Do you know it was the mothership?" asked Teron.

The question stopped Duggan in his tracks. "It seemed the most logical option. It was close by when Corai was shattered. I've gone with the assumption they're carrying a more advanced version of the *Crimson*'s Planet Breaker. Maybe they have enough power to use it at a far greater range."

"I have another idea," said Teron. "I've got people working on confirmation, but I'm halfway convinced I'm correct."

Duggan wasn't sure what Teron had come up with. When he thought about it, he realised there were so few variables, the only other option was an obvious one. "The pyramids?" he asked.

"It could be," said Teron. "We've assumed them to be nothing more than glorified oxygen generators. What if they can also function as a weapon?"

"That doesn't explain how they knew where to fire, sir."

"Perhaps it does. What if these alien artefacts are linked together in such a way that they are capable of detecting the others? What if the Dreamers came through the wormhole to look for their missing pyramid?"

"Why destroy it, then?"

"That's what we don't know. As it stands, we're in a position of even greater uncertainty. The Ghasts blame us for the loss of their world, while the Dreamers pursue expansion. I would much rather be facing only one of these foes."

"What does the Confederation Council plan?"

Teron curled his lip. "They plan to bicker and argue until we are ruined!" he said. "It was impossible for them to come up with a suitable plan when we were only fighting the Ghasts. Now we are facing two enemies, it is as though the Council are frozen like statues. Whilst they fight over which filling to have in their sandwiches, a number of different factions are attempting to grab power for themselves!"

Duggan had never seen Teron so animated, nor display such overt anger. "Is our funding safe?" he asked, bringing the Admiral back onto firmer ground.

"For the moment. I also find myself with a short window of opportunity in which I can act unmolested. If I can't unearth the truth of what's happening, I dread to think what the Council will decide in the absence of proven facts."

"Reading between the lines, I take it you are planning to refrain from military action against the Ghasts?" said Duggan.

"You could always read a situation as well as anyone, Captain Duggan. That's exactly what I'm going to do. Our spacecraft are on high alert, but I have instructed them to avoid conflict wherever possible. If that means they run from a fight, so be it. I am coming around to the belief that the Ghasts have been completely honest during the peace negotiations."

"You are not a man to sit back and wait," said Duggan.

Teron laughed gruffly at being found out so easily. "I like to explore many options in parallel," he said. "I'm sending you on a mission to speak to someone on my behalf."

"A Ghast?"

"Yes – I've been dealing with him during the negotiations. I've spoken to him directly since the declaration of war and he wishes to meet."

"What does he want?"

"I don't know. The Ghasts put great store in face-to-face communication – we learned that very quickly. If they feel it's something important, they won't accept anything other than everyone being in the same room."

"They'll deal with me? I'm not known for my skills in negotiation."

Teron laughed again. "I can't send anyone else, John. This is strictly off the record. If it goes wrong, there'll be nothing I can do to help you. Gol-Tur knows I'm not coming – you'll need to try and impress him. They're stubborn bastards, the Ghasts."

Duggan shrugged. "I'll do what I can to help fix this mess. Could it be a trap?"

"There's a chance. I can't see what they'd have to gain by it. Either way, I'm not going to commit significant metal to it."

"I shouldn't need guns if I'm there to talk."

"I'd prefer to provide you with them nonetheless. Unfortunately, you'll be going in one of our Anderlechts."

"I thought the Ghasts liked to see demonstrations of strength?"

"Gol-Tur is old and he's not stupid enough to be impressed by fleets of warships." Teron smiled. "That's what he told me."

"When am I going?"

"As soon as you leave the room. There's an Anderlecht in one of the trenches at Tillos and I've acquired it. Everything will be in place before you can find a car to take you there. I'll send over a detailed set of instructions for you to read in flight."

"Understood."

"If you get back from this, there might be a surprise waiting for you, Captain Duggan. A surprise you will love and a mission you will hate."

"No point in me asking what that means?"

"None."

The meeting had reached its conclusion. Outside, someone knocked impatiently on the door to indicate the next meeting was due to begin. Duggan rose to leave and then stopped. He wasn't sure what gave him the idea, but as soon as the thought appeared, it latched on and wouldn't let go.

"Sir?"

Teron looked distracted, like he'd already switched over to the next item on his never-ending schedule of business. "What is it?"

"There's Gallenium on Atlantis, isn't there?"

"I believe so – very little which is easy for us to extract. Why?"

"The Dreamers must have a way of finding the stuff. A way that isn't random."

Teron gave Duggan his full attention. "You think they might come here for it?"

"It would explain the anomaly the stats guys uncovered."

"I'll look into it," said Teron. He looked worried and Duggan was certain the Admiral would put other matters aside until he'd checked out the possibilities.

Duggan left the room, elbowing his way through the group of attendees waiting outside the meeting room. They tutted and stared but Duggan didn't even notice.

CHAPTER SIXTEEN

"IT'S CALLED THE *ES* PROXIMAL," said Chainer.

Duggan steered the hovercar between two slow-moving cranes and pointed them towards their destination. It was early evening and the light was fading. The warship they'd seen in trench three when they'd landed at Tillos was still in the same place. Its hull was scarred and the protective lacquer had long since been scoured away, leaving the alloy armour a dull, unreflective grey. The Proximal was one of many such warships in the Space Corps – an ageing and unmodified workhorse, gradually drifting into obsolescence. It was all relative, of course - the warship packed enough weaponry to destroy a dozen large cities. Thirty years ago, it would have given a Cadaveron a run for its money. As technology had moved on, these older vessels of the fleet had been left behind. The basic design remained sound and eventually it would likely be re-fitted with newer, better weaponry. Until that day came, it had little significance as a front-line warship.

"I think I preferred the *Rampage*," said Breeze.

"It was definitely a bit more impressive."

"If we have to fire the weapons, we've failed the mission," said Duggan.

"One of *those* missions, is it?" asked Chainer. "And you're not going to trust us with the gory details until we've hit lightspeed, are you?"

"Got it in one," said Duggan, keeping his eyes ahead.

"Should I update my will before we take off?" asked Chainer.

"I check mine every time we land," joked Breeze.

"If you've got anything to leave behind, they're paying you too much," said Duggan.

"Having kids is what eats up the salary," said Breeze. "I've got three of them and they're always hungry."

"I thought you lost custody fifteen years ago?" said Chainer.

"Yeah. It was my wife I fell out with, not my children. I couldn't see them going without. When I die, I'll leave a tiny house and a bank account with a few dollars."

"No regrets?" asked McGlashan.

"I'd be a fool if I said I didn't. I've got no more regrets than any other man. And my children think their old dad is doing something worthwhile."

"Maybe I need to find someone and have a few kids," said Chainer. "It sounds like fun."

Breeze shook his head in mock disbelief. "You keep telling yourself that, Frank. Besides, I hear that too much hi-stim affects a man's ability to father children."

"Really?"

"Yes, really."

Breeze was a master at keeping a straight face and he didn't flinch under Chainer's stare. "I have no idea if I believe you or not."

"As you wish."

Duggan was happy to tolerate conversation amongst his crew, though he rarely took part in the small talk. As the hovercar travelled silently over the Tillos airfield, he wondered if it was time he opened up a bit more. The crew knew when it was time to behave and he didn't often need to step in and remind them. He asked himself what would happen when the war was over – would he see them again, or would he let them drift away until all that remained were memories? *Am I stupid enough to let it happen?* It was becoming increasingly apparent that he was being tested for promotion, hence Admiral Teron giving him a lot of personal attention. *Can a man have friends and family while he remains committed to his duty? I should speak to Lucy.*

They arrived and Duggan left the car parked up near to one of the lifts which served trench three. The upper half of the Proximal towered over them, extending for a kilometre to both left and right. The four of them descended in the lift and then climbed the central boarding ramp to enter the vessel. McGlashan did a quick check on one of the wall consoles.

"Empty apart from us. Were you expecting troops?"

"I don't know what I was expecting," said Duggan. "I was pretty much told to go and get us on our way."

"I can't believe they couldn't find a few soldiers at such short notice," she said. The Space Corps respected its soldiers, but would happily send them out on even the highest-risk missions – that's what they were for. It was unusual to find the warship empty. Then, there were footsteps behind – many footsteps.

"Lieutenant Ortiz reporting for duty, sir."

Duggan turned to find her standing in front of a contingent of armed men and women. They were grim-faced and Duggan recognized a few of their faces.

"Glad to see you, Lieutenant. Is this everyone?"

"This is who I was instructed to bring, sir. Forty-three of us in total."

"Less than a full complement," said McGlashan.

"Every one of us fights like four, sir," said Ortiz, producing a salute so crisp it would have made her old drill instructor weep tears of happiness.

"Welcome aboard," said Duggan in a loud voice. "Get to your quarters at once. We're leaving in less than fifteen minutes."

"Move it!" shouted Ortiz. "Captain Duggan does *not* like to hang around!"

There were two exits from the airlock. Ortiz took her troops through one, while Duggan and the crew left through the other. The interior of an Anderlecht was rather more spacious than that of a Vincent class, which wasn't to say it was spacious as such. The corridors were as wide as one-and-a-half persons, making it easy to pass, but impossible to walk shoulder to shoulder. The bridge was appreciably larger and this one had seating for eight. Automation advances combined with an experienced crew meant that four was sufficient to operate an Anderlecht at more or less peak efficiency. If Lieutenants Massey or Reyes had been available, Duggan would have brought them along. In their absence, he felt that a new face would have resulted in more disruption to outweigh the benefits they'd have brought. This wasn't cynicism on Duggan's part and there was neither pride, nor stubbornness involved in the decision.

The Proximal's engines were powered up and ready to go. The crew spent several minutes running through a number of top-level checks to test for anything obvious the maintenance teams had overlooked. As usual, they'd done a thorough job and everything was in order.

"Admiral Teron promised clearance. Do we have it?" asked Duggan.

"Yes, sir. They've emptied the area around the trench and we can go whenever we're ready."

"No time like the present," said Duggan. He tapped in a command to start up the autopilot. Seconds later, the Anderlecht rose clear of its dock, producing minimal turbulence. As it climbed, the autopilot increased the power and the warship accelerated at an ever-increasing pace.

"Have you got the coordinates?" asked Duggan.

"Yes sir. This is going to be a long trip."

"I expected as much," said Duggan. "How long?"

"Ten days. It's outside Confederation space – sort of mid-way between the Helius Blackstar and the closest of the Ghast worlds."

"We can't get halfway in ten days!" said Chainer. "Not in this old thing."

"I tried to boil it down to a few words that would let you grasp the general direction we're heading," said Breeze.

"Initiate lightspeed when you've finished your conversation," said Duggan.

"Aye, sir!" said Breeze at once.

A minute later and they were away. The Proximal winked off the Tillos sensors and vanished into the depths of space.

"Dead on Light-H," said Breeze. "Nothing unexpected and no secret modifications to the engines to give us some extra speed."

"I'm disappointed," said McGlashan. "I was getting used to Admiral Teron springing new tech on us."

"Give me a run-down of our armaments," said Duggan. He was forced to concede that he was also disappointed. The thrill of the new never left him.

"Ten Lambda batteries, six Bulwarks," she replied. "Bang on normal. Our shock drones are two generations out of date and we're carrying no nukes."

"We'll get the shit kicked out of us if we fly into any trouble," said Chainer.

"It would be nice to be assigned a ship and be able to stick with it," said Breeze. "Preferably something better than the Proximal."

"Just two years ago we were happy with the Detriment," said Duggan.

"We only thought we were happy," said Chainer. "My eye is easily turned. I want the *Crimson* back."

"It'll be stuck in a dock somewhere with its weapons and core stripped out and a swarm of technicians shoving their diagnostics equipment where it's not welcome," said McGlashan.

"Do you think it'll fly again, sir?" asked Breeze.

Duggan recalled Teron's passing comment about the *Crimson* being elsewhere. There'd been no chance to think about it since, but there was something in how the Admiral had spoken which made Duggan think there were no plans to dismantle that particular spacecraft.

"It'll fly," he said.

"He knows something," said McGlashan.

"Not so," said Duggan. "Call it an educated guess."

"I can see this line of questioning isn't going anywhere. Can you tell us where we're heading instead?" asked McGlashan.

"I've been asked to negotiate with the Ghasts," said Duggan. "If any of you laughs at the notion, I'll have you tied to a Lambda and fired into space."

"I wouldn't dream of laughing, sir," said Chainer with an admirably neutral expression. "Why are we negotiating, instead of fighting? Not that I mind, you understand."

"There's a good chance this is a misunderstanding. The Ghasts have lost Vempor."

"Lost? As in destroyed?"

"Yes. They've quite naturally blamed us, since we've done it to them before."

"After they provoked us!" said Chainer.

"That's not quite the point. We haven't attacked Vempor and the only possibility remaining is an attack by the Dreamers."

"The mothership was weeks away from Vempor when we saw it!" said Chainer.

"We think it's something to do with the pyramids the Dreamers have been leaving behind. They could be using them as weapons."

"Do we have any idea how many of those things there are?" asked McGlashan.

"None whatsoever. The mothership could conceivably hold a good number, as well as those warships that keep appearing where we don't want them."

Duggan filled them in on the details. They had many questions and he had few answers to offer in return. The conversation eventually ran dry and the crew returned to their duties, whilst Chainer took himself off for some sleep. The thrumming of the air conditioning and the scent of electricity made Duggan feel like he was home once more. After a time, it threatened to lull him into somnolence, so he headed away from the bridge, with no particular goal in mind other than to kill some time.

CHAPTER SEVENTEEN

TEN DAYS LATER, they arrived. The *ES* Proximal shuddered slightly under the deceleration as its mainframe switched across to the gravity engines. The life support systems shielded the crew from the effects and they hardly registered any physical symptoms from what had occurred.

"Anything out there?"

"I'll tell you shortly," said Chainer. "There's definitely nothing close by."

"Are we early?" muttered Duggan to himself, knowing there hadn't been a specified time for the meeting to take place – only an agreement for it to happen here as soon as possible. He had a quick check through the sensor feeds. They were in the middle of nowhere, many days sub-light travel from the closest solar system.

"Void, void and more void," said Chainer.

"The perfect place for a secret rendezvous," said McGlashan.

"Am I allowed to let the *Juniper* know we're here?" asked Chainer.

"Hold off for the moment, please," said Duggan.

"I hope it won't be long," said McGlashan. "I've had enough of waiting."

Duggan couldn't recall McGlashan ever showing much in the way of impatience, so assumed the trip had really dragged for her. "We don't know where Gol-Tur is coming from, nor what sort of ship he's in."

"It'll be bigger than this one," said Chainer. "We're always outgunned."

Duggan opened his mouth to speak, but was cut off by an urgent exclamation from Breeze.

"Fission signature! Right on top of us!"

Duggan swore. "How close?"

He was provided with an answer before he could give any thought to evasive action. Without further warning, forty billion tonnes of Ghost battleship appeared next to the Proximal, heading on a collision course. Duggan tried frantically to pull the Anderlecht away. He would have been much too slow, except that whoever was piloting the Oblivion realised the danger and brought the warship to a halt, a scant eight kilometres distant. The shock of what had happened didn't shut Chainer up for long.

"In all my years in the Space Corps, I can say with absolute certainty I have never had that happen to me."

Duggan's heart was pounding, not so much at the threat of an unexpected death narrowly avoided, but at the idea that fate could have finished this mission so easily. If the Proximal had been destroyed, Admiral Teron could only draw one realistic conclusion about what had happened. He looked at the starboard sensor feed – the display with filled with kilometres of cold, deadly battleship. It utterly dwarfed the Proximal and outgunned it dozens of times over.

"Hail them," he said.

"Too late, they're hailing *us*. It's Subjos Gol-Tur from the Oblivion class *Trivanor*."

"Subjos?" mused Duggan. "How senior is someone with that title?"

"Could be a limitation of the translation module," said Chainer. "It should have provided a best-guess approximation."

"I've run a check," said McGlashan. "Whoever Gol-Tur is, he's *very* high up in the Ghast command."

"Good. Someone who can make decisions."

"They're waiting, sir," said Chainer. "Would you like me to bring him through?"

"Yes please. On the bridge speakers."

When the Ghast spoke, there was a rough edge to his voice. He sounded different to Nil-Far and the age was unmistakable.

"Captain John Nathan Duggan," he stated. "I have heard your name, destroyer of Lioxi." It was unclear if there was judgement in the words – the Ghasts were not the same as humans and it was difficult to be sure how they viewed events around them.

"Fleet Admiral Teron has sent me to speak with you."

"Yes. I see your spaceship has a shuttle. I will send you the codes for our aft docking bay and will speak to you as soon as you arrive."

"Agreed," said Duggan.

"He's left the channel," said Chainer.

"They don't piss around much, these Ghasts," said Breeze.

"Just how I like it," growled Duggan. "Commander McGlashan, you have control of the Proximal. I'm leaving immediately."

"Sir," she said in acknowledgement.

"This is what we've come for. Wish me luck," said Duggan, heading out through the bridge doorway. If there was a response, he didn't hear it.

Not all Anderlechts were equipped with a shuttle. The Proximal was once such craft, which was presumably why Teron had decided it was suitable for this mission. The transport was a cramped, archaic model with a stale smell to the interior. One of the lights in the cockpit flickered incessantly and there was an unknown, sticky green substance on one of the control bars. Duggan didn't like to think what it was and wiped it away with a cloth someone had left on the floor. Everything about the Proximal pointed to slow decline, in sharp contrast to the activities taking place elsewhere across the Space Corps.

In minutes, the shuttle had broken away from its docking clamps. Duggan let the autopilot do the work for him on this occasion. He wasn't in the mood to fly the thing himself. The *Trivanor*'s pilots had set the battleship on a parallel course to the Proximal and at a very low speed. There was no way the shuttle would be able to pass safely between the two if they were travelling quickly. The cockpit was fitted with a large display which had been designed to look like a windscreen. Duggan stared out gloomily – the *Trivanor* looked even newer than the *Dretisear*. Any hope the Ghasts had slowed the pace of their shipbuilding was clearly misguided.

"Everything okay, sir?" asked McGlashan. Her voice sounded tinny through the wall speaker.

"It's good so far. The *Trivanor* is impressive."

"Better than anything we've got, so try not to piss them off too much."

Duggan laughed. "I'll do my best."

"What are you expecting to get from this?"

"Admiral Teron didn't know and I'm sure I don't know either. Both sides are talking and that's a good enough start."

The tiny computer on the shuttle followed its pre-programmed course down to the millimetre. A blue-illuminated docking bay came into view, a tiny square on the vast flank of the *Trivanor*. There was more than enough space for the transport to set down easily and it landed on the solid floor in the bay. The outer door slid shut. Duggan sat for a moment, wondering how he would know when it was safe to disembark. The light didn't change and there were no display screens along the bay walls. The shuttle sensors informed him of a change in pressure outside, but it wasn't safe enough for him to leave yet. He was just about to open a comms channel to the *Trivanor*'s bridge, when a Ghast voice pre-empted him.

"Captain Duggan, you may leave your vessel."

He didn't speak in response. The shuttle sensors confirmed there was a breathable atmosphere outside, so he left the tiny cockpit and triggered the release for the exit door. The door opened outwards with a faint hiss. At the bottom and to one side, two Ghasts waited, dressed in grey. They weren't carrying any weapons – presumably Gol-Tur wasn't concerned at the idea of having a lone human running loose around the battleship if Duggan was stupid enough to attempt sabotage.

"Come," said the first, indicating a direction with a sweep of his hand – it was one of many human-like gestures the Ghasts possessed.

The interior of the *Trivanor* was hardly any different from Duggan's memory of the *Ghotesh-Q*, which he'd been aboard briefly a few months previously. He was taken along a wide, well-lit corridor, with consoles attached to the walls at regular intervals. There were other Ghasts present – they attended the consoles or they walked purposefully towards whatever destination they'd been given. Duggan's escort didn't greet their fellow crew, nor did they speak to each other. They knew exactly where they were headed and they turned left and right along a series of corridors. Duggan wasn't fooled by the changes of direction – it was easy to tell that the battleship's interior was compact. Older Ghast warships had a lot of wasted space. The *Trivanor* had nothing spare, freeing up room for engines and weapons.

Without there being an extensive change in his surroundings, Duggan became aware they'd entered a new area of the warship. The walls and floors were still unadorned, but the doors were a different colour – blue instead of grey. It was also quieter and there were fewer signs of the crew. Duggan's escort stopped outside one of the doors. There was a series of symbols painted on the surface in black, the meaning of which was unclear. Neither of the two Ghasts did anything so crude as knock. In fact, they made no attempt whatsoever at communication with the occupant. Nevertheless, the door slid aside without a murmur.

"Inside," said one of the Ghasts, motioning with his hand.

Duggan stepped between them and crossed the threshold without fear. His overriding emotions were excitement and anticipation. The door closed behind and he looked around the room. The lighting was as blue as the rest of the warship, but here there were signs of a humanlike desire to make a home away from home. The room was square, with walls twenty feet long and a covering of hard, blue tiles on the floor. Screens covered two walls, displaying status readouts for the ship. To Duggan's surprise, there was a plant in one corner of an unfamiliar type. It was tall, blue-tinged and spindly. The plant looked unmistakeably well cared-for. His shock was doubled when he noted the presence of wood – the first he'd seen amongst the Ghasts. There was a dark wood desk, large and square, with two unoccupied chairs on the nearest side. The chairs didn't look any more comfortable than the other Ghast furniture.

Sitting at the far side of the desk was a Ghast. It was a male – Duggan couldn't recall ever seeing a female – and he stared at Duggan with piercing eyes. This Ghast looked much like all the others Duggan had seen, talked with or fought, except this one was clearly very old. Lines spread across the skin of his cheeks like fractures left in stone from a spacecraft's landing.

"Captain John Duggan. I am Subjos Gol-Tur. We will talk."

Duggan had learned not to wait for an invitation to sit. He pulled one of the two spare chairs into position, trying not to show the effort it cost to do so. He lowered himself into it, finding it as unsuitable for sitting as he'd expected.

"Subjos Gol-Tur," he acknowledged. "There are many things to discuss."

CHAPTER EIGHTEEN

GOL-TUR DIDN'T BEAT around the bush. "It seems fitting for Admiral Teron to send the man who destroyed Lioxi to discuss the loss of Vempor."

"The Confederation has not attacked Vempor."

"Admiral Teron said as much. However, our home world did not shatter without reason."

"The Confederation is not sure it believes your planet is gone."

"Does not believe? Why would we lie?" There was a dangerous glint in Gol-Tur's eye.

"Amongst humans it is not unusual for enemies to lie to each other, in order to obtain an advantage."

"Yes, this is something we have learned. I do not approve."

"Nevertheless, there is little trust between humans and Ghasts. We have no proof that Vempor is gone and there are people amongst the Confederation Council who are asking why we are being blamed for something we didn't do. Since they do not trust the Ghasts, they believe your declaration of war is proof you were never seriously interested in peace."

"A war we didn't start in the first place," said Gol-Tur with a mirthless, rasping chuckle. "A war I've fought in since the outset."

This was the second time Duggan had heard a Ghast point the finger of blame at the Confederation for starting the war and the history books were starting to look a little less trustworthy. Duggan knew each side in a conflict would justify their actions and from the Confederation's perspective there was no doubt who was to blame. The Ghasts evidently had a different set of facts to refer to.

"Now is not the time to visit the past," said Duggan.

"Indeed it is not," said Gol-Tur. "The past is gone and the future is waiting to be written."

"Do you want a resumption of the war?"

"No!" said the Ghast. "We have known almost two generations of nothing else. Our industries have built naught but warships and guns. The air in our atmosphere stinks with the acrid smoke of our smelters. We have sunk much into this conflict and many of us grow tired of it!"

"Many?"

"There are some amongst us who have never experienced peace, or were too young to remember it. They wish to strike back against the Confederation in order to punish you severely for what you have done."

"We did not destroy Vempor, but if war begins again, the Confederation will not hesitate to destroy your other worlds. We have the weapon and the means to deliver it."

"Who did destroy Vempor, if not the Confederation?"

"The third species," said Duggan. "I witnessed them shatter a planet in their search for a rare material which they use as a power source."

Gol-Tur stiffened at the words – the Ghasts were unwilling liars and poor at concealing their emotions. He rose from his seat, standing well over seven feet tall. He was not stooped in spite of his age and he crossed easily to one of the display screens, which he studied for a moment. Duggan tried to make sense of the scrolling lines of symbols, but could glean nothing from them.

"The point of impact was on site Originator-A," said Gol-Tur. "We thought it was well-shielded from detection, but it appears not. They have come for us."

"What do you mean?" asked Duggan.

"I may tell you at some point," said Gol-Tur. "Not today."

"This is why we do not trust the Ghasts," said Duggan. "There are unknowns which appear significant to us, yet you make efforts to keep them hidden. The greater your efforts, the less the Confederation will trust you."

Gol-Tur looked away from the screen. "If that is the result, then so be it. Tell me, Captain Duggan – amongst humanity, are secrets not permitted, even between friends?"

"They are," said Duggan, aware of Gol-Tur's meaning. "Things are not so simple here and I reject your example. Would your site Originator-A perhaps be a pyramid with base dimensions of one-point-five kilometres?"

"I do not wish to say."

"The same type of object the Dreamers have been leaving on planets around Confederation space? There was one on Vempor. Can you imagine how damaging that was to the trust we have been trying to build? This is not a case of minor secrets between friends. There are significant facts which are being actively hidden."

"What do you suggest, Captain John Duggan? Our two sides are once again at war. There are things we are not willing to disclose. How can we alter the current state of affairs?"

"If you accept the Dreamers to be the ones who destroyed Vempor, you must agree to a new truce. The Space Corps is keeping its fleet at a distance and as far as I'm aware, there has been no new bloodshed."

"Not so. We have destroyed two of your Anderlecht cruisers in the last three days. In addition, a Hadron has badly damaged one of our older Cadaverons and two of our light cruisers. This is not what I would call keeping your fleet at a distance."

Duggan struggled with his temper. It was the Ghasts who'd redeclared war, so it was they who were to blame for the consequences. "It is not too late, damnit!"

"I am willing to accept the Confederation are not responsible for the loss of Vempor," said Gol-Tur. He returned to the desk and sat, his sharp eyes never once leaving Duggan. It looked like the Ghast had finished speaking, but after a pause he spoke once more. "I came here to see if we can resolve the problems we face. In the spirit of that endeavour, I will trust you with some information in the hope it will be enough."

"Go on."

"There is history between the Ghasts and the race you call the Dreamers. It is something we believed we had escaped many hundreds of years ago. When they first appeared at the Helius Blackstar, we didn't know who or what had come. Now, your words have made things clear. I believe you when you say the Confederation is not responsible for what happened at Vempor. The Dreamers have arrived and they are looking for us. We didn't think they could locate our artefact, yet they have proven us wrong."

"They came through the wormhole looking for the Ghasts?"

"That is almost certain. They seek to destroy us utterly."

"These pyramids are linked, then?"

"They can detect each other across vast distances, yes."

"I have studied the locations of the Ghast worlds – your planets are not clustered. How will they find you?"

"They will find us," said Gol-Tur. The translating device the Ghast wore on his chest struggled to cope with something in his voice which Duggan recognized as sadness. "There is also a site

Originator-B on Sinnar. Why they have not located and destroyed that, I don't know. It is all a matter of time from now."

The Ghost reached under his desk for something. Duggan was a good enough judge of character that he wasn't expecting Gol-Tur to lift up a gun, but he wasn't a good enough judge to predict the appearance of the clear decanter which the Ghost placed on the table. A deep red liquid swirled within. He reached down again and two delicate crystal glasses joined the decanter. Without asking Duggan if he wished to partake, Gol-Tur quarter-filled each glass. The Ghost picked up one and brought the glass to his nose for a moment, before he took a delicate sip.

"This *Grask* was drawn on the day of my birth."

Duggan reached for his glass – it was chill, as though it had been kept artificially cold. He took a sip of the liquid, expecting it would take a layer from the skin of his throat. It didn't – the Grask was cold, yet with infinite layers of complexity. The taste lingered on his tongue and would linger in his memory for much longer. "What are we to do?" asked Duggan.

"A resumption of the truce is the only reasonable outcome for our two species."

"We have the makings of an accord, Subjos Gol-Tur. I will return to Fleet Admiral Teron with the details of our conversation. Will you call off hostilities? Our two sides can work together against the common enemy. If we can establish a new truce it gives us an opportunity to forge a lasting peace."

"If only it was so easy," said Gol-Tur. His eyes went distant. "Amongst your negotiating party, there was a man named Jin Buckner. I recall his face quite clearly. His manner was as bland and inoffensive as most of the other members of the negotiating group. Whilst engaging in small talk, Jin Buckner once made it known that he had an excellent memory. *Photographic* he called it."

Duggan didn't know quite where the Ghost was heading with

this, but he knew he wasn't going to like the conclusion. Gol-Tur continued.

"It wasn't especially difficult for us to have him ingest a certain drug we use against our criminals. It was more difficult to separate him from the others in his party, but we managed it eventually. I'm sure with persistence we'd have been able to extract a considerable amount of useful information from him. In the end, there was not the time."

Duggan looked at his glass and then at Gol-Tur. "Have you given me the same?"

"No, you are drinking nothing but Grask."

"What did Jin Buckner tell you?" asked Duggan, keeping his voice neutral.

"The location of your planet Atlantis. He was born there, apparently, so knew the exact coordinates."

"What about our other planets?"

"Bits and pieces. Some almost complete, others of little value. Enough for us to speculate and no more."

Duggan had guessed the reason Gol-Tur was telling him this. "You have warships heading towards Atlantis?"

"We do. They were authorised to make full speed towards your planet after the engagement between our Cadaveron and your Hadron. The journey will take them many days at light-speed, during which we are unable to contact them with alternative orders."

"How many days?"

"Eleven or twelve. Once they arrive, they will launch incendiary devices into the atmosphere and then depart to search for other Confederation worlds."

"Can you stop them?" asked Duggan, before asking the question he was more worried about. "Are you willing to stop them?"

"You have much to learn about us," said Gol-Tur. "I have told you I wish there to be a new truce. I will order it as soon as you leave this room, with the understanding Fleet Admiral Teron will do the same. I have provided information which might give you time to prepare your defences against the vessels we have sent to enact the ruin of Atlantis. I will ensure there are instructions awaiting our warships as soon as they exit lightspeed, ordering their immediate withdrawal."

"You sound like you're doubtful those orders will be obeyed."

"The man in charge of the lead ship is not sympathetic towards peace. He may prefer to overlook his orders, even though it will cost him his life."

Duggan swore. "How many warships have you sent?"

"Seven, including the Oblivion class *Kuidenar* and *Dretisear*. It will be enough."

"What else besides the battleships?"

"Two Cadaverons and three Kravens."

Duggan tried to hide his dismay. There was enough firepower there to devastate the planet with conventional arms, without having to use their atmosphere bombs.

"Is Nil-Far with them?" asked Duggan.

"Nil-Far remains Captain of the *Dretisear*, though he does not lead the seven."

Duggan looked into the alien face of the Ghast opposite. He was different to any human, yet somehow the same. There was a link between the two of them, faint and weak, but present nonetheless. There was much more Duggan wished to learn, but he accepted today wasn't going to be the day where the remaining blanks would be filled. There was a chance Gol-Tur was telling him nothing but lies. Admiral Teron had seen enough in the Ghast to think his dealings would be honest and Duggan felt the same.

"This could be a difficult situation to extract ourselves from, Subjos Gol-Tur."

The Ghast nodded his head once. "Such is war and such is

peace. When neither side wishes its extinction, there will be a way, no matter how hard."

"We are concluded for the moment. I wish to return to my ship."

"Your escort is waiting outside of my door. I know you will inform Fleet Admiral Teron about what is coming to Atlantis as soon as you return to the Proximal. Afterwards, I suggest you make haste towards Atlantis to add your guns to whatever defence you can muster. If our warships ignore their orders, you are free to fire upon them without prejudicing our truce. I do not think you possess the means to stop the *Kuidenar* if its captain is determined."

"I hope we can resolve our differences. The Dreamers are a foe we should face together."

"Yes, Captain Duggan, they are. I dread to think what they might have become."

Duggan paused mid-stride towards the door when he heard those words, but Gol-Tur didn't say anything more. He left the room, finding two guards waiting for him. They were as uncommunicative as he'd expected and they walked off towards the hangar bay without a word. Duggan was grateful for the silence, since he had much to think about.

CHAPTER NINETEEN

THIRTY MINUTES LATER, Duggan was back on the bridge of the *ES Proximal*. McGlashan was the one to ask what had happened, as if she'd been nominated for the duty.

"We've got good news and some very bad news," he told her. She opened her mouth to ask another question and Duggan raised a hand to forestall her. "I need to get a message to Admiral Teron. Use my authority to force open a channel."

"He's unavailable, sir," said Chainer.

"I don't care where he is or what he's doing, get him on the comms!"

When Teron finally spoke, he didn't sound angry – there was only worry in his voice. "I need you to get to Atlantis at fastest speed, Captain Duggan," he said, before Duggan could speak.

"I will, sir. You've heard about the Ghast fleet already?"

There was a sound from Teron, which Duggan took to be the Admiral assimilating new information and joining a few dots. "That's what it is, then? I've had to take time out of an emergency meeting to speak with you. The Projections Team's latest report arrived less than an hour ago. The chance of us losing Atlantis has jumped to over ninety-nine percent, according to this. The stats guys hardly ever predict above ninety percent chance for anything, since they think it'll make them look foolish if they get it wrong."

"The Ghasts know where Atlantis is, sir. They have seven warships inbound, with a mission to destroy the planet with incendiaries. What's the breakdown on the report?"

Teron swore loudly – a sure sign he was feeling the pressure. "Eighty-five percent likelihood the Ghasts will be responsible. The remaining chance attributed to a Dreamer attack."

"Gol-Tur has agreed to a truce. He's ordered the withdrawal of the fleet heading for Atlantis. The message won't reach them at lightspeed and their senior captain isn't predisposed towards peace. He may well choose to ignore his orders."

Teron swore again, took a deep breath and cursed twice more. "Fill me in and quickly. I have a meeting to return to and you need to be on your way."

Duggan sketched out the details of his discussion with Gol-Tur. Teron listened without a word, remaining so quiet it would have been easy to think he was gone. When Duggan finished, the silence continued for a short while until Teron broke it.

"Thank you, Captain Duggan. Bad mixed with good. Return to Atlantis at once and pray that we have time for sufficient of our warships to reach the planet before the Ghasts."

The silence returned. Duggan looked at Chainer, who nodded to indicate Teron was gone.

"Prepare our return to Atlantis, Lieutenant Breeze."

"Yes, sir," said Breeze. "The Oblivion isn't sticking around either. Their engine output has jumped several million percent."

The Ghast battleship was gone twenty seconds before the Proximal was able to make the jump into lightspeed, illustrating the gulf between the two warships. There was no sensible reason to compare an old Anderlecht with a new Oblivion, but it didn't stop Chainer grumbling about the quality of the hardware he was sitting in.

"What a load of crap," he said.

"It was the best the Corps could find in the time available," said Duggan, wondering why he'd bothered to respond. There must have been something in his tone which stopped Chainer from saying anything more and the Proximal soon began its own journey.

"It's going to be a long ten days," said McGlashan.

"And the bridge replicator is playing up," said Chainer, still looking to complain about whatever was closest to hand. "I've got to walk all the way to the mess room."

"Perhaps it's a message, telling you to cut back," said McGlashan with an innocent smile.

"I travel better with a full stomach, thank you very much."

"I think we need to keep our focus," said Duggan, stepping in early. It was unlikely an argument would start and he had no doubt the talk was simply a distraction from the threat facing Atlantis. No one said anything for a while, though Duggan could feel the tension. Eventually, it was Breeze who asked what everyone was thinking.

"Reckon we can stop them, sir?"

Duggan sighed. He'd known the question was coming and he didn't want to answer it. "No," he said at last. "If the Ghasts are determined enough, an Oblivion is big enough to fly through almost anything we might fire at it. When they destroyed Charistos and Angax, there was no build-up. Their spaceships appeared, flew to within fifty thousand klicks and dropped their warheads on opposite sides of the planets. There was little time for an interception – I believe we had a few Gunners that were close enough to launch, but from what I read about it later, there was nothing we could have done."

"Nil-Far seems okay, though? For a Ghast," said Chainer.

"He's not our friend, Lieutenant. He's a competent officer in their navy and I'm sure he'll follow orders. It's the captain of the *Kuidenar* I'm concerned about."

"Do you think the new truce will survive if they destroy another of our planets?"

"I've asked myself the same thing, Commander. I don't see how it can. There'll be people who know the truth, but even the truth won't be enough for some. It would be a hard knock for the Confederation to take and I'm not sure I'd blame anyone who wanted to continue fighting."

"It's a shame we need the Ghasts, eh?" asked Chainer.

"For at least another two years, I'd say," said Duggan. "I suspect we can replicate the Shatterer technology already and it'll just be the matter of setting up a production line and modifying our warships. A few months and our fleet will pack a much bigger punch than it does now. It'll be a while after that until all our suitably-sized ships carry them."

"Then we need energy shields and disruptors," said Breeze. "I think your two years is on the optimistic side, sir."

"It may well be, Lieutenant. Time will be against us for the foreseeable future, though every step we take is something to applaud."

"From what Gol-Tur said about the Dreamers, it sounds as if they're a bigger bunch of bastards than we first thought," said Chainer.

"He said little and implied a lot," said Duggan, scratching his chin in thought. "The impression he left me with was that the Dreamers have an extensive empire. A *very* extensive empire."

"Now they're coming for us."

"It seems like the Ghasts have never been the real threat at all," said McGlashan, her eyes dark and brooding. "The war up till this point has only been to prepare us for what is to come."

There was something troubling about her words, as though she had a prescience that came to the fore at the most unexpected of times. "The Ghasts remain the most immediate threat, Commander."

"I disagree, sir. They might destroy Atlantis and they might not. I think that whatever the outcome, there'll be no return to war between us. It's these new aliens, sir – they are going to push humanity harder than the Ghasts ever did. We're on a war footing now and everything we do is aimed towards advancing our technology and our hardware. When it's over, we'll look at this time and give thanks that we had the opportunity to prepare."

"When it's over," repeated Duggan.

"I've got to assume we're going to win, sir," she grinned. "No warmongering aliens are going to get past us, are they?"

"Absolutely not," said Duggan. "As soon as we've got a thousand *Crimson*s in the fleet, we'll beat the crap out of anything that comes through the Blackstar."

"Man, I'd love to be back on the *Crimson*," said Chainer with a faraway expression.

"Not the ES *Terminus* or *Rampage*?"

"Nah, they had no soul. Maybe the second-generation Galactic class will have the soul. Don't get me wrong – they're solid enough. With a bunch of Shatterers and a set of stealth modules, they'd be a match for most anything this side of a Dreamer mothership. Until then, I think I'd prefer the *Crimson*."

"It's not an option, Lieutenant - we'd better get used to it. The *Crimson* no longer matters. Things have changed and not just for me - for all of us. Since Admiral Slender was killed, we've been trusted with the top-rank missions and we've pulled through every time. That's how it'll be in the future. No more pissing about in a Vincent class and scrapping with Ghast Hunters – now we'll be given the resources to go with our responsibilities."

"Does that mean I'll get a pay rise?" asked Chainer.

"Nothing more than your annual one percent," said Duggan, not losing step. "What I'm saying is that we should congratulate ourselves for what we've achieved. This is our chance to shape what's coming. We're going to see the Space Corps' new technology before most other people and I want us to be proud that we've been given the opportunity."

"I am proud, sir," said Chainer. "I was proud even when we were on the Detriment. Everything that's happened since makes me determined to be better than I have been in the past. I don't want to let anyone down and whatever happens, I'll do my best to beat whatever we come up against fair and square. If I can't win fairly, I'll fight dirty."

"Me too," said Breeze.

"And me," said McGlashan.

Chainer's serious mood evaporated as quickly as it arrived. "A couple of medals wouldn't go amiss, either," he said. "I'm sure I deserve a handful after all the crap I have to put up with from you lot."

"Have I got the power to rank strip a Lieutenant?" asked McGlashan.

"No, Commander, but I do. I can also recommend a pay freeze on the basis of poor performance."

"Since we're safely at lightspeed, I think I'll take myself off to the mess room for an hour," said Chainer, pretending he hadn't heard.

The light-hearted end to the conversation had the desired effect and Duggan found he was able to put his worries aside for the moment. He was glad, since he had no desire to spend ten days with his mind endlessly turning. He realised he needed to find a better way to deal with the contrast between the high-adrenaline moments and the quieter downtime. The time in flight was meant to be spent recharging his batteries and calmly preparing for the sudden bursts of activity. In reality, the excitement was more often than not an escape from his brain's restlessness and turmoil. There was only one person he felt comfortable enough speaking about it with and he brought the subject up in the mess room, late one morning.

"I think it's just how you are," said McGlashan. "Are you worried about it?"

"I don't know," Duggan admitted. "It seems like I can never find peace. What do you do?"

She shrugged. "The answer is easy enough for me to say, though it probably won't help you. I just don't let it become an issue. Mostly, I read. You'd be surprised how calming it can be."

"I never liked reading much. Except for the stuff I'm required to read to keep up to date with the job."

"You should try it." She gave him a knowing look. "In reality, you're stuck with how you are, John. In peacetime, there'll be other channels along which you'll be able to divert your energy. Except there'll be fewer highs and lows. You'll be able to take each day as it comes and the decision on what to do will be yours alone. Here, you're trapped, with little control over what happens and when."

"You're right, as ever," he conceded. "I like talking with you, Lucy."

"You should practise it more," she said. "Outside of work."

He looked at her and saw the seriousness in her face. "I'd like that. I can't promise when there'll be a break from this."

She laughed. "We're in demand!" she said. "We'll be stuck on a ship every day for the next ten years! Denied every request for shore leave!"

"No if I can help it," he said. "It would be nice to have a life."

"The life you never had and never knew you wanted?"

"The life I'm starting to think about more and more."

"Good," she said, touching his hand briefly. "There's hope for you yet." She stood up and stretched. "That's my time over. I'll see you back on the bridge."

"I meant what I said."

"I know," she replied, heading away.

CHAPTER TWENTY

IN THE FINAL few hours before the *ES* Proximal reached Atlantis, the crew stayed on the bridge, uncertain what they might find when they exited lightspeed. If Gol-Tur's estimation for the arrival time of the Ghast fleet was correct, there would be an extra day or two in which to prepare. Not that they needed extra time – a Space Corps warship was always ready for conflict. When Duggan considered the situation, a part of him wished they'd arrive only a few minutes before the Ghasts. It would save a lot of agitated waiting.

"Any time now," said Breeze, letting the others know it wouldn't be long.

"The skies are going to be busy," said Chainer. A couple of days ago he'd pulled up the locations of the other Space Corps warships and calculated which ones could reach Atlantis in time. There would be far more spaceships in the vicinity than the planet's ground facilities could cope with. It was a good thing most warships could remain in flight almost indefinitely and only needed to land for refitting or to change personnel.

"Here we go," said Duggan, watching as the external sensor feeds settled down.

"We're two hours out from the planet," said Breeze.

"There's nothing close to us," said Chainer. "Checking the fars - it may take a minute."

A view of the distant planet appeared on the main screen – a sphere of lush greens and deep, beautiful blues. It looked tranquil as it rotated with imperceptible slowness. Its single, tiny moon showed as a light-grey circle far away to the right.

"They haven't got here yet," said McGlashan. "Everything looks normal."

It was a relief but not one the crew dared speak about, in case by doing so they brought misfortune upon the place. They looked at the image, unable to take their eyes away from it. There was no way to discern what was in orbit using the naked eye and Duggan drummed his fingers while he waited for Chainer to speak.

"What do you see?" he asked eventually.

"I'm awaiting connection to the Tillos central comms network for the fleet warships in the area. In addition, we've had handshakes from twelve fleet warships so far, sir. There are likely to be many more as we come closer."

"What sort of hardware are we talking about?"

"Three Anderlechts and nine Gunners."

"Not enough to take out one Oblivion," said Duggan. "I'm going to take us towards Atlantis." It was usual to scan the surroundings before making such a decision. Duggan was reassured there was no immediate threat, so he increased the Proximal's speed to maximum and kept them pointed straight towards the surface.

"Seventeen more Gunners, one more Anderlecht and the ES Terror showing up on the local network," said Chainer.

"Still not enough," muttered Duggan. He'd seen the disparity between the latest Oblivions and the best the Space Corps could produce. He wasn't sure there was enough firepower available to stop a pair of Oblivions if their captains were intent on destroying Atlantis. The Ghast battleships would certainly be destroyed in the process, but they didn't need very long to launch their incendiaries. If they got close enough to the planet, they could ensure the deaths of billions.

They were still an hour away when Breeze picked up the fission signatures of incoming warships. "There's something coming, sir. Half a million klicks away from us – it's big, whatever it is."

"One ship or several?" asked Duggan, looking over his shoulder at Breeze.

Breeze blew out an audible breath. "Two ships, sir. They're ours – the *Archimedes* and the *Maximilian!*"

"They've sent the best," said Chainer.

"There's no way they'd chance anything other than a full-scale response," said Duggan. He was glad to see the *Archimedes* and the *Maximilian*, but was concerned they'd be nothing more than easy targets for the Ghast Shatterers.

"Sir, I've got Tillos station on the comms. They want to speak to you. It's Colonel Jabran."

"Fine," said Duggan, indicating that Chainer should bring the colonel through.

"Captain Duggan? You've have priority clearance to land and have been instructed to do so immediately." The man's voice was laden with the stress of the wider situation.

"Who gave you those orders?"

"They were put in place before you departed last time."

"There have been no updated orders in twenty days?"

"None."

"There is no need for us to land."

"The mainframe will disconnect you from the local ship-to-ship comms network if you don't comply."

Duggan felt like putting his head in his hands. The Tillos mainframe couldn't prevent the Proximal from communicating to the other ships individually, but it could prevent access to the central comms network through which all the local fleet ships would coordinate their response to the Ghasts. It wouldn't be a disaster, but would be an extreme inconvenience that could put the Proximal and other ships at risk. "Who is in charge of the *Archimedes*?"

"Admiral Franks. She's to lead the fleet against the imminent threat."

"We'll be ready to land in less than one hour," Duggan replied. "Colonel Jabran, I want you to find someone who can countermand those orders and I want you to do it immediately." He made a cutting motion with his hand, to let Chainer know to end the connection.

"Want me to speak to someone on the *Archimedes* for you?" asked Chainer.

"Yes please, Lieutenant. I'd like to speak directly to Admiral Franks." He sat down to wait. "I don't plan to sit this one out on the ground."

"Sir, Admiral Franks is unavailable," said Chainer. "The *Archimedes* has only been able to repeat the previous orders - we're to land at the earliest opportunity and await further instruction."

Duggan gritted his teeth. This wasn't what he'd anticipated to find on his return and he had little choice but to follow the last orders for the Proximal and hope he could obtain new ones before the Ghasts came.

Over the course of the next hour, another fifteen Gunners broke from lightspeed, along with a further four Anderlecht cruisers. Duggan was sure they'd keep arriving, up until the very last minute. When the Ghasts arrived, there'd be enough Space Corps warships waiting to blow them to pieces. Unfortunately, it wasn't certain if the Ghosts could be stopped before they were able to launch their own weapons at the planet.

"The Ghosts are not going to get away from here if they decide to fight," said Breeze. "Not that any of us want it to come to that."

"A fight would be the worst possible outcome," said McGlashan. "The Oblivions are about the only thing capable of putting a hole in a Dreamer warship. If we knock two of them out because of a misunderstanding, it'll cost both sides dearly."

They came ever closer to Atlantis. Duggan adjusted their course until they were in a rapidly-decaying orbit which would bring them quickly to their destination. The blue depths of the Tavan Ocean swept away beneath them, its size belittled by the speed of a modern spacecraft. After another few minutes, the Tillos base appeared on the horizon. Its mainframe connected with the Proximal's and Duggan handed over direct control to the automatic docking systems.

"We're being taken into dock two," said Chainer. No one was especially interested, but he felt obliged to go through the motions of keeping everyone informed.

Duggan was stewing over what he assumed was incompetence somewhere along the chain of command. He pulled himself away from his dark thoughts. "What've they got down there?" he asked, only half-interested in the answer.

"One ship - the *ES Lightning*, sir. It's still in trench one. They must have forbidden any other landings."

"I'm not surprised in the circumstances," said McGlashan.

"What does the *Lightning* look like?" asked Breeze, peering at one of the feeds.

"It looks ready to be stripped down and recycled," said McGlashan.

"There are plenty of people working on it."

"It's always the same when a warship comes in. As soon as one's on the ground, they'll give it a thorough checking over."

"You can't accuse them of cutting corners," said Chainer.

"No, you could never point that particular finger at them," said Duggan, willing to give praise even when he was being badly treated himself. "There were times when the funding wasn't there, but you could always be confident the fleet warships were fully maintained."

The base mainframe brought them in fast. It was required to follow procedure, but it was permitted to break the rules in certain circumstances, such as when the inbound ship was damaged and needed immediate attention. The Proximal was in full working order, so Duggan assumed the existing orders dictated the highest-priority landing. Admiral Teron had likely been the one to leave those orders and he'd have wanted Duggan available for his next mission as soon as possible. Duggan huffed and puffed, watching as they dropped through the muggy air at speed, only slowing down at the last possible moment. The base computer was precise and they landed without a thump.

"Now what?" asked McGlashan.

"We've not had an order to disembark, have we?" asked Duggan.

"No, sir."

"Patch me through to Tillos."

"I've got one of their comms guys here," said Chainer after a short delay.

"What are our orders?" asked Duggan.

There were a few moments of confusion in the base control station. "I'm not sure, sir," said a woman from the comms building. "We're getting Colonel Jabran."

Jabran came a few minutes later. "What is it?" he asked testily." The stress was getting to him.

"We've been subject to a high-priority order to land and now we're sitting on our behinds waiting to hear what happens next," said Duggan, with an equal degree of impatience.

"That would appear to be the case," said Jabran. "There are no more orders."

"We can't disembark?"

"Not until I get the go-ahead."

"Can we take off?"

"The mainframe will strip away your central comms access if you do so before we receive a follow-up order."

"You're saying the orders specifically asked that we remain on the Proximal?"

"No, Captain Duggan, they did not. However, my last order concerning the Proximal came directly from Admiral Teron and he stated only that he required a priority landing for you."

"This is a ridiculous situation," said Duggan. "Don't you have the authority to override your own control systems?"

Jabran hesitated. "I'd rather wait, Captain Duggan. I won't interfere with the Fleet Admiral's orders."

"This is stupid!" roared Duggan. "Damnit man, can't you see that?"

"If Admiral Franks gives me permission, I will override the base control systems. Or the Fleet Admiral, of course."

"Admiral Franks is busy, Colonel Jabran! She has dozens of ships to coordinate. This is *your* station, not hers."

"I have stated my position," said Jabran flatly. Duggan recognized the tone of a man who'd dug his heels in and had no intention of budging. He gave the signal to Chainer for the comms channel to be closed.

"Piss off," said Duggan after a moment. He wasn't usually prone to displays of petulance, but couldn't think of a more suitable response to the situation.

"This is crazy," said Chainer. He looked baffled.

"Try and get me through to Admiral Franks again."

Chainer tried. "She's still unavailable, sir."

"Get someone to pass on a message, then."

"What about Admiral Teron, sir?" asked McGlashan. "He could get this sorted out."

Duggan had already thought about speaking to Teron. If he did so, it would mean going above Admiral Franks' head, which she might think disrespectful and Duggan didn't want to risk it just yet. It could potentially be a day or two until the Ghasts arrived, so there was a bit of time before he was required to take more direct action.

Duggan shook his head at the whims of fate. If the Ghasts arrived unexpectedly early, it would take precious extra minutes to get the Proximal up into space. While a single, ageing Anderlecht was unlikely to make a significant difference to the outcome, it still possessed enough firepower that it was better-placed in a high orbit than sitting on the ground. With a sigh of frustration and impatience, Duggan sat back and waited.

CHAPTER TWENTY-ONE

DUGGAN HAD INITIALLY EXPECTED a delay of a few minutes. Those minutes stretched to an hour and then two. All the while, Space Corps warships circled the planet high overhead and the Ghasts came ever closer. Duggan tried twice more to get in touch with Admiral Franks and was met with the same lack of success as before.

"I can force open a channel, if you like?" said Chainer eventually.

Duggan had reached the stage where he was angry. He was reluctant to allow his anger to dictate his response, so he shook his head. When he felt the need, he'd go direct to Teron. "We're waiting another hour and then I'll resolve this," he said.

Ten minutes passed and Duggan couldn't recall an occasion when time had moved so slowly. Each second was excruciating and he suppressed the urge to leave the bridge in order to stretch his legs and relieve some of the tension. In the end, he was glad he didn't, since Commander McGlashan said something which led his mind to a new idea.

"When you spoke to Gol-Tur, he mentioned they'd obtained the coordinates of Atlantis from one of our envoys," she said.

"That's what he told me. Jin Buckner was the man's name – it's not someone I've heard of," said Duggan.

"I looked up his records when you first mentioned him," she said. "Out of curiosity, nothing more. It seems he was a military man for nearly twenty years."

"That wouldn't surprise me in the slightest," said Duggan.

"And he'd memorised the coordinates for Atlantis," she stated.

"Apparently so," Duggan replied, wondering where she was heading with this.

"Which of the two sets of coordinates do you think he gave?" she asked.

An internal alarm sounded in Duggan's head, letting him know McGlashan was getting onto something significant. "I don't know," he said.

"The planetary ones or the navigational ones?" she pressed.

"If he told them the navigational coordinates, there's a chance we'll be able to intercept them much further out," he said. He felt a sudden excitement, without yet knowing the best way to take advantage of this important possibility.

"When I was at the academy, we were only ever shown the navigational coordinates," said McGlashan. "The planetary coordinates appeared in the datafiles, but we were never asked to refer to them. It was all about how to ensure your warship arrived a safe distance away from your destination."

Duggan's excitement grew. Every planet logged by the Space Corps, populated or not, had two sets of coordinates. The planetary coordinates were the precise location of the planet itself. The navigational coordinates were a short distance away from the planet and were meant to be where an arriving spaceship targeted itself when it broke out of lightspeed. The navigational coordinates were a set distance away from the planet and were designed as a safety buffer. As technology advanced, lightspeed travel became much more accurate and most spacecraft openly ignored the navigational coordinates, in order to arrive much closer to their destination. Nevertheless, the Space Corps continued to use navigational coordinates and expected its captains to observe them.

"The Ghasts could arrive two or three hours further away than they're expecting," said Breeze.

"Won't they just do a short lightspeed hop to carry them the rest of the way?" asked Chainer.

"Almost certainly," said Duggan. "However, there'll be a delay during which they'll have to make a decision and then prepare for the jump."

"A short delay," said Chainer.

"It gives us something to go on," said McGlashan.

"Sir, I've got Admiral Franks on the comms," said Chainer.

"At last. Bring her through."

Duggan had met Franks only a single time before, but he recognized her slight drawl at once. "Captain Duggan," she said, tiredness evident in her voice. "I'm sorry it's taken so long to respond. There have been one or two failings which prevented the details of your message getting to me. There has been a lot to organise."

"Do we have clearance to launch, Admiral?"

"Yes, of course. I've provided Colonel Jabran with the authorisation codes he needed. You should be free to join us in the next few minutes."

"Admiral Franks, I notice you've set up the defensive shield close to the planet."

"We anticipate the Ghasts will exit lightspeed no more than an hour away. Our current position gives us time to intercept."

"Sir, with respect, a Space Corps warship would arrive an hour away, since its crew would have sufficient knowledge to be able to do so. It's my belief the Ghasts will aim to arrive close to the navigational coordinates. They are ignorant of our conventions when it comes to space travel."

Admiral Franks was quick on the uptake. "They might arrive several hours distant. You think we should aim to intercept at the navigational coordinates?"

"That was my first thought, Admiral. Then I realised that only one of their warships would need to make a short lightspeed jump towards Atlantis and then it could deliver its payload without challenge. Even if we split the fleet, there are risks."

"Thank you for your insight, Captain Duggan. The fleet will remain where it is. If the Ghasts have access to the planetary coordinates, we'll have a chance to defeat them if we stay where we are. A small chance is better than no chance at all."

"I think that is the best plan. However, with your permission, I would like to fly to the navigational coordinates in order to attempt communication with the Ghasts when they arrive – to ensure they are aware of Gol-Tur's orders."

"Your request is denied, Captain Duggan. If they are in a warlike frame of mind, they may well decide to shoot first rather than listen. Once they've committed to violence, the chance of them backing down is diminished."

"I agree, which is why I'd like clearance to take the ES *Lightning* - the stealth modules will keep us hidden and prevent the Ghasts launching their missiles at us. At the very least, the arrival of their fleet at the navigational coordinates will be easier to detect if we have a ship in the vicinity. It might take several minutes for our warships to spot the Ghasts when they're a few hours distant."

"The ES *Lightning* isn't ready to fly. They're in the process of refitting it."

"It got us from Corai to Atlantis. If its critical systems have been left in place, I'm willing to take the gamble."

"But am I willing to take the gamble?" she replied, not expecting Duggan to respond. Admiral Franks made up her mind. "Very well. I'll authorise the release of the *ES Lightning* from its dock. If it'll fly, get out there and see if you can speak to the Ghasts. Whatever happens, keep close to them and inform the *Archimedes* as to their precise location."

"Thank you."

"What makes you think they'll listen to you?"

"I don't know if they will," admitted Duggan. "Nil-Far is with them and he's loyal to his superiors. There's a chance I'll be able to sway him."

"It isn't Nil-Far we should worry about, is it?"

"I'll take that as it comes, sir."

"Very well. Do your best, Captain Duggan."

As soon as Admiral Franks had gone, Duggan surged to his feet. "Come on, let's get going."

"Do you think they've patched up the *Lightning* enough?" asked Chainer.

"We'll soon find out. Speak with Tillos and make sure they know exactly what is happening."

"What about the guys below?"

Duggan opened a channel to Lieutenant Ortiz. "The Ghasts are coming to Atlantis and I've got two choices for you. Do you want to stay on the ground and see what happens when they drop incendiaries into the atmosphere, or do you want to come with us to the *ES Lightning* which may well break into pieces when we take off?"

"We'll come with you, sir," she said without hesitation.

"You're going to be standing on each other's toes. There are forty-three of you and bunks for less than twenty."

"They can take turns."

He hadn't for a moment expected her to stay on the planet. "Get to the forward boarding ramp. You've got about five minutes."

"We'll be there in three," she said.

Duggan led the crew away from the bridge, towards the forward boarding ramp. The urgency of the situation added impetus to their dash through the narrow corridors of the Proximal. True to her word, Ortiz had the ship's complement of troops ready to leave. One or two looked as if they'd been recently woken from sleep, while most were alert and ready for action. Duggan exchanged words with one or two as he shouldered his way to the release panel for the ramp. With a grinding scrape, the ramp dropped away from the hull and thick, humid air washed in from outside.

"Move!" shouted Ortiz.

They moved, quickly and efficiently off the ship. The lifts groaned under the weight of the soldiers and crew, who crammed themselves into the metal cylinders. At the top, there weren't enough vehicles to take them across to the *ES Lightning* in the adjacent trench. The lucky ones, including Duggan and his crew, got themselves a car. The others had to run the kilometre or so to the *Lightning*'s berth. The hull was a mess of activity – luckily the maintenance and repair crews were moving away from the warship, instead of towards it.

"If there's anyone too slow to get off, they'll have to come with us," said Duggan.

"Might be a few of them would prefer that," said Breeze.

"I very much doubt they know what's coming," said McGlashan.

"Yeah, I suppose not."

"Poor bastards," said Chainer. "We're not going to let them down."

"No," said Duggan, desperately hoping he could make it true.

There was little of the *ES Lightning* visible above the top of the trench. Duggan pulled the car up as close to the edge as he could manage and sprinted for the lift. While he ran, he cast his eyes over the battered warship. They'd started the repairs and most of the dents in the armour had been filled with alloy. The once-molten metal had hardened, but hadn't yet been shaped and blended into the surrounding areas of the hull. The effect was one of misshapen lumps, with a mismatch of dull grey and gleaming silver.

"It doesn't need to look good in order to fly," panted Chainer as he joined Duggan in the lift, alongside a dozen others.

There were plenty of people at the bottom of the trench. They carried diagnostic equipment and portable interfaces to allow them to control the cranes and repair robots. Most of the technicians looked worried and one of them – a senior man by his uniform – stopped Duggan.

"You know what you're getting into, don't you?" he asked.

"No. Tell me."

"We've made the hull structurally sound, though you might not think so to look at it. Unfortunately, there's a persistent problem with the life support modules. We've brought them all back online, yet they keep shutting off at random intervals. We've run extensive tests without finding out the cause. In these cases, we'd usually do a complete replacement and package the damaged units off to the factory for a total strip-down."

"Why haven't you done so?"

"Time, Captain. We've not had the time."

"If it'll fly, we have to take the chance."

"It'll fly. For how long, I can't guarantee. Why is it so important? Give us a few more days and we'll have the old replaced with new."

"This can't wait," said Duggan. "We need everyone off the

ship at once. We're leaving as soon as I can get to the bridge and warm everything up."

The technician gave him a curious stare. "In that case, I wish you good luck."

CHAPTER TWENTY-TWO

THE BRIDGE WAS in a worse state than they'd left it. Whoever had been working here had gone in such a hurry they'd not had time to clear away a collection of dirty trays and cups. Chainer could be surprisingly fastidious and he gathered them into a pile, which he placed in one corner.

"They've not removed the tray Commander McGlashan stuck over the warning alarm," he said, taking his seat. "They've managed to get the light turned off, though."

Duggan brought his console online and checked through a few of the onboard systems. "There're plenty of amber warnings here," he said. "I'm preparing us for an emergency departure. I want a detailed breakdown of which areas give the greatest concern."

"We're still on backup comms," said Chainer immediately. "That shouldn't cause us significant problems since we'll be staying reasonably close to the other warships of the fleet. There'll be a second or two delay at most."

"The life support modules are green," said Breeze.

"I wouldn't trust what you see."

"I won't. Just letting you know what the current status is, sir. There's reduced output from the engines as well. Nothing too significant."

"What about the stealth modules?"

"They're in perfect working order."

Duggan nodded. He sent the command to the ship's AI for it to start up the engines. The entire spaceship rumbled and shuddered for a few seconds before settling into the familiar hum. Gauges moved towards their operating positions and various status screens showed rolling lists of updates.

"I can't see any signs of imminent failure," said McGlashan.

"Except the life support," said Chainer.

"Are the external gantries clear?" asked Duggan.

"They're moving the last one away now."

"Lieutenant Ortiz, please confirm you're in place."

"Everyone present and accounted for, sir."

"Excellent, we'll be departing shortly."

"Sir, we've got unexpected guests onboard," said Breeze, examining the life support display.

"Use the internal comms and tell them to leave," said Duggan.

"It's mice, sir. Three of them."

"I hate mice," said McGlashan. "I thought the Space Corps was meant to have strict anti-vermin controls in place?"

"Someone can deal with it when we get back," said Duggan. "Let Lieutenant Ortiz know. It might keep the soldiers occupied."

"Shooting mice?" asked Chainer. "They'll love that."

"I wasn't planning on gunfire, no," said Duggan drily. "I'm sure they can come up with a less dangerous method to root out our uninvited rodents."

It wasn't long until the *ES Lightning* was ready to go. The hull was clear, but there were still repair crews in the vicinity, hurrying to put distance between themselves and the warship. Duggan had no desire to cause injury, so he activated the autopilot. The engines hummed with increased intensity and the spaceship lifted slowly from its trench. As soon as it was clear, the autopilot rotated the vessel until it was pointing towards the navigational coordinates for Atlantis. All the while, it continued to climb, through the low-lying clouds and into the clear sky above. Blue turned smoothly into black as they climbed above the lower atmosphere. Duggan took over the controls and increased the engine output. In other circumstances, he'd have pushed them immediately to one hundred percent. He was wary of doing so, given how much damage the *Lightning* had recently sustained. There was no need for worry – the warship's engines reached their maximum available output without drama.

"Are we doing a quick hop to get where we're going or are we sticking to the gravity drives?" asked Breeze.

"We'll do a hop," said Duggan. "The AI core on the *Lightning* should be able to get us close. I wouldn't want to risk it with the Proximal."

"I'll communicate our plans to the *Archimedes*," said Chainer. "We're patched into the local comms network."

"What's the total ship count?" asked Duggan.

"The *Archimedes*, the *Maximilian*, the *Rampage*, nine Anderlechts and fifty-eight Gunners."

"It'll be carnage – on both sides."

"Everyone loses," said McGlashan. "Most of all the people on Atlantis."

"If this goes wrong, the Dreamers will find significantly less opposition from both ourselves and the Ghasts," said Duggan. "So let's make sure it doesn't go wrong."

"I'm ready to start the countdown," said Breeze.

"No point in hanging around," said Duggan.

They made the jump at a low lightspeed. Several seconds at

Light-A was enough to carry them almost four hours conventional travel away from Atlantis. The *ES Lightning* reappeared in an area of normal space that contained no hazards to spacecraft, this being the primary reason for setting the navigational coordinates here.

"We landed on the button," said Chainer. "Within a few thousand klicks."

"Activate the stealth modules," said Duggan.

"The engines need to recover from the jump, sir. It'll be about two minutes."

"Fine, do it when ready."

"I've completed the close-in scan and there's nothing visible," said Chainer. "If this is where the Ghasts are coming, we've arrived first."

"We could be waiting for a whole day or more if Gol-Tur's estimates were accurate," said McGlashan. "I'm not sure I've got the patience left in me."

"The *Archimedes* has acknowledged our arrival, sir. They have nothing else to report."

"Keep checking the area, Lieutenant. If there are no Ghast ships in close, look further afield."

"I'm on it."

"I'm activating the stealth modules, sir," said Breeze. "Uh-oh."

"They've failed?" asked Duggan sharply.

"Not the stealth modules, sir – they're working fine. I've just got my first red light on the life support."

"Any obvious cause?" asked Duggan, knowing what the answer would be.

"It'll take me a while until I'm certain, but the early signs are it's a recurrence of the problem we had on the way back from Corai."

"Just like the technician warned," said Chainer.

"The Ghasts don't normally keep us waiting," said Duggan. "I'm sure they won't disappoint us this time."

"You're wrong, sir," said McGlashan. "They only arrive when we *don't* want them to. Since we want them to come as soon as possible, I can safely say they'll be late."

Duggan smiled. "I don't think I'll offer you a bet on it, Commander."

It was a good job for Duggan that he didn't put any money on the outcome. They remained in place, close to the navigational coordinates of Atlantis. Chainer scanned the local space continuously, in case the Ghasts had already appeared an unexpected distance away. In the meantime, Lieutenant Breeze kept watch for an energy surge which would herald the arrival of a warship from lightspeed. He detected several small signatures, each of which was associated with the appearance of a Space Corps warship close in to Atlantis. As the hours ticked by, a second of the life support units failed and amber warnings appeared on two more.

"The modules failed at a progressively faster rate when we returned from Corai," said Breeze. "The guys at Tillos have only run diagnostics and then reset the entire system. Whatever the underlying cause, they've not fixed it."

"They didn't claim to have done so," said Duggan.

"I know, sir. I'm telling you why the failures are coming faster. We're running out of time."

"Can you give me an estimate of how long we have?"

"At this rate? Ten hours maximum. After that, I'd be worried about us being crushed by high sub-light acceleration and lightspeed would be a definite no."

"We can crawl back to base if needs be," said Duggan. "Even if it takes us weeks."

"It *will* take weeks."

Duggan opened a line to Lieutenant Ortiz. "Our life support

is failing – we estimate ten hours until the units are unable to protect us from the effects of acceleration. After that, the air goes and the heat. How many suits are there onboard?"

"Twenty for the troops, ten spares and four for the crew is the usual number, sir. There'll be thirty-four in total."

"Thirteen short of what we need. Gather them up and keep them close at hand."

"Should I send four up to the bridge?"

This was no time for martyrdom. "Yes, please. As soon as you can."

When Ortiz was gone, Duggan swore loudly. "I should have left some of them behind!"

"I thought you were fairly clear when you described the risks, sir," said Chainer.

"You can't predict the future, no matter how much you might want to," said McGlashan.

Duggan knew they were right and their words should have brought him reassurance. However hard he tried to come to terms with it, he couldn't help but blame himself. McGlashan saw the anguish in his face and came over, under the pretence of looking at one of his viewscreens.

"Sometimes there is no right answer and all roads lead to death," she said quietly. "It takes strength to keep going."

"I know it," he said. "It's hard."

"It might never happen," she said. With that, she returned to her seat, leaving Duggan with his struggle.

McGlashan's words hadn't resolved the matter, but Duggan took strength from them. In his younger years, he'd never let the possibility of failure lead him to inaction. As he grew older and his responsibilities increased, it became progressively harder to jump in without thought for the results. *Damn I really am getting old,* he thought. For some reason, the idea made him smile inwardly and the clouds cleared from his mind. After that, he sat patiently for the next six hours. He was normally the one with the pent-up energy, but this time he felt like an oasis of calm amongst the others. Chainer fidgeted and drank coffee, while Breeze shifted endlessly in his seat. The life support units continued to fail, until Duggan wondered if he'd need to call off his self-made mission.

"Get your suits on," he ordered at last. "We can leave the helmets for later. Message Lieutenant Ortiz and let her know."

"She says they're already wearing them, sir," said Chainer.

It took a few minutes to struggle into the spacesuits. When it was done, Duggan felt only slightly more secure. Then, with two hours left before the predicted failure of the life support units, the Ghast fleet dropped out of lightspeed.

CHAPTER TWENTY-THREE

"LOOK at the size of those bastards," said Chainer, showing a zoomed-in view on the bulkhead screen.

They stared. A single Oblivion was wonder of menace, backed up by colossal firepower. Seeing two of them together, accompanied by an escort of Cadaverons and Kraven light cruisers was an awe-inspiring sight. The Space Corps was catching up rapidly, but for the time being, the Ghasts were building better warships.

"The closest is fifty thousand klicks away and the furthest another thousand on top of that," said Chainer.

"Any indication they've detected us?" asked Duggan.

"No, sir. They're just sitting there at the moment."

"Let the *Archimedes* know we have visitors."

"Aye, sir."

While Chainer sent his message, Duggan studied the formation of the Ghast ships. Mentally he found it a struggle to avoid thinking of them as the *enemy* fleet. The *Dretisear* still showed battle scars from its encounter with the Dreamer warship – the Ghasts had either lacked the time or the inclination to remove the imperfections. There was no doubt from looking at it that the battleship was otherwise at one hundred percent of its operating capabilities. The *Kuidenar* was exactly the same size and design as the *Dretisear*, though its hull had a pristine, highly-polished surface. There was no record in the Space Corps of an encounter with the *Kuidenar* and it was clearly one of their newest warships.

"They appeared at the same time and they're clustered within a few hundred klicks," he said. "I wonder if they've discovered a way to coordinate more accurately when they're at lightspeed."

"Could be," said Breeze.

"This is the moment of truth, folks. If Gol-Tur is as good as his word, the captain of the *Kuidenar* will be aware of the order to withdraw."

"They won't be ready for another lightspeed jump yet," said Breeze. "I'll let you know as soon as there's a fission signature."

"There'll be no way to tell if they're getting ready for a long journey or a short one by that stage," said Duggan.

"True. They could decide to go home or to head for Atlantis and there'd be no way to know what their intentions are."

"We need to act," said Duggan firmly.

He took his seat and grasped the control bars. Power surged through the *ES Lightning*'s gravity engines and it sped towards the Ghast fleet. Even with the huge power draw from the stealth units, it had enough in reserve to close the distance rapidly.

"If they decide to head off at anything like their maximum velocity, we'll be left behind," said Breeze. "I'm not sure I like our chances if we have to drop stealth in order to keep up."

"Nor me," said Duggan. "Lieutenant Chainer, please put me in contact with the *Dretisear* and get Nil-Far. I want the narrowest broadcast you can manage, so the others don't pick it up."

"They're all narrow when they come from a warship, sir." He caught Duggan's stare. "I'm contacting them now!"

It took a few moments before Chainer received a response. "I think they're confused about why they can't see us. I'm sure they'll soon have a good idea of our approximate location from the strength and direction of our comms signal."

"They're unaware we've developed stealth technology. It might give them pause for thought. Repeat the request – I want to speak to Nil-Far."

This was the crucial moment and Duggan clenched his fists as the seconds ticked by. He wanted a chance to talk with Nil-Far before the rest of the Ghast fleet was aware of the ES *Lightning*'s presence.

"Come on!" he said.

"Got him!" said Chainer.

"Put him on the bridge speakers. Now!"

Nil-Far spoke, his rasping, alien voice floating in the air in front of the bulkhead screen. "Captain John Duggan," he acknowledged. "I see the Space Corps has successfully implemented a cloaking device."

"What are your plans, Nil-Far?" asked Duggan, unwilling to waste precious seconds discussing Space Corps secrets.

"We will destroy your world in retaliation for the destruction of Vempor."

"You've been given the order to withdraw. I personally spoke with Subjos Gol-Tur."

"I have received no such order."

Duggan gritted his teeth. "You must listen to me. The Dreamer pyramids are all connected somehow. There was one on Vempor – I saw it with my own eyes. They do more than just create oxygen – they can destroy worlds. I have seen it happen. I don't know why there was such a pyramid on Vempor, nor why there is one on Sinnar, but the Dreamers know how to find them. Do you hear me? The Confederation is not responsible for this!"

"The Ghast fleet is moving towards Atlantis, sir! They've gone straight to full sub-light speed!"

"What are your plans, Nil-Far?" said Duggan, struggling to keep calm.

"Dax-Nide leads this mission. He has ordered an assault upon the Confederation planet. The *Dretisear* and *Kuidenar* are equipped with the weaponry to eradicate anything living upon the surface."

"We are not enemies!" Duggan shouted. "You have been ordered to withdraw, damnit! You need to speak to Dax-Nide and tell him to stop!"

"I am not aware of an order to withdraw, John Duggan."

"Then speak to Subjos Gol-Tur!"

"If such an order existed, Dax-Nide would have communicated it to me."

"Gol-Tur told me that Dax-Nide is vengeful. I repeat, we are *not* responsible for the loss of Vempor. If you go through with this, the Dreamers will destroy Sinnar anyway and the Confederation will be forced to use its Planet Breaker on the remainder of your worlds! This is a situation which can have no victors, unless you get Dax-Nide to stop this attack!"

"He's cut you off, sir."

Duggan thumped his fist down. "I will not allow a false accusation to kill billions!"

"They're way ahead of us already, sir. It's still going to take them a long while to get to Atlantis," said Chainer.

"Let the *Archimedes* know at once. Recommend immediate and full assault directed at the *Dretisear* and the *Kuidenar*. The others aren't equipped with the incendiaries."

"Are we sure?"

"The Ghasts don't lie. The atmosphere bombs have low

range – we should have the opportunity to intercept and destroy their battleships," Duggan said.

"What are we going to do?" asked McGlashan. "If we de-cloak, we'll be an easy kill."

"We need to wait until they're out of Shatterer range – then we'll do a lightspeed hop in front of them."

"We saw the *Dretisear* launch from one-point-five million klicks," said McGlashan. "They're travelling at the speed of their slowest Kraven, so we need to wait twenty-five minutes. That's assuming they don't have a longer range and we don't know about it."

"I'll take the risk," said Duggan. "We're going to head directly away from Atlantis in order to put some extra distance between us and the Ghasts. Let's see if we can cut that time to below twenty minutes."

"The Space Corps fleet is moving to intercept, sir," said Chainer. "We're pretty far out but I can see enough to build up a picture."

"There's going to be the sort of confrontation we've never seen in the war to date," said McGlashan, with one eye on the sensor feeds.

"Commander McGlashan is right, sir," said Chainer. "This is going to be terrible, whatever the outcome."

"It hasn't happened yet," said Duggan. "What sort of forma-tion are our warships in?"

"Gunners in front, Anderlechts after, followed by the *Rampage* and *Maximilian* flanking the *Archimedes*. They're tight together – only a few klicks between each ship."

"Good," said Duggan. "The Gunners will act as a shield against the Shatterers. The Ghasts can't fire them very quickly, so with any luck they'll detonate a few against our smaller vessels."

"Sucks for them," said Chainer.

"We know it, Lieutenant, but it's the best approach."

Duggan kept a close eye on the distance counter. The numbers rolled across his screen in a blur, yet without increasing anything like as quickly as he wanted.

"We're cutting it fine with the life support," said Breeze.

"You should consider the option of landing on Atlantis, sir," said McGlashan. "Leave it to the other guys and gals to sort things out up here."

"I acknowledge your comments. We're staying out a little while longer."

"Yes, sir."

"Keep trying Nil-Far. Something tells me he's the key to this."

"No response from them, sir. They're closed to our comms requests. According to the local network, there's comms traffic from the *Archimedes* to the *Kuidenar* and the *Dretisear*, asking them to desist with their actions and withdraw. So far there's been no response."

"We're at a million and a half klicks," said Duggan.

"Giving it five extra seconds for luck," said Breeze. "Okay, the stealth modules are powered down."

"Fire us in towards the planet as soon as we're ready. I want us as close as possible."

"Won't be too long. Fingers crossed we live through it."

"It's that bad?" asked Duggan.

"Getting there – the life support is going to fail in the near future."

"I only need this one jump."

"On the plus side, if we die, there'll be no time for pain."

"Great," said Chainer. "That makes me really happy."

"Three, two, one..."

The *Lightning* disobeyed the laws of nature and reappeared a moment later, twenty thousand kilometres above the surface of Atlantis. The entry and exit transitions were rough, leaving the crew retching and nauseous.

"I don't want another one like that," gasped Chainer, trying to pull himself together.

"Be thankful you're not dead," Breeze said, steadying himself with one hand.

"I need to know what's going on," said Duggan, shaking his head to clear it.

"The whole of our fleet is continuing dead-ahead towards the Ghasts," said Chainer. "Admiral Franks has left a handful behind."

"Damned if she does and damned if she doesn't," said Duggan.

"What do you mean?" asked Breeze.

"If she sits and waits, the Ghasts might be able to punch through and launch their incendiaries. If she intercepts, the Ghasts could try a lightspeed jump that takes them between the fleet and the planet. If she splits her forces into two, each group will lack the firepower to knock out the Oblivions."

"Our warships don't show any sign of slowing down," said Chainer.

"They will," said Duggan. "Admiral Franks is doing the only thing she can do, which is to try and position herself in a place that's far enough away from the planet if the Ghasts come head-on, yet close enough to attack if the Ghasts attempt a lightspeed jump past our fleet."

"They're holding the aces," said Breeze.

"A planet is an easy target, Lieutenant. We found that out ourselves at Lioxi."

"What's next for us?" asked McGlashan.

"We're carrying no weapons, so the only thing we can do is put ourselves in the way. Any objections?"

"Nope."

"Let's do it."

With the stealth modules deactivated, the *ES Lightning* was devastatingly fast. The warship burst away from Atlantis, gaining quickly on the rest of the Space Corps fleet. Duggan wasn't sure if he imagined it, but there was a faint sensation of acceleration. If the gravity drives could produce this feeling, the life support system was definitely on the border of a total failure.

The Ghasts were an hour away when Duggan guided the ES *Lightning* to take its place amongst the collection of Vincent class fighters protecting the larger warships of the Space Corps fleet. The captain of the *Dretisear* didn't respond to further requests and the Ghast battleships continued on their course. Duggan and his crew waited.

CHAPTER TWENTY-FOUR

AT A DISTANCE of one-point-five million kilometres, the Ghasts launched their Shatterer missiles.

"There is a total of twenty missiles incoming, sir," said Chainer. "Six from each battleship and four from each Cadaveron."

"Approximately six minutes until impact," said McGlashan. "They've targeted the first line of Gunners."

"Are we one of them?"

"Negative, sir."

"At one launch per minute, there'll be none of us left by the time we can fire our Lambdas," said Chainer.

"Teron likes to keep something up his sleeve," said Duggan. "Maybe the *Archimedes* and *Maximilian* have got Shatterers of their own."

"If that's the case, they're holding on to them," said McGlashan.

"So this is it?" asked Chainer. "We have to sit here and wait until the Ghasts choose us as a target?"

"Yes, Lieutenant, we wait."

"There's got to be a better way, sir."

"I'll let you know when I think of one."

"The Ghasts have launched a second wave of missiles. That's another twenty." McGlashan looked up. "One of them has got our name on it."

"Understood," said Duggan.

"I can't stand being helpless," said Breeze. "I don't mind losing as long as I get to stick two fingers up at my enemy."

"Message Lieutenant Ortiz. Tell her to prepare for impact. Keep your spacesuit helmets close by."

"Done."

"Activate stealth. If nothing else, it'll tell us if we can shake off an inbound missile."

"The stealth modules are active."

"Where's our missile going?"

"We haven't moved, sir, so it's difficult to tell if we've confused it."

Duggan shifted the ES Lightning a few kilometres from its position, taking great care to avoid the other warships in the vicinity. "Well?"

"No luck. The Shatterer has altered its course and it's coming straight for us."

"Deactivate stealth," said Duggan, returning the ES Lightning to its previous position.

"I wonder if the Ghasts have any idea what a stupidly good weapon they've come up with," said Chainer.

"Unexpected consequences," said Duggan. Then, without warning, an idea came to him. It was fully-formed and detailed, with perfect clarity – something to even the odds. "There is a better way," he said, responding to Chainer's statement from a few minutes before. "Get me Admiral Franks."

"The comms man I've reached won't pass me through," said Chainer. "He's too stubborn."

"Whatever it takes, get me through to her now."

"Okay, I'll see what I can do to bypass their comms team." It took him a short while. "Here she comes, sir. She doesn't sound happy."

Admiral Franks spoke. She was flustered and irritated. "Captain Duggan? I don't have time for this."

"I appreciate that Admiral, but I need to know - are our warships expected to wait here while the Ghasts pick them off from a million klicks away?"

"The details of our planned response were communicated to every warship, Captain Duggan."

Duggan looked at Chainer and was met by a shrug and a shake of the head. "Did that include the *ES Lightning*, sir?"

"I assume so. Do you have anything you need to tell me, Captain? I have a fleet to command."

"Are we going to wait until the Ghasts destroy us with their Shatterers?" he repeated.

Admiral Franks sighed, betraying a mixture of several emotions. "Not exactly, Captain. The *Archimedes* and *Maximilian* have been equipped with experimental countermeasures. We have the capability to intercept some of the inbound missiles."

"How experimental and how many interceptions?"

Duggan had a way of wringing the truth from others, even his superiors. "The Splinter missile system is untested except in trial conditions. The *Archimedes* and *Maximilian* each have two batteries of two."

"What is the success rate on the Splinter missiles?"

"No greater than thirty percent."

"Less than three minutes until the first Shatterer impacts," said McGlashan, her voice raised to ensure everyone heard. "And there's a third wave on the way."

"I have another idea, Admiral," said Duggan. "Instruct each

of our warships to make a lightspeed jump as soon as they're targeted. Tell them to emerge as close to the Ghast fleet as they can and fire at the two battleships."

"Our spaceships will be destroyed."

"One Shatterer is enough to finish off a Gunner, Admiral. The crew on the targeted ships are already dead. This way they have a chance to hit back – to do something to weaken our opponents, instead of waiting to die."

"The Splinter missiles might be enough." The tone of her voice spoke volumes – she didn't believe it for a second.

"Give the order, Admiral. Before it's too late."

"Very well, I'll give the order."

"She's gone, sir," said Chainer.

It didn't take long for the new instructions to be disseminated around the fleet.

"There are multiple power surges around us," said Breeze. "Thirty-seven fission drives coming online."

"Why not sixty?"

"The Ghasts have doubled up on some targets, sir," McGlashan explained. "I don't know if that was intentional on their part."

"Are our ships going to get away in time?"

"They'll have something like a minute to spare," said Breeze.

"What about us?" asked McGlashan. "We've got nothing to fire."

Duggan took a deep breath. "We can't let them have all the fun. We're dead if we stay and dead if we go."

"I never liked those lose-lose situations," said Chainer. "There's no point in us activating stealth when we reach the Ghast fleet, I suppose?"

"I'm afraid not, Lieutenant. We're trying to distract them, not hide."

"That's what I thought. I hoped you'd come up with another plan to get us out of here alive."

"Not this time," said Duggan sadly. He turned to Lieutenant Breeze. "Our fission drives warm up a little quicker than the ones on the other Gunners. They've had enough of a lead on us. Get us ready to go. As close to the *Kuidenar* as you can manage – we'll crash into them if we have to."

"I'm warming them up for their last ride, sir."

Duggan leaned back in his chair. His mind was clear and calm. He wasn't scared of death – it wasn't something he wanted, but he knew he'd had more than his share of escapes when another man would have died. *Perhaps it's time for someone else to have my luck,* he thought. The idea was comforting.

"Sir? The last of the life support units has failed," said Breeze. "If we make the jump we'll be plastered less than a micron thick across the rear wall of the bridge."

"Shut the fission drives off!" said Duggan.

"Done, sir. With ten seconds to spare."

"Two minutes until the Shatterer reaches us," said McGlashan.

"Best get your suit helmets on," said Duggan. "Speak to Lieutenant Ortiz and make absolutely certain none of her guys forget. Tell them to pray for the ones without."

"I've activated the emergency alarm in the mess area and their sleeping quarters. They'll get the message," said Chainer.

"All thirty-seven of our targeted warships have gone to light-speed," said Breeze. "We've got more beginning their preparations."

"What about the inbound Shatterers?" asked Duggan, feeling a momentary concern that the missiles would somehow turn and pursue their targets.

"They're heading in a straight line, sir. Two or three will hit Atlantis – the others will go out into deep space."

"That's some relief," said Duggan. He turned his attention to the tactical screen, which showed the Ghasts as red dots of varying sizes. Around them, Space Corps warships appeared as much smaller green dots, with a single larger dot to represent the Anderlecht class *Surgical Strike*. Hundreds upon hundreds of missiles appeared, moving in all directions. "This is going to get messy," he said.

"Twenty-seven of our warships arrived close enough to engage," said McGlashan. "The remaining ten aren't able to launch yet. They've fired off another twenty Shatterers. They've targeted the *Rampage* and the *Archimedes*. There's a second one coming for us."

"This is going to crap," said Breeze.

"Just how we like it, Lieutenant," said Duggan.

"Less than one minute until the first Shatterer reaches us."

"Where are those countermeasures Admiral Franks mentioned?" asked Chainer to no one in particular.

Duggan didn't bother to reply. With the failure of the *ES Lightning*'s life support, there was no point in trying to take evasive action - even sub-light acceleration would kill the crew and soldiers within a second. So, Duggan watched the tactical screen, trying his best to make sense of the chaos. Missiles appeared and vanished, having connected with their targets. New missiles joined them, criss-crossing the tactical display, with computer-generated numbers and letters assigned to them as the *Lightning*'s AI did its best to assign details and priorities to a thousand different objects.

"Vincent Class *ES Lion* confirmed destroyed," said Chainer. "Also the *Spinner* and the *High Flyer*."

"The *ES Rampage* has gone to lightspeed," said Breeze.

"They've lost one of their Kravens."

"Damnit, it's the battleships we need to stop!"

"Thirty seconds until the first Shatterer impacts with us,"

said McGlashan. "There are launches from the *Archimedes* and *Maximilian*, sir. I don't recognize the missile type – presumably it's the Splinter countermeasures."

Duggan closed his eyes briefly, the confines of the helmet hiding him away from everything. Amid the confusion, his brain felt curiously detached. There was no panic, only sorrow at the losses on both sides. He knew he was helpless to affect the situation and for once it didn't matter. He'd done his best and now it was up to other people to do what they could. The feeling of acceptance and calm didn't last long.

"Sir?" said Chainer with barely-suppressed excitement. "I'm getting a message from Nil-Far. He wants to speak to you!"

CHAPTER TWENTY-FIVE

"NIL-FAR, CALL THIS OFF!" said Duggan before the Ghast had a chance to speak.

"Dax-Nide has chosen to disobey orders, John Duggan. You were correct – Subjos Gol-Tur asked for us to withdraw."

"Why are you still attacking our ships?"

"Dax-Nide will not back down and he will not listen to me."

"Pull the *Dretisear* back!"

"I cannot. Dax-Nide must give the order."

"What?" spluttered Duggan.

"You do not understand our command structure."

"A Splinter missile made a successful interception with our inbound Shatterer," said McGlashan. "The next is due in one minute."

Duggan didn't have time to feel relief at the news. "Nil-Far, if Atlantis is destroyed, there will never be peace between the humans and Ghasts! Don't you understand? We all lose, except the real foe who has come against us."

"I wish it were otherwise."

"Why don't you do something to change it?"

"It would be a betrayal."

"The *ES Rampage* has destroyed one of the Ghast Cadaverons," said McGlashan. "The *Rampage* is damaged but still firing at near full capacity."

"We've lost Vincent class *Razor*, *Trance* and *Livid*," said Chainer. "As well as the Anderlecht *Vignette*."

The names came – warships, men, women lost in a withering, unceasing bombardment of plasma warheads. Duggan glanced at his screen. The *Lightning*'s AI was tracking so many targets it was pointless trying to make sense of it all. He looked away and tried to focus on the one thing he could control.

"I understand betrayal, Nil-Far. Saving your species is not a betrayal."

"The *Dretisear* and *Kuidenar* are readying their fission engines," said Breeze.

Duggan's heart jumped in his chest. "What are your plans?"

"Dax-Nide has ordered us to leave the others of our fleet behind. He has instructed a short-duration lightspeed journey towards your planet."

"Stop this, Nil-Far. Withdraw and leave the *Kuidenar* to us."

"Goodbye, John Duggan." The connection to the *Dretisear* was cut.

On the *Lightning*'s bridge, the bulkhead screen changed to show an image of the two battleships. The Ghast vessels were difficult to see amongst the blossoms of plasma flares and the raking trails of Vule cannon fire. Duggan squinted until he could make out the dark outlines of the *Dretisear* and the *Kuidenar*. Lambda warheads detonated against both warships, the explosions bursting and expanding into brilliant white, before fading and becoming lost in the endless storm of countermeasures. Duggan was gripped with the certainty that these two warships were unstoppable. Whatever the efforts of the Space Corps fleet, it wouldn't be enough to prevent them delivering their payload of incendiaries into the atmosphere of Atlantis. They were incarnations of death – come to set the universe on fire and the conflagration they brought would ensure the end of humanity and Ghasts alike.

As Duggan watched, the shape of a Gunner hurtled through the clouds of flares surrounding the *Kuidenar*, the rear third of the Space Corps ship glowing blue from the heat of a Ghast missile strike. Streaks of Vule slugs converged on the approaching vessel, punching deep holes through the ruined ship's armour.

"They're trying to ram the *Kuidenar*," said McGlashan in disbelief.

"Please make it," said Chainer.

Chainer's plea was in vain. The *Kuidenar* fired a hundred or more conventional missiles from its port-side batteries. So close were the two vessels that it was over before Duggan's brain could register what had happened. When it was finished, the Vincent class was gone – torn into a hundred thousand pieces and hurled across the sky. Some of the remains collided with the battleship, all along the four-and-a-half thousand metre length of its hull. Still the battleship came, relentlessly, its speed undiminished.

"That was the *ES Hood*," said Chainer.

"A Splinter missile got our second Shatterer, sir," said McGlashan. "There's nothing more inbound."

Duggan looked up dumbly. *A best-case success rate of thirty percent,* he thought. *One chance in nine they'd get both. Best-case.* A tear rolled down his cheek, its existence hidden from the others of the crew. The tear wasn't for him or anyone he knew by name – it was for the men and women on the *ES Hood*, who had given everything and been killed at the last, their sacrifice in vain. *And it seems as though nothing can touch me, no matter how badly I play my hand.*

"The *Kuidenar* and *Dretisear* have jumped, sir," said Chainer.

"Where are they?"

"Checking." Chainer looked up, his face drained of colour. "They've gone close to Atlantis – they're just shy of one hundred and thirty thousand klicks above the surface and moving at full speed."

"Fifty-seven seconds until they reach delivery range at their current speed," said McGlashan.

"Have we got anything there?" asked Duggan.

"There are half a dozen Gunners closing and it looks like they've got the Proximal up in the air."

"It's over," said Breeze quietly. "They'll hardly make a scratch on those two battleships."

"What about the *Maximilian* and the *Archimedes*?" asked Duggan.

"The Ghasts jumped straight past them, sir. We have nothing big in range."

"The *Archimedes* and *Maximilian* are warming up for a short hop towards the battleships," said Breeze. "They're going to be too late to stop the Ghasts launching."

"It'll get them away from the Shatterers," said McGlashan.

"Not much use for the people on Atlantis," said Chainer.

"We need those two warships intact, Lieutenant."

The sensor feeds remained on the Ghast warships. The *Kuidenar* and *Dretisear* were both damaged – their hulls glowed in patches of orange and reds, and plasma fires still burned brightly on their armour plating. Sporadic bursts of countermeasures sprayed into space, as if the captains of the vessels were concerned they would be subjected to a surprise attack. *By a vessel in stealth,* thought Duggan.

"They're within a hundred thousand klicks," said Chainer, his voice thick with emotion. "Those bastards."

"I hate them, yet..." said McGlashan.

"They're fine warships," said Duggan, saying what McGlashan had not dared.

"Coming to eighty thousand klicks."

"This is the point of no return. For all of us. The numbers we lose today will be a fraction of the deaths to come," said Duggan.

"Aye," said Breeze, unable to wrench his eyes away from the battleships. The closer they came to Atlantis, the smaller they looked – two tiny dots set against the tranquil oceans and endless forests.

"I still can't grasp that we have the technological ability to do this," said Chainer.

"And the stupidity to put it to use," McGlashan replied.

"Sixty thousand klicks. They'll launch soon."

"The *Archimedes* and *Maximilian* will be too late whatever happens from here," said Breeze.

"I've detected a launch from the *Kuidenar*, sir," said Chainer. "It's some kind of cylinder. Right over the main land mass."

Duggan's heart fell. He'd known it was coming, but that didn't prevent the inconceivable shock of being witness to the deaths of billions. He'd been thrust into that role before and had never wanted to see anything like it again. "How long till impact?"

"It's moving fast - twenty seconds, give or take," Chainer replied.

Duggan felt he should say something, though his mind refused to conjure up anything that seemed respectful enough. *Sometimes it's better to say nothing at all.*

McGlashan cleared her throat – a trait she had to indicate when she was uncertain. "Sir? There's been a Shatterer launch from the *Dretisear*."

"What?"

"It's targeting the incendiary bomb."

There was no time to form a response – at that moment, the situation changed from madness to complete pandemonium.

"The *Dretisear* has launched a full broadside at the *Kuidenar*," McGlashan continued. "I'm tracking three hundred conventional missiles, two Shatterers and an increase in counter-measures. The *Kuidenar* has responded in kind."

"The *Archimedes* and *Maximilian* have jumped," said Breeze.

"Where are they?" asked Duggan.

"They've come in real close to the Ghasts, sir. Well within Lambda range."

"Get me Admiral Franks!"

The connection was made almost instantly. "Captain Duggan? This is not the time."

"Don't fire on the *Dretisear*!"

"Too late, Captain. The order has been given."

Duggan swore loudly. "Nil-Far is not our enemy!"

"Full Lambda launch from both the Hadron and the *Archimedes*, sir," said McGlashan. "That's just about a thousand missiles."

Duggan slumped into his seat and put his head in his hands. "What's the status on the atmosphere bomb?"

"It's just been intercepted by the Shatterer," said McGlashan.

Duggan couldn't raise a smile. The image on the bulkhead screen showed the two battleships as they traded missile fire. Dozens of warheads detonated against their flanks, ripping the armour and twisting it into new forms. In moments, the outlines of the spaceships were lost in the inferno. At one point, the intensity faded briefly to reveal them both, still firing at each other.

"They must have done something to harden the outer armour," said Breeze in disbelief.

"Nothing can survive that," said Chainer.

"Get me Nil-Far."

Chainer looked up. "If he's alive, sir."

Nil-Far *was* alive – when he spoke, his voice displayed no more emotion than usual. "Captain John Duggan. My time is short."

Duggan could have said many things, about how the Ghast had prevented a war, or how many people he'd saved on both sides. He was sure Nil-Far had come to his decision based on this and more, and didn't need to hear them served up to him. "Thank you," was all Duggan said.

"The *Kuidenar* is breaking up," said McGlashan. "It's still firing."

"How long until the Lambda wave hits?"

"Right about now."

The previous ferocity of the engagement was dwarfed by what came. The Lambdas plunged through the Ghast counter-measures. Hundreds of them thundered against the battleships, before exploding into pure, cleansing heat. The light burned into Duggan's eyes and left echoes across his retinas. When it faded, the *Kuidenar* and the *Dretisear* were no more. Huge chunks of molten alloy spread across the sky and tumbled onwards to the surface of the planet.

The *Archimedes* and *Maximilian* fired again, sending their missiles to pursue the remains and smash them into smaller pieces. The debris was too thick to be so easily dispersed. Many pieces burned up before they crashed into the surface of Atlantis. Others survived – much-reduced in size - and landed in the ocean, while a few others struck the great belt of forest that stretched for thousands of kilometres to the north and south of the planet's equator. The inhabitants of the planet had been saved from death, but tens of thousands would die from the tidal waves or the seismic shocks resulting from the impacts. *They may never learn the truth,* thought Duggan.

Everything was silent for a time. There was no chatter on the comms and no one on the ES *Lightning's* bridge spoke. Duggan idly noted that the remainder of the Ghast fleet had been destroyed at some point in the last few minutes. The fighting had exacted a great toll on the Space Corps fleet – the majority of the Gunners and Anderlechts had been destroyed and the ES *Rampage* was badly damaged.

Eventually, Duggan felt he needed to say something. "Come on, let's get this ship home."

CHAPTER TWENTY-SIX

THE JOURNEY to Atlantis took several days. Without a functioning life support system, Duggan was unable to utilise the *ES Lightning*'s acceleration to anything like its full potential. At the other end of the journey was a need to slow down. There were a number of calculations involved in order to ensure they were as efficient as possible. Duggan lacked the motivation to work it out for himself, so he handed control of the warship to the AI. While they flew at a pitifully slow speed, the other surviving vessels, including the *Archimedes* and *Maximilian*, went to lightspeed. The Tillos base was hopelessly under-equipped to deal with so many repairs at once and the fleet was sent elsewhere. Nevertheless, there was a number of spacecraft which were deemed too have suffered too much damage, and these were directed to the Tillos airfield.

During the flight, no one made contact with the *Lightning*, except for the usual routine checks. This suited Duggan fine, and he spent his spare moments checking the incoming reports from Atlantis. The information was garbled and incomplete, but a number of coastal towns had suffered from tidal waves. There had been several earthquakes, though these had fortunately occurred far from the planet's main populated areas. Overall, it wasn't clear how many had died – certainly it would be much less than what the captain of the *Kuidenar* had intended. The media reports talked about the results of this *natural disaster* and Duggan wondered how long they'd be able to keep it under wraps, assuming that was the intention.

After a time, the *ES Lightning* came close enough to Atlantis for the autopilot to request clearance to land and begin the descent. Those onboard who had lacked suits were still alive, much to Duggan's relief. The warship had retained enough heat and oxygen for them to live, though it had been a close-run thing.

"Tillos escaped the damage," said Chainer.

"Looks like," responded Breeze, not giving the matter any attention.

"They've brought the *Rampage* here," Chainer continued. "I'm surprised they had space for it."

"It's a tight squeeze in the dock," said McGlashan, looking across with partial interest.

"They've got an Anderlecht and two Gunners parked up to one side on the landing field. There are two empty docks – you'd think they'd use them."

"They've given us one of them?" asked Breeze.

"Yeah, dock number three," said Chainer.

"It shouldn't be surprising. There probably aren't a great many stealth modules available across the entire Space Corps. They probably cost more to manufacture than an entire Anderlecht," said McGlashan. "They'll want this ship ready for action as soon as possible."

"It's going to be a struggle for them to sort us out and the *Rampage* at the same time. Maybe that's why they've left the second dock empty."

"And they'll likely have to send the *Rampage* elsewhere to complete the repair job," said Duggan. "That's a big spaceship."

"What do you think Admiral Teron is going to say about what's happened?" asked McGlashan.

"I don't know," said Duggan. "He'll be angry at the loss of life, but will already be making plans for what happens next."

"When will you speak to him?"

"Soon, I'm sure. There'll be something else for us to do – there always is."

The *ES Lightning* landed gently. The personnel onboard made haste to leave, grateful to get away from the place which had so nearly become their coffin. The air outside was as humid as before, though Duggan breathed it in eagerly.

"Where to?" asked McGlashan. "I've received specific orders that I'm not to make myself available to the personnel pool."

"Me too," said Chainer.

Breeze simply nodded to show he'd been given the same instructions.

"In that case, we're going to be heading off sooner than I anticipated," said Duggan. He squinted towards the distant buildings. "We'll speak to someone in the base headquarters."

They took the closest vehicle and wended through the inbound repair teams. A few minutes later, a bemused Duggan was heading towards Meeting Room 73. The rest of his crew were left to fend for themselves in the lobby area, where it hadn't taken Chainer long to find a food replicator. After a further five minutes, Duggan was seated within the overly-familiar walls of the meeting room, staring expectantly at the video screen. The face of Admiral Teron appeared, a little too close to the camera for comfort.

"Sir," said Duggan in acknowledgement.

"Who the hell is that?" asked Teron with great irritation.

Duggan turned in his seat to find an unfamiliar man walking

into the room, carrying a cardboard folder. This man stopped, realising something was amiss. Colour drained from his cheeks when he saw who was on the video screen.

"Sorry," he said, hurrying out.

"What are these people playing at?" grumbled Teron. "I ought to ban meetings."

Duggan didn't wish to involve himself. The Admiral was in a bad mood and Duggan had a suspicion he was soon to find out why. "How do things stand between us and the Ghasts?"

"Do you know something? We've made greater strides towards peace in the last few days than we managed in all of the preceding weeks."

"That doesn't surprise me."

"Nor me. Where before we lacked motivation, now we're driven."

"The peace would have been too uneven prior to the attack by the *Kuidenar*," said Duggan. "Now we know they have the location of Atlantis, we need a settlement as much as they do."

"And who knows what other secrets they might be keeping?"

"Have we formally agreed a truce?"

"Yes, we have. I would expect us to agree upon an early draft document for a permanent peace within the next week or two."

"That's quicker than I was expecting."

"It'll be the details that take months. I personally trust the Ghasts – when they tell me something, I generally believe them. When they don't tell me something, that's an answer in itself."

"So everything is good?"

"We're getting there." Teron still didn't look pleased. "Tell me, Captain Duggan. How did Admiral Franks perform in the engagement?"

Duggan hadn't been expecting the question and floundered for an answer. "We won, sir."

"That's a stupid answer and you're not a stupid man."

"I was buying myself time to add some diplomatic bells and whistles to the answer," he replied truthfully.

"Forget about that. I want your honest opinion."

"Some good, some bad. She was in charge of one of the largest ship-to-ship engagements of the entire war and she held everything together when others would certainly have failed. However, the overall impression I got was of timidity. The Ghasts had us on the back foot, that's for sure, but she allowed them to dictate. We could have done more."

"She spoke very highly of you. I think the result might have been different if you hadn't suggested deep fission jumps to the approaching Ghast fleet."

"It was to Admiral Franks' credit that she didn't let pride stop her from acting on my advice."

"Thank you for your appraisal. The Space Corps did well in trying conditions and we acted as a team to defeat our foes."

"I agree, sir."

Teron pushed something around on his desk. It was off-camera, so Duggan couldn't tell what it was, but he got the feeling he was about to hear the news Teron had been putting off telling him. He was right.

"As soon as I received a reliable report about the result in the skies of Atlantis, I contacted the lead analyst in the Projections Team and asked for a re-run of their report regarding the fate of the planet."

Duggan felt a constriction in his chest. "And?"

Teron lifted up one of the familiar brown folders and brandished it angrily like it was a photograph of a mass-murderer. "Still nailed-on at ninety-nine percent chance of destruction."

"The Ghasts?"

"Not this time. Now there's no mention of the Ghasts in the report. Now they're predicting the Dreamers to be the sole cause. I asked them to run and re-run the simulation. Each time it comes out the same, with a variance of a tenth of one percent."

"What's changed?"

"I recalled you mentioning the presence of Gallenium during one of our previous conversations. I had meant to let the stats team know about it at once, but unfortunately other things intervened and I forgot. If Atlantis was free from traces of Gallenium, the chance of destruction drops to about one percent since our engagement with the Ghasts. As soon as you put Gallenium into the simulator, the chance goes straight to ninety-nine percent."

"It could still be an anomaly – a fault in the simulation," said Duggan stubbornly.

"I don't deny the possibility, but I can see by your face you know what's coming."

"What's the time frame?"

"Three months. A *maximum* of three months."

"Do they specify which Dreamer vessels they expect to enact the destruction?"

"I didn't request that much detail."

"The mothership," said Duggan.

"It was there at Corai to gather the resource they'd harvested. When they come, the mothership will be with them."

"You have a plan."

"I told you before, there is always a plan. In this instance, it's closer to desperately clutching at distant straws. If we faced a lesser foe, I'd be ecstatic with what we've got. Now?" He shrugged.

"Tell me about it, sir."

"The Space Corps research labs have been working on something. Tell me, John. Did you notice a warship in trench two when you came in to land?"

"No, sir. There was only the *Rampage* and that was in the end dock."

Teron nodded knowingly. "There *was* something in trench two. It landed less than an hour before you brought the *ES Lightning* in."

"Another stealth ship?"

"Yes, another one."

"The new tech performed outstandingly against the Dreamers, but without weapons we can't do much other than stare at our opponents. Assuming I'm to be assigned to this second ship, are you asking me to try and crash into our enemies?"

"If that's an opportunity you can take, then I would expect you to do exactly that." Teron lifted his hand to cut off Duggan's next question. "This time we aren't sending you out so helpless."

"Have we overcome the limitations imposed by the power draw?"

"Not yet. The issues we've talked about remain unresolved. What it boils down to is that our current use of Gallenium isn't efficient enough. Therefore, once we install the stealth modules on an armed warship, there is insufficient engine mass to propel the ship when the power draw is taken into account. There are other issues as well, which prevent us from establishing a few cloaked warships as static batteries to surprise any aggressors."

"Where does that leave us?"

"There is one ship in the fleet with enough power to run the stealth modules *and* retain a full complement of weaponry. Quite a large complement of weaponry, as it happens. There's a mission for you and your crew, John. I hope you're well-rested, since I need you to depart at once."

Something clicked in Duggan's brain and he knew exactly which ship it was that Admiral Teron had prepared for him. "The *Crimson*," he said.

CHAPTER TWENTY-SEVEN

DUGGAN ELBOWED his way through the crowds of people waiting outside Meeting Room 73, his mind in a spin. Teron wanted the mission to begin without delay and he'd promised to fill in the details once Duggan and his crew were boarded. The Admiral had remained cagey under questioning and Duggan guessed there were a few aspects of the planning which still needed ironing out. He located his crew easily enough – they were lounging in padded seats in the main lobby area. Chainer was lifting a can of hi-stim to his mouth when he saw Duggan approach.

"I've only had one," he protested.

"It doesn't matter, come on," said Duggan, marching past in the direction of the exit doors. The others scrambled to their feet, throwing out questions like confetti.

"No rest for the wicked, eh?" said Chainer.

"Nope."

"Where are we going?"

"I don't know," said Duggan.

"Which ship have we been given?"

"The *Crimson*."

"You're kidding?"

"Do I look as if I'm kidding?"

"Where is it?"

"Trench two."

There were the sounds of feet drawing to a sudden stop. "It's been there all along and we didn't see it?"

"Keep up, please. We need to be away."

"Is it armed?"

"Heavily armed, so I'm told."

"What are we going to fight?"

"The Dreamers."

"Shit."

The stream of enquiries dried up after that. Duggan flagged down a passing car and gently encouraged the lone occupant to vacate it. The four of them climbed inside and sped off towards the seemingly empty trench two. When they came closer, the imperfections of the stealth technology were apparent – there was the hint of an outline above the lip of the dock. When Duggan looked at it straight-on, he saw nothing, but when he turned his head to the side, his peripheral vision could see shapes and lines. These hints were elusive and when he attempted to pin down the outline of the warship, his eyes failed him.

"How are we going to get inside if we can't see it?" asked Chainer, once they were in the lift.

"I'm sure there'll be someone waiting for us at the bottom, Lieutenant."

There was a greeting party – a team of dour-faced scientists of some rank, each carrying a hand-held analysis device. "Captain Duggan, I assume?" said the lead man.

"Yes," said Duggan. "Is it ready?" While he spoke, he looked over the man's shoulder. From so close, the *Crimson*'s cloak created a shimmering in the air. He thought he could detect a high-pitched whine that he wouldn't have otherwise associated with a spacecraft and there was the smell of something in the air, charged alloy mixed with heat.

"Whenever you are. Are these all you're taking?"

Teron hadn't said anything about troops – he'd told Duggan to get into the air and nothing more. "I haven't seen the roster. If we're the only four on it, this is everyone."

"I'm not interested in the roster, Captain. I'm a scientist, not a gun-toting grunt."

"Maybe you should show a bit more respect," said Chainer, unusually bold.

Duggan held up a hand to stop any more comments. The scientist looked as if he wanted to say something else, but he saw Duggan's face and held his tongue.

"I'll disengage the cloak and you can go onboard," said the man. "My team have left everything powered up and there should be no one left on the ship."

"Thank you," said Duggan.

The scientist lifted his tablet and made a couple of gestures. Without noise or ceremony, the ESS *Crimson* appeared before them, compact and laden with promises of death. From here, it was impossible to see the whole of the ship – Duggan didn't need to; the memory was etched forever in his brain. The boarding ramp was down and he walked towards it, the ill-tempered scientist already forgotten. The others followed, their faces tilted upwards.

"Never thought I'd see this again," said Chainer.

"Nor me," said Duggan truthfully.

The *Crimson* had been subjected to extensive research since they'd recovered it over two years before. That didn't mean it had changed much – in fact, everything looked the same. They reached the bridge, expecting to see new equipment to update the old. There were a few bits and pieces – the original monitors had been replaced and there were some additional control panels, which gleamed in bright contrast to the old.

"Not much different," said McGlashan. "Most of this stuff is more than fifty years old now. You'd think they might want to pull it out and swap in the latest tech."

"The interfaces are solid enough," said Duggan. "The same basic design we've used for decades. It's the back-end where the work takes place."

The scientist was true to his word and the consoles were powered up and ready to use. Chainer dropped into his seat and scanned the facilities available to him.

"We've been improved," he said. "New sensor arrays and a few more added to the total."

"The engines are the same as they ever were," said Breeze. "More grunt per metre cubed than anything else in the fleet."

"Have they installed anything to protect against engine scrambling?"

"I'm not sure. I'll let you know when I find out."

Duggan turned to where Commander McGlashan was sitting. She stared intently at the weapons consoles, her brows lowered in thought. When she spoke, it wasn't to let them know about their offensive capabilities.

"When do we find out where we're going?" she asked. "The ship is ready to fly as soon as we get the word."

"I'm waiting for Admiral Teron to give the nod."

"Do we have to sit in the dock?"

"I suppose not," said Duggan. "Strap yourselves in, I'll take us into orbit."

"I haven't finished my pre-flight checks, sir!" said Chainer.

"You won't need to," said Duggan with confidence. "I can guarantee you this warship has been subjected to the most rigorous inspections you can imagine."

With that, Duggan took his seat. The leather chair crackled

beneath his weight and gripped him comfortably. The screens around him were green and each monitoring gauge settled perfectly where it should be. He'd seen spaceships fresh out of the dock with more variance in their onboard systems than this.

"Do we have clearance?"

"Absolutely," said Chainer.

"I'm activating the autopilot," said Duggan. He grinned. "There's too much ground traffic to risk a manual take-off."

The autopilot dribbled power to the engines and lifted the *Crimson* effortlessly off the ground – one-point-five billion tonnes of weapons, engines and armour. Up it climbed, into the darkening sky of Atlantis. The ground crews below paused to look, sensing this was a sight they might never witness again. Even the most experienced amongst them had no idea what the departing warship was – their eyes told them it was an obsolete relic from the past, fit only for the museum. A few of them guessed at the truth, without knowing why they were so sure the *Crimson* was far more than it appeared.

At fifty thousand kilometres, Duggan instructed the mainframe to establish an orbit.

"Not much about, sir. A few Gunners and the Proximal are in a low orbit," said Chainer. "Is the planet safe now?"

Duggan realised he hadn't told them anything yet. "No, Lieutenant, the planet is no safer now than it was when the Ghast fleet arrived."

"The Dreamers?" said McGlashan, guessing easily.

"The Space Corps stats analysts believe they're coming here."

"Why are there hardly any warships to protect the place?" asked Chainer.

"Anything we had close enough to get here was sent against the Ghasts." He mentally stumbled, since he wasn't quite sure himself why there were so few spacecraft in the area. "I don't know, is the short answer. Maybe they've already given up."

"I've finished checking through the weapons systems," said McGlashan, a familiar gleam of excitement in her eyes. There was something else, too – fear.

"Am I going to like what you're about to tell me?"

McGlashan didn't get a chance to answer.

"I've got Fleet Admiral Teron on the comms," interrupted Chainer.

Duggan gave a motion to indicate he was ready to speak.

"Captain Duggan, my apologies for leaving you hanging. I see you've taken the *Crimson* up."

Teron was very-well informed, since there was no way he could have known simply by talking over the comms. "Yes, sir. I thought it prudent to make a head-start. Can you provide us with some details of what's expected?"

"Can your crew hear me? Never mind, they deserve to know." The words were ominous.

"They perform better when they know what they're facing, sir."

"You get all the crap, Captain Duggan and this time is no exception. I trust you and I trust your crew. Atlantis is doomed, according to the reports. I'm not a man who believes in fate, which I why I'm giving you this job – if there's anyone who can defy the odds, it's you. I'm also not a man who gambles, but this time I'm taking a big one. You're carrying irreplaceable hardware. I'd like it back, though in my heart I accept it's not going to happen."

"Sir, I thought you didn't like beating around the bush either."

Teron laughed with relief as he realised Duggan wasn't going to hold anything against him for what was to come. "Quite right, John. I need you to find the Dreamer mothership and I need you to destroy it before it reaches Atlantis. There's Gallenium on Pioneer as well – I don't know if you're aware. The Projections Team gave me the bad news about that planet just this morning."

"The *Crimson* can't beat the mothership, sir."

"You have to do something. If you don't destroy it, lure it in a different direction. Anything but let them come here."

The recent conversation in Meeting Room 73 had given advance warning that something was coming, but with no indication the requirements would be quite so demanding. In his mind, Duggan had thought he was being sent on a trial run to take out one of the lesser Dreamer warships. Now he saw that Teron had given him a task which was infinitely more dangerous.

"Alone?" he asked.

"We could send every single warship we have and they'd be destroyed in minutes – seconds, even. You know this is true."

Duggan didn't try to deny it. "Yes, sir. I know it's true."

"I'm working on something. Whether it'll happen in time, I don't know. I can't even say if it'll be significant."

There was no point in prying. Teron liked his secrets. "Where are we headed?"

"The Tillos mainframe has uploaded the details – scant as they are."

"I can see them."

"Good luck, Captain Duggan, to you and your crew. I thank you for the services you've rendered to the Space Corps."

"Thank you, sir."

"Goodbye."

"He's gone," said Chainer.

"That sounded like a farewell to people who are already dead," said Breeze.

"It was, Lieutenant."

CHAPTER TWENTY-EIGHT

DUGGAN SPENT a few moments skimming through the information which had arrived from the Tillos base. "Set a course for Kidor," he said.

"Kidor again?" asked Breeze, entering the destination into his console.

"There's no mothership there," said Chainer, a glimmering of hope in his voice.

"Just a Dreamer battleship," said McGlashan.

"It's the one connection we have to those alien bastards," said Duggan. "We're going to destroy that battleship and the pyramid in the hope it brings the mothership in to take a look."

"We're expected to defeat their second most powerful ship in order to call out the most powerful? It doesn't get any better, does it?" asked Chainer.

"We've come through worse before, Lieutenant."

"No, we haven't," said McGlashan.

"You might be right," Duggan conceded with a chuckle.

"I'm definitely right."

"We've gone to lightspeed," Breeze informed them, in case

they'd missed the subtle transition. "It'll be two days to Kidor at Light-V."

Duggan nodded to acknowledge the information, his eyes not leaving McGlashan. "Give us a run-down on what we're carrying, Commander. It would be nice to know what stick we have to beat our enemies with."

"This is where it gets good," she said. "At least if we were facing a Cadaveron it would be good."

"Come on," said Chainer, impatient to hear.

"There are more Lambdas than last time – we're up to twenty-four clusters of twelve with a fast-launch option. They've added two more Bulwarks, taking us to twelve. It's a new type I don't recognize, but the manufacturing date is two months ago, so they're fresh out of the plant."

"What about the disruptors?"

"They've re-installed them. On top of that, there are eight nuke launchers and eight missiles per tube. They're modified Lambda propulsion sections like we had on the Galactic class and the warheads have a yield of slightly more than two gigatons each."

"Are they going to break down again?"

"Your guess is as good as mine. These are a newer revision if that provides any reassurance."

"Not really. What else?"

"This is where it gets good and bad. The good thing is we have two Shatterer missile launchers, with eight warheads for one tube and seven for the other."

"Why the odd number?" asked Chainer.

"I think I can guess," said Duggan. "We're using parts they've salvaged from the *Ransor-D* Cadaveron, or possibly that tube we pulled from Everlong."

"Here was me hoping they've perfected the technology," said Chainer. "Only to find we're using stolen Ghast parts."

"I assume the Shatterers were the good news," said Duggan. "What about the bad?"

"The Planet Breaker, sir. It's installed, unlocked and ready to use."

"Damn," said Chainer.

"Teron was right in more than one way when he said he was taking a gamble," said Duggan. "If we lose the *Crimson*, it'll cut off the Confederation's access to a means of catching up with the Dreamers' tech levels."

"We can hope they've extracted enough to make blueprints in the labs," said McGlashan.

"This is a lot of weight we're carrying," said Breeze.

"That we are, Lieutenant."

Duggan sat down to think. He was accustomed to having things held back – he readily accepted he wasn't so important that he needed to be told everything there was to be told. Here, there was no holding back. The *Crimson* had been loaded with every available resource available to the Space Corps. If the ship was destroyed, there was a chance it might set the weapons labs back a dozen years or more. There was something else to add to the responsibility he'd been given, which Lieutenant Breeze shortly announced.

"The Dreamer core is installed and online," said Breeze. "I didn't realise until I'd completed my checks."

"Another asset we can't possibly afford to lose," said McGlashan.

"Atlantis is the only asset we can't afford to lose, Commander. The Space Corps have drawn lines in the sand and it's up to us to keep our enemy on the other side of those lines."

McGlashan nodded to show it was something she understood. "We'll give it our best shot."

Duggan left the bridge and made his way to the gym. On the way, he passed through the mess area – it was strange to find it absent of life, though the smells of stale replicator food remained. The mess was usually the most frequented area of a spaceship outside of sleeping hours. Duggan couldn't foresee a necessity for the *Crimson* to land but he'd been wrong before. This time there was no choice – the engagement with the enemy would have to be resolved without surface combat.

He sat on one of the gym's two treadbikes. The rumble of its gears helped him focus his mind and although he couldn't help but think about what lay ahead, he found he was more relaxed than he had been for a long while. He reflected that each of his recent missions had merely been part of a much greater whole. This time it was an all-or-nothing attempt to force an outcome. The odds of success weren't good – in fact they were exceedingly poor – but there was an opportunity here to buy some time for the Confederation. He was under no illusion about what would happen if they pulled off a shock victory against the Dreamer mothership – more of the aliens would certainly follow through the wormhole. Still, it seemed unlikely they had many more warships of such overwhelming power in their fleet, so the loss of just one would give them a real bloody nose. Most importantly, the Space Corps would definitely be interested in salvaging the wreckage left behind.

"You're daydreaming," said a voice, cutting through his reverie.

"It was pleasant thoughts for a change, Commander," he said.

"Wondering where to hang your medals when we come home triumphant?" she asked with a grin.

"When I've been given a normal mission, I concentrate on the possibility of failure. Not because I'm pessimistic, simply because I like to anticipate whatever is in my power to do so. Then I get accused of dwelling too much on failure." He smiled. "With the odds stacked so heavily against us, I find it impossible to think about anything other than success."

"How do we accomplish this outstanding achievement which is so clearly mapped out in your head?"

"I'll think of something," he said.

"Do you have a plan?" There was a note in her voice which told him she was hoping for an answer.

"I apologise if I sounded dismissive. This is a tough job we've been given and the fact that I've come to terms with it does not mean everyone else feels the same."

"It's not *that* bad." She ran fingers through her hair. "Maybe it's close to being that bad. I've known fear and doubt in the past, but they've never bothered me. You've always got us out of trouble, John."

"And this time you don't think I can do it?"

"I don't think you've been dealt a fair hand."

"The player with the lowest cards can still win, Lucy."

"If you've got a royal flush, you're not going to fall for the bluff and you're definitely not going to blink first."

He climbed from the treadbike and looked at her. Unable to prevent himself, he reached out and pulled her close, wrapping his arms around her. She stood quietly, her face looking up at his.

"I told you I'd think of something and I will," he said quietly.

"I don't want to die before I get to know you," she said.

"No promises," he said. "Not when I can't keep them."

"I know. Do your best, that's all I'm asking."

"That's something I can promise."

He stepped back and held her stare. The fear remained in her eyes, but there was also determination to beat what was to come. Whatever demons she struggled with, they'd met their match in Commander McGlashan.

"I need to get back to the bridge," he said. "Are you staying here?"

"Yes, sir. I've got a couple of hours left on my break and a workout on the treadbike will do me good."

"Fine, I'll see you back there."

He headed along the twisting, turning corridors of the *ESS Crimson*. The hum of the engines was soothing and he ran his fingertips along the smooth alloy walls as he went. He fancied he could sense the warship's eagerness to face battle – like it was straining to be unleashed upon whichever opponents the crew faced. There was many a captain who succumbed to the lure of attributing human desires to their spaceships. Duggan usually felt attuned, but not to the degree he did at that moment. He asked himself if his new-found feelings for Commander McGlashan had opened his mind, or if it was simply because he was certain that death awaited them in the coming days.

He reached the bridge. Breeze and Chainer were there, hunched and unmoving before their consoles, their faces illuminated by blues and greens. Neither of them spoke a greeting, so lost were they in their own thoughts. For once, Duggan was grateful to be left alone and he took his seat. A timer informed him there were still forty-three hours until their expected arrival at Kidor. He wasn't surprised to find his usual longing to arrive was mixed with a desire for the clock to remain forever frozen where it was.

As he waited, he couldn't stop thinking about Commander McGlashan - the warm comfort from holding her, the smell of her hair and the look in her eyes when she accepted his embrace.

CHAPTER TWENTY-NINE

"FIFTEEN MINUTES until we enter local space," said Breeze. "On most other ships that could mean *any time from now,* but on the *Crimson* I think we can be fairly certain it'll be fifteen minutes."

Duggan expected Lieutenant Chainer to come up with a wisecrack, though nothing was forthcoming. The mood on the bridge was good – the adrenaline-fueled pretence that all was well. Duggan was familiar with the charade – he'd seen it many times before and taken part in it himself. It was infinitely better than misery and barely-suppressed dread.

"What happens if the Dreamer battleship isn't here?" asked Chainer.

"In that case, we'll do the Ghasts a favour by destroying the pyramid for them."

"Where will we go after that?" Chainer persisted. "We'll have nothing else to go on by then and no clue about the enemy's location."

"True," said Duggan. "We'll have wasted nothing apart from a couple of days spent with the threat of death hanging over us.

That's no different to any other mission. If the battleship is gone, we'll report in to Admiral Teron and he'll probably send us somewhere else. Eventually we'll find something that wants to shoot us down and we'll get our chance to show how mistaken they are for trying it."

"I see."

"Don't act so shocked, Lieutenant," said McGlashan.

"I'm not shocked. I know we're at the whim of luck – it's got to the stage where I'd rather get things over with now, instead of waiting and waiting. Eventually we're going to come up against that mothership and I don't want it hanging over me forever. It's like when I have to visit the dentist, I prefer to get an appointment straightaway, rather than wait for a couple of weeks."

"No one gets tooth decay these days!" said McGlashan.

"Yeah well, you know what I mean, don't you? No one likes going to the dentist, and I don't enjoy knowing I could die at any moment."

"That's a real Chainer-ism," said Breeze. "Using a nonsense example to back up an obvious point."

"I like to think I put across an eloquent argument," said Chainer.

"While I appreciate the philosophical discourse, gentlemen, I feel we should spend the next few minutes in preparation."

"I've spent the last two days in preparation, sir," said Chainer. Nevertheless, he rotated in his seat until he was square-on with his console again.

Breeze did the same. "Five minutes to go," he announced.

"The time has come for us to show what we can do," said Duggan. "The ES *Terminus* and *Rampage* were a step up for us, but compared to the *Crimson* with its stealth modules, those two were much less effective weapons. The Dreamers have limited forces in Confederation space and each time we knock out one of their warships, they lose an irreplaceable resource. I'm sure we're aware this won't be the last we see of them – even so, that doesn't lessen the significance of what we're trying to do. This is about buying time. The more time we buy, the greater our victory will be. If we get two years out of this, we'll have earned the chance to advance our own technology in order to reduce the gap between us and our opponents. We can't let Atlantis fall."

One by one, they stood and saluted. Duggan saw the fire in their eyes and knew there was no fear which would prevent them from doing their best. He returned the salute and thanked them for what they'd done so far.

"We're out of lightspeed," said Breeze.

"Kidor dead ahead."

Duggan didn't hesitate and he increased their sub-light speed to maximum. The *Crimson* reached a velocity of almost nineteen hundred kilometres per second – a speed which exceeded anything else in either the human or the Ghost fleets.

"Activate stealth modules," he said.

"Done."

"Engines at fifty percent," said Duggan. "The *Crimson*'s far better equipped than the *Lightning* to carry this technology."

"There's nothing close or on the fars," said Chainer. "Unfortunately, we've come in on the blind side. I can't see the pyramid site from here."

"I'll bring us over and around," said Duggan. "It shouldn't be too long at the speed we're holding."

"As soon as I see anything, I'll shout, sir."

"What happens when we fire our weapons?" asked McGlashan. "Does it interfere with our cloak?"

"No," replied Breeze. "The power draw from launching our missiles is comparatively tiny. We'll be able to maintain stealth."

"Except the missiles themselves aren't cloaked, so the enemy will be able to identify our location fairly easily by watching where the warheads appear from," said Chainer.

"Unless we move quickly and erratically," Duggan added.

"It'll help, sir. It won't fool them for long."

"The disruptors draw from the fission drive, right?" McGlashan asked.

"Yes they do, Commander. That might stop us making a quick escape if we need one but it shouldn't interfere with our ability to stay hidden."

Minutes passed and the image of Kidor became gradually larger on the viewscreen. Duggan had been concerned that memories of his failure here would continue to haunt him. They did not, and when he stared at the slowly-rotating sphere of rock, he felt only determination.

"Oxygen levels at twelve percent on parts of the surface," said Chainer. "If we extrapolate, it's probably more or less breathable close to the pyramid."

"How long until you can see what you need to see?"

"Any moment now, sir."

"Keep looking."

Chainer's estimation was an accurate one. Barely ten seconds passed before he spoke again. "There it is!" he exclaimed. "That's the pyramid, exactly where we left it."

"What about the battleship?"

"If it's in an orbit I might not see..." He stopped himself mid-sentence. "Nope, there it is. Seventy or eighty thousand klicks above the pyramid and circling the area."

Duggan picked up a hesitation in Chainer's voice. "What's wrong, Lieutenant?"

"I don't think it's the same ship, sir. This one is smaller."

Duggan swore. "There's definitely only the one ship? Or could there be another somewhere close by?"

"Your guess is as good as mine. We did say that a battleship was an awful lot of hardware to leave here. Maybe it was called off to perform another task."

"I don't like surprises. I'll bring us closer until we're directly above and at a million klicks. That should be far enough for us to watch without being easily seen."

They were soon in position. The stealth modules allowed for a completely different approach to combat. Without them, the Dreamer warship would have spotted them from well beyond a million kilometres away. Now, Duggan could wait patiently until he was sure it was a good time to strike.

"It's my belief that the battleship is gone and has been replaced by one of their cruisers," said Chainer. "The warship down there is the same as the others we've seen before."

"Could the battleship be in a slow orbit?"

"If it is, they're moving with much less speed than I'd expect, sir. Not that I have a vast wealth of experience in how the Dreamers usually operate. They could have landed for a sight-seeing tour for all I know."

Duggan chewed on his lip. "We're not in such a hurry that we need to rush in at the first sight of the enemy," he said.

"They'll detect us at some point, sir," said Chainer. "At that stage, we'll have lost our ability to launch a surprise attack."

"Can you provide an estimate of how long it might take them?"

"I wouldn't like to try. The battleship and mothership didn't take long, but it comes down to distance, capability and plain old chance."

"They could detect us at any time, in other words. We'll give it another five minutes and then we'll go in for the attack. Report any change in the enemy behaviour at once."

"Of course."

The five minutes went by without the battleship making an appearance and without the enemy cruiser deviating from its course. Duggan didn't wait a second longer and aimed the

Crimson directly at the Dreamer warship. His skin prickled and his mind was in perfect focus. "Let's get those bastards," he said.

"Six minutes until we're close enough to use the disruptor. Want me to disable the homing modules on the missiles?" said McGlashan.

"Yes please," Duggan replied. "How long until we're right on top of them?"

"Eight minutes."

The planet came closer and the enemy ship remained teasingly in place – a large, red dot upon Duggan's tactical display.

"We're in disruptor range," said McGlashan.

"Hold fire."

The seconds went by. Lieutenant Breeze cleared his throat a few times, the only sign of tension amongst the crew.

"We're less than a minute away," said Chainer.

"Let me know when," said McGlashan.

"Hold fire."

"I can confirm their energy shield is powered up and active," said Breeze.

"I wasn't expecting anything else, Lieutenant."

The numbers on the distance counter were a blur as the gap between the *Crimson* and the enemy vessel diminished.

"Sir?"

With fewer than ten seconds left before they reached the Dreamer ship, Chainer spoke, his voice steady and matter-of-fact. "They're changing course, sir."

Duggan faced McGlashan. Whatever fear she'd once felt was gone, leaving the familiar excitement of battle clear in the set of her face.

When the range dropped below three thousand kilometres, he spoke. "Fire."

CHAPTER THIRTY

"DISRUPTOR FIRED," said McGlashan. "Shatterer tubes one and two away, along with ninety-six Lambdas and four nukes."

As soon as the words left her mouth, Duggan turned the *Crimson* sideways and into a violent roll, to bring more of its missile tubes to bear. McGlashan didn't need to be told twice and she fired as soon as her console advised her it was possible. Another ninety-six Lambdas and two nuclear missiles followed the first wave.

"Their shields are down, sir," said Breeze. "Our fission drive is at sixty percent of its maximum."

Duggan changed course again, to allow another four of the *Crimson*'s missile clusters to fire. The warship felt clumsier than usual because of the stealth modules, but compared to the *Lightning*, it was agile and fast. Everything happened at once and by the time his crew provided updates, the fight was almost over.

"Shatterers one and two have impacted," said McGlashan. "The nukes have detonated close by and I'm reading twelve Lambda strikes."

"Fourteen," said Chainer to correct her.

"Their energy output has plummeted to effectively zero," said Breeze.

"I'll bring us close up – keep firing," said Duggan. "Don't let up."

"Yes, sir."

Duggan took the *Crimson* away from the rapidly-expanding sphere of gamma rays which engulfed the enemy warship. The Space Corps' vessels were exceptionally well-shielded, but he didn't want to risk staying too close given the monumental quantities of radiation in the area.

"Forty-Eight Lambdas away. No sign of a counter-launch from the enemy."

Chainer focused one of the sensor arrays on the cruiser. The feed was grainy and blurred from the radiation, when it would have otherwise been a perfect image. The Shatterer explosions faded, leaving two white-hot holes through the enemy warship's armour. In places, the alloys still burned from the ferocity of the blasts. A number of smaller holes showed where the Lambdas had scored hits.

"Their engines are coming back online," said Breeze.

"What about their shield?"

"Not a chance. Not while they stay within this radiation."

"Seventeen more Lambda strikes," said McGlashan. "I've launched seventy-two more and another two nukes."

Plasma explosions appeared along the entire length of the Dreamer warship's flank. Towards the rear of the vessel a five-hundred-metre section of struts and plating detached itself from the superstructure. The enemy vessel accelerated slowly and ponderously, but even this was sufficient to rip away another damaged piece from its port side.

"It's breaking up already," said Breeze, wonder in his voice.

"Take away their shields and they're fragile," said Chainer. "Who needs armour when you've got shields?"

The light from the plasma cleared, providing the *Crimson's* crew with a glimpse of the extensive damage they'd caused. The Lambdas were designed to penetrate armour before they exploded, and against the cruiser they had caused a terrible amount of destruction.

"They must have hardly anything left," said Breeze. "Their engine power is all over the place. They've not even got enough for their particle beam."

"And we must have knocked out whatever controls their missiles," said McGlashan.

At that moment, the final two nuclear warheads detonated and fifteen more Lambdas cascaded against the cruiser's flank. The vessel was ripped into three and the pieces thrown apart from each other.

"There's still engine output from the largest of the three sections," said Breeze. "It's uncontrolled."

"They're done," said Duggan. "Cease fire."

It was over – a series of secondary explosions occurred in the depths of the cruiser's hull. Then, there was a single, catastrophic blast which turned the whole of the *Crimson's* bulkhead viewscreen into vivid white. By the time the sensors had adjusted and filtered out the plasma light, there was nothing left which could be identified as a warship. A hundred thousand pieces of wreckage spun and turned as they followed their random courses. One such piece came within a kilometre of the *Crimson*, travelling at such a velocity that it caught Duggan entirely by surprise. It didn't seem important, somehow.

Chainer was the first to find his tongue. "Crap," he said, the single word expressing a dozen feelings.

Duggan blew out the breath he'd been holding. "I can hardly believe it," he said, his eyes fixed on the bulkhead screen.

"I'll bet they've not been on the receiving end of something like that for a long time," said McGlashan. "Serves them right."

"Get on the comms to Admiral Teron or one of his team and let them know what's happened," said Duggan, bringing himself back to matters at hand.

"Yes, sir."

"I'm bringing us into a position directly above the pyramid. We're going to knock out their shield and then blow them to pieces."

The fight had been a short one, but it had carried them away from the site of the Dreamer artefact. Duggan turned the *Crimson* about and set a course that would bring them a few thousand kilometres above the location of the object.

"Admiral Teron acknowledges our success," said Chainer. "We're to proceed as planned."

"Understood," said Duggan.

"Sir?" asked McGlashan. She didn't usually use the word as a question unless she was concerned about something.

"What is it, Commander?"

"What if we destroyed the cruiser before they could signal their distress?"

Duggan laughed. "We may have done. That's why we're going to allow the pyramid plenty of time to send a message. I have no doubt Lieutenant Chainer has been watching them like a hawk."

"I certainly have, sir!" said Chainer. "They've sent nothing I recognize as a distress signal so far."

"There's no way they could have missed what we've just done to their warship, is there?"

Chainer shrugged. "I have no idea what facilities they have in those pyramids. I doubt they have a comprehensive set of sensor monitoring equipment."

Duggan swore. "So there's a chance the enemy doesn't know we've destroyed their cruiser?"

"I didn't want to be the one to say it while everyone was

happy," said Chainer. "I'm glad we didn't give the cruiser an opportunity to fire back at us if that makes you feel any better."

"Not really," said Duggan. He stood and walked twice around the bridge, while the others watched expectantly. In spite of his concern, it was almost certain the enemy warship had sent off a warning signal before it had been destroyed. In fact, it would have been a sign of gross incompetence if they had not. Even so, Duggan would have preferred to know for definite, since it would make the waiting much easier. As it was, he had to deal with the worrying notion that he'd accomplished an excellent victory, whilst simultaneously cutting off the only lead to the Dreamer mothership. With no way to resolve the situation, he turned his attention to the one thing he could proceed with.

"Commander McGlashan, fire one of our nuclear missiles at the pyramid below. I want them drenched in radiation to keep their shields offline."

"Hold!" said Chainer urgently.

"What is it?"

"I think I've picked up a reading from the pyramid, sir."

"A distress signal?"

"I don't think so. They're sending a regular high-speed pulse into space using a method that isn't suitable for carrying complex data."

"Talk sense, man!" said Duggan, impatient for Chainer to get to the point.

"I thought I was, sir," said Chainer. He saw Duggan's face and quickly continued. "This is more like a network handshake than a bunch of aliens having a chat."

"It's an automated check-in?"

"I think so. They're sending the signal approximately a hundred times per second. It's changing slightly each time."

"Coordinates!" said McGlashan.

"Could be, Commander. The signal is going to the same

receptor each time, to let the recipient know exactly where this particular pyramid is at that moment in time."

"Was there such a signal coming from the pyramid we found on Trasgor?"

"No, sir."

"Why did you describe the signal as being like a *network handshake?*"

"I've done this job for a long time. That's what the signal is, sir."

"If there was no signal from Trasgor, might that imply whatever network this pyramid on Kidor is part of, it wasn't completed until recently?"

"That would be the obvious conclusion, though it wouldn't explain what the purpose of the network is," Chainer replied.

Duggan knew exactly why the Dreamers might want to build a network of linked power sources. The primary purpose of these artefacts wasn't to generate oxygen at all.

"Can you trace the signal?" he asked.

"If you want me to," he said. "It's going a long way into space, but we've got a lot of decent kit onboard so it shouldn't take long to pinpoint the destination."

"I'm going to wait right here at your shoulder, Lieutenant, so please be quick."

"Here we go. The recipient is located on a previously-mapped planet in the Garon sector. At lightspeed, it shouldn't take us too long to reach it."

"Want me to set a course?" asked Breeze, guessing Duggan's likely orders.

"Shortly, Lieutenant. There's a small amount of business still to conclude here." He turned his attention back to Chainer. "What's the name of this planet, out of interest?"

"Tybalt, sir. It's called Tybalt."

Duggan nodded once, wondering if fate was playing tricks on

him. The planet shared a name with the Anderlecht cruiser he'd captained many years ago, before an explosion in one of the missile tubes had killed the son of the Space Corps' head man. Duggan had spent many years shaking off the effects of that particular accident.

"I will not be guided by superstition," he said, more to himself than anyone else. He noticed Commander McGlashan staring at him, as if she was concerned about what his reaction might be. "Fire the nuke," he said.

CHAPTER THIRTY-ONE

IT DIDN'T TAKE long to destroy the pyramid. The close-range detonation of a two gigaton nuclear warhead shut down its shield immediately. After that, a barrage of Lambdas ensured the pyramid would never function as a power source again. There were gauss emplacements set in a perimeter and Duggan ordered these to be destroyed as well. He was aware it was a waste of ammunition, but the destruction gave him a feeling of satisfaction.

"Let Admiral Teron know where we're going," said Duggan, looking at the still-glowing ruins of the pyramid.

"You can let him know yourself, sir. He's on the comms."

"That's nicely-timed," said Duggan.

"Captain Duggan, since I'm talking to you I assume you haven't left Kidor yet?" Teron sounded stressed in a way that was rarely apparent in his voice.

"Yes, sir. We've had one clean kill and also destroyed the pyramid the Dreamers left behind."

"Time is running out. Where is the mothership?"

"I don't think it's coming, sir. However, we've located signs of

Dreamer activity on a planet called Tybalt. We were about to make best speed towards it."

"Tybalt, you say? Give me a moment to look at the charts." The line went silent, before a muffled curse was heard from the other end. "You need to get there as soon as possible. Leave without delay. How long will it take you?"

Duggan raised an eyebrow in the direction of Lieutenant Breeze.

"Twenty-one hours, sir," said Breeze loudly.

"I've already arranged reinforcements, though I didn't know where to send them until now. You'll be joined at Tybalt by everything we can muster, but I must warn you it'll be longer than twenty-one hours until they arrive. If you're still alive, you'll be in charge, Captain Duggan."

"What's wrong, sir?" asked Duggan.

Teron sighed wearily, giving an indication of the burden he was carrying. "The Tillos base picked up a signal a few hours ago on a wavelength they don't normally monitor. They had no idea what it was and it didn't last long enough for them to trace its precise origin. They were, however, able to narrow it down to an area of the Garon sector in which Tybalt happens to be located. The woman who detected this signal passed details of the event up the chain of command until someone with enough authority cross-checked it against a database of what we've learned about the Dreamer communications. Do you need me to spell out the rest for you?"

"No sir. The Dreamers have pinged Atlantis and we have to assume they're making preparations to destroy it."

"This is it, John. If they aren't stopped, we're going to lose another planet. We may have been wrong to think they were coming directly to Atlantis. They must have a weapon situated on Tybalt. Find it and destroy it."

"They still know where our planet is, sir."

"We can only deal with what is in front of us. Destroy that weapon first. If there's anything left of the *Crimson*, get it to Atlantis in case they decide to perform the task from close range."

"Yes sir. If that's all, I'll give the order for our departure towards Tybalt."

"Please do," said Teron. The faint hum of the comms connection ended.

Duggan smiled grimly at Breeze. "You heard the Admiral."

Breeze disengaged the stealth modules and a short while later, the *ESS Crimson* burst into lightspeed. Duggan didn't bother to take his seat for the transition, so full of nervous energy was he.

"Our victory against the cruiser didn't count for anything," he said.

"Since when did war go smoothly?" asked McGlashan.

"I shouldn't lose sight of that, should I?" he responded.

"Why all this messing around with pyramids?" asked Chainer. "If they've got Planet Breakers, why do they need to bother with what appears to be a network of power sources across half of the sector?"

"Travel time," said Duggan, mentally slotting the pieces into place. "This must be what they do when they come to conquer somewhere new. I'm certain that each pyramid feeds into a central weapon system, which they can use to take out any of their enemies from afar. Why bother spending time travelling from place to place when you can set something like this up? Once the weapons network is in place, they can use it to control a huge area of space."

"It must be a damned huge area, if they could take out Vempor," said Breeze. "The Ghast home world was an enormous distance away."

"It makes you wonder how far away the Dreamers live," said McGlashan. "Presumably they have established these weapon arrays elsewhere, yet were unable to use them to target planets in the Confederation and Ghast sectors."

"What was the name of the second Ghast planet with a pyramid on it?" asked Chainer. "Sinnar, was it?"

"That's the one," Duggan told him.

"Why haven't they destroyed Sinnar in the same way they destroyed Vempor?"

"I don't know, Lieutenant. Perhaps the weapon array takes time to charge up before each use. Also, Gol-Tur told me the Ghasts had shielded their pyramid. Maybe the one on Sinnar is better shielded than the one on Vempor."

"Why didn't the Ghasts simply destroy their pyramids if they present such a risk?" asked Breeze. "Or bury them a long way down?"

"I don't have answers," said Duggan. "And the Ghasts have been less than forthcoming."

"Look where that's got them," said Chainer.

"They're entitled to secrets, whether or not we agree with their choice to keep things hidden from us," said Duggan.

McGlashan looked angry. "There's nothing good that can come from this, only more death and misery for everyone in the Confederation. Even if we manage to drive our enemies away this time, they'll return, better-armed and with greater numbers than anything we can stand against."

"Are you up for the fight, Commander?"

"Damn right I am, sir. That doesn't mean I want it to happen, though."

"None of us want it. The end of the road gets further away with every step we take. That doesn't mean I'm going to stop putting one foot before the other."

"Nor me," she replied. "I'm going to do everything I can to send them running. And then I'm going to chase after them, killing every one of them I find until they have no hope of threatening us again." The anger in her face was clearly visible.

"Hold those thoughts and they'll serve you well should you ever lose hope," said Duggan.

"And be thankful we're in the only Space Corps warship that has any chance of forcing a victory," said Breeze. "Think of the poor people who can't do anything other than look into the skies every morning and ask themselves if today is the day they're going to die, without an opportunity to prevent it."

The conversation ended, amicably as it always did. The crew were too experienced to allow even the most heated of arguments to descend into unpleasantness. Duggan rarely had to step in and warn any of them to watch their tongues. It helped that they were friends when off duty, not that they'd seen much in the way of shore leave recently.

When his break was due, Duggan sat in the mess room with a tray of steak and fries in front of him.

"You're always in that seat."

Duggan looked up at the voice, unsurprised to see McGlashan there. "I'm a man of habit."

She sat opposite and gave him a wide smile. "It's not even the closest seat to the doorway or the replicator."

"It's roughly eight paces from each," he said.

"You've counted?"

"Maybe."

"What's important about the number eight?" she persisted. "I'm determined to learn exactly what makes you tick." There was a serious question underlying the light tone of her voice.

"If the room were full of soldiers, this seat would be close enough for me to be part of the group, yet not so close that they'd think I was trying to be their friend."

"How do you feel about me sitting so close?"

"Pleased."

"That's it? Pleased?"

He laughed. "We're on duty. You need to stop asking me to reveal too much of myself. The ship's captain must remain aloof. I believe I read that in a handbook somewhere."

"Is that a direct order? Sir?"

"You can ask me whatever you want," he said.

"Why are you in such a good mood?"

"Am I?" he asked. "I suppose I do feel less burdened than usual."

"Yet here we are, facing the greatest danger we have ever faced. Our lives are at risk and so much at stake!"

"I know that," he said. "It's the same as it ever was, except this time it's a bit worse."

"A bit worse?"

"A lot worse," he conceded. "However, for once in my life I have the answers to the questions. Ever since we were sent to find the *Crimson*, we've had vital information withheld from us. Now, here we are, flying out to meet the latest threat to humanity's existence and I feel I've got the answers."

"Which are?"

"Murderous aliens are coming to kill us, while we try to defeat them using a warship cobbled together from bits and pieces of the technology they left behind on one of their previous visits. It's like it's come full circle."

"Not yet, it hasn't. Once we've beaten them, then it'll be a full circle. Until they decide to send fifty motherships through the wormhole."

"I thought I was meant to be the cynical one," he countered.

"You've got me there."

They remained for a few minutes, until Duggan discovered that his tray of food was finished. He stood, just as McGlashan did the same. They headed into the corridor leading towards the bridge. Before he could stop himself, Duggan put his arms around her shoulders and kissed her mouth, wondering why he hadn't done it sooner.

"You could get fired for doing that on duty," she said quietly, smiling up at him.

"I didn't want to die with the chance missed."

"I won't tell."

They returned to the bridge. If either Chainer or Breeze noticed a change, neither of them let on.

CHAPTER THIRTY-TWO

"WE SHOULD BREAK out of lightspeed in ten minutes," announced Lieutenant Breeze.

"Tell me about the solar system," said Duggan. He'd already looked, but wanted a recap.

"It's unusual in that there are only two planets orbiting an otherwise-unremarkable sun," said Chainer. "Neither planet has a moon."

"Presumably moons get in the way of firing whatever weapon they've chosen to install there," said Breeze.

"The planet Tybalt has a comparatively fast rotation about its axis and in turn it completes a full orbit of its sun in fewer than one hundred days," Chainer added.

"All of which provides the likely reason for the continued existence of the Ghast planet Sinnar," said Duggan. They'd spent the last few hours talking about it.

"Yes, sir. Their opportunity to fire will be limited by the position of the sun and the rotation of the planet. We don't have enough data to predict when they will be able to fire at Sinnar, assuming that is their intention."

"And we believe this limitation makes it highly likely the Dreamers will attempt to establish at least one additional weapon array."

"At least one," said Breeze. "More likely two or three more, depending on what factors are important to them."

"I wonder how much of the universe they conquered before they turned their attention towards us," said McGlashan. "They might fill a thousand planets."

"There's no point thinking about it," said Breeze. "When you're talking about infinity, there's always going to be someone bigger and stronger than you."

"The trick to survival is escaping their notice," Chainer added.

The conversation had drifted from its course, but Duggan couldn't stop himself from making a comment. "That sounds too fatalist for my liking. We've proven time and again that we can alter our future. I will never believe I can't change what's to come."

"Perhaps we should delay this conversation until we're in a position to let it run its course," said McGlashan.

"That would probably be for the best, since we've just arrived," said Breeze mildly.

The words galvanised them into action. Without taking stock of their surroundings, Duggan fed maximum power to the *Crimson*'s engines, until the ship was travelling at full speed. "Activate stealth as soon as you're able," he said.

A short while later the engines dropped to fifty percent, but since they'd achieved a velocity of nineteen hundred kilometres per second there was nothing in the vacuum to slow them down. With the *Crimson* hidden by its concealing shroud of technology, Duggan diverted his attention to the remaining priorities.

"What's out here? Give me the details."

Chainer had begun his area scan the moment they'd exited

lightspeed. "Nothing close by, sir. We're two hours away from Tybalt. I'm getting you a picture on the main screen."

A grainy image of the planet appeared – greys and browns streaked with bands of black.

"Can you see anything on the fars?"

"The first sweep has found nothing. It doesn't matter, since we know there's something here, don't we?"

"That we do, Lieutenant. I'm going to take us directly towards the surface. If you don't find what we're looking for I'll take us around in a high orbit once we get closer."

"I've detected a surface object, sir. Another pyramid."

Duggan felt strangely disappointed. "Are you sure? Part of me was hoping to see something a bit more..."

"Exciting?" asked McGlashan.

"*Interesting,* would be more accurate."

"You've seen one pyramid, you've seen them all," said Breeze.

"Commander McGlashan, can you help me out on the sensors?" asked Chainer. "I've got a priority communication from Admiral Teron."

"Bring him through, Lieutenant," said Duggan.

Teron dispensed with the niceties. "I'm glad you've arrived. We're running out of time. There's to be no playing about, Captain Duggan. I want you to operate the Planet Breaker as soon as you're in range of Tybalt. That is a direct order and I want to be sure you understand it."

"I understand, sir. We're approaching the planet now. Once the Planet Breaker becomes available, we will use it at once."

"Good," said Teron, the relief palpable in his voice, as if he'd handed over a great responsibility. "I hope you know I don't give this order lightly. This is the part of my job I find most difficult to come to terms with."

"There's probably no other way, sir. Even if there was an alternative, there might be additional risks."

"It gives you the greatest chance of returning home, John."

"That was never the fear, sir. I have a hunch the mothership is elsewhere, so we'll have that to come."

"I had hopes it would be destroyed in the shattering of Tybalt. Don't wait around to see if it shows up – if the mothership isn't close by, your orders stand."

"Yes, sir. Are the reinforcements coming?"

"They're on route and at lightspeed. They'll be needed if the mothership arrives."

"It'll come, sir. What ships are inbound? They won't stand a chance."

"The *Archimedes* and the *Maximilian* will arrive within four hours. We've learned from our past encounter. The enemy particle beams won't be nearly so effective this time. The Ghasts are sending two ships. They were in the same place as ours – drumming out a peace in a solar system nobody's heard of."

"It's good they're committing their own warships."

"They've got the same motivation we have. They don't want to lose Sinnar."

"What are they sending?"

"You already know the *Trivanor*. The *Sandarvax* will be less familiar. It's impressive, John – makes me glad we'll be on the same side."

"The more the merrier."

"Destroy the planet. It's the only way to save Atlantis and Sinnar. If it flushes the mothership out, so much the better. Let's hope they don't know how to fight in the rubble of a shattered world."

"I'll keep you updated. Goodbye, sir."

With Teron gone, Duggan looked at each of the other crew members in turn, trying to gauge their mood.

"It was always likely to come to this," said McGlashan.

Duggan nodded. "Yes. I suppose I knew it."

"There's no one living there," said Breeze.

"The Planet Breaker has got a thirty second warm up and a range of approximately fifty thousand klicks. Are we firing when ready?"

"That we are, Commander."

"There could be valuable intel if we do a quick orbit, sir," said Chainer. "It would be nice to know how they've constructed this super-weapon."

"Thank you, Lieutenant, but we'll follow Admiral Teron's order to the letter. I would hate to be responsible for the loss of Atlantis because we delayed for ten minutes."

"Okay, sir. I'll continue scanning as we approach to see if anything else turns up."

Duggan did his best to get comfortable while the *Crimson* tore through local space towards its destination. He couldn't settle and shifted constantly, until he finally stood up and paced around.

"There's a second pyramid, sir," said Chainer. "It's a few thousand klicks to the north of the first one – it's only just visible."

"Run a scan over an area the same distance to the south of the first pyramid."

"Yep, there's a third one," said Chainer after a moment of concentration. "And a Dreamer battleship in a high orbit."

"Has it detected us?"

"No, sir. It's following a course that I believe will allow it to monitor the entire surface of the planet."

"It shouldn't make a difference to what we have planned," said Duggan.

"It had to be here, didn't it?" asked McGlashan.

Duggan grinned. "I'm starting to feel as if it's my nemesis. How high is their orbit?"

"Thirty thousand klicks, sir."

"I don't suppose we can run a simulation to predict the likelihood of their destruction once we use the Planet Breaker?"

"I could program you one in a few days," said McGlashan. "My non-scientific instinct tells me they stand a realistic chance of being smashed to pieces."

"That's what my equally non-scientific guts tell me," said Chainer.

"If we assume an equal placing about the surface, how many pyramids are down there?"

"Nine," said Chainer promptly.

"They've invested a whole lot of resources in this place," mused Duggan. "I wish I understood the reasons better."

"Let the analysis teams worry about it, sir," said Breeze. "We've got enough on our plate."

The viewscreen image of Tybalt became steadily more clearly-defined as the *Crimson* approached. Duggan wouldn't have usually spent much time looking at such an uninteresting place, but he felt an obligation to commit its details to memory. *If I'm going to destroy it, I should at least have the decency to look at it first.*

The enemy battleship continued orbiting, altering its trajectory with each circuit in order that it could monitor each of the emplacements on the ground. Chainer watched it carefully, but found no evidence to suggest the enemy were aware of the inbound *ESS Crimson*.

"I don't want to be too close to that warship when we come into the Planet Breaker's firing range," said Duggan. "I'd rather get in and out. If the bastards live through the destruction, we can join the *Archimedes* and *Maximilian* in trying to shoot them down."

"We'll be at fifty thousand klicks in five minutes," said Chainer. "The enemy will be around the other side of the planet by then."

"Good. There's no reason for us to delay."

The bridge fell silent, except for the subdued humming of engines and electronics. There was something humbling about being in charge of a weapon with such monumental destructive power and none of the crew wished to disturb the quiet by speaking anything irreverent.

"We'll be in range in one minute," said McGlashan. "I've activated the Planet Breaker warm-up routines. Thirty seconds and it'll be ready to fire."

"Hold till fifty thousand klicks."

"The Planet Breaker is charged up and able to fire on your command, sir. Twenty seconds until we're in range."

It was a long twenty seconds. Duggan didn't take his eyes away from Commander McGlashan's face. He saw the apprehension and the excitement. She knew this weapon was an abomination, yet there was an allure – the infinite power to destroy at the press of a button. Encompassing it, her overriding emotion was sadness, along with the hope she wouldn't be judged for taking part in what was to come.

"Now," said Duggan.

CHAPTER THIRTY-THREE

THE PLANET BREAKER hadn't been fired for many months. It didn't matter – the shriek of its charge-up was etched into Duggan's brain forever. The sound built to a howl and the walls of the bridge shook with the force of a vibration which felt as though it might tear the *Crimson* apart. When he thought his ears could take no more of the punishment, the sound ebbed away so quickly that it left his head and ears ringing. Through it all, he maintained a death grip on the spaceship's control bars in preparation for turning away from the doomed world.

The expected did not come to pass.

"What the hell?" asked McGlashan. "How long did it take to work last time?"

"It was instantaneous," Duggan replied. "You didn't misremember."

"There's a power spike from the closest pyramid," said Breeze. "A trillion percent increase." He sounded bewildered at the number. "There are lesser spikes from the other visible pyramids, sir."

"Fire again," said Duggan.

"Not a hope, sir," McGlashan replied. "I have no idea what the charge-up time is, but it's not going to fire again any time soon."

Duggan swore loudly and thumped his fist against the arm of his chair. "What's going on? Someone tell me what happened!"

"The pyramids must have absorbed the energy from the Planet Breaker, sir."

"How did they know what to do?"

"I doubt they guessed what we had planned," said Breeze. "We know hardly anything about the weapon or our opponents. Perhaps where they come from everyone has a Planet Breaker and they developed defences to prevent their use."

"What if we destroy the pyramids?"

"I imagine that would do the trick. There are nine pyramids plus a weapon array with unknown capabilities and defences. I doubt our opponents are going to sit idly by as we destroy each in turn."

"They certainly aren't," said Chainer. "Here's their battleship coming over the horizon."

"Are they coming directly at us?" asked Duggan sharply.

"Not directly. They must have a good idea where we are, since they'll not be too far off."

"Let's get away," said Duggan.

He spun the *Crimson* around and accelerated in a random direction, keeping at fifty thousand kilometres from the surface.

"What now?" asked McGlashan.

"This isn't what I had planned," Duggan replied, failing to answer the question. "I don't know what now."

"The enemy battleship has changed course and dropped to fifty thousand klicks to match us," said Chainer.

"Have they got a lock on?"

"I don't know, sir. Their course matches ours exactly and they're closing to three thousand klicks."

"Damnit! Have the stealth modules suffered damage, or did they just get lucky?"

"The stealth modules are fully operational," said Breeze.

"They could have learned something from our last encounter," McGlashan suggested. "They chased us for long enough."

"They didn't catch us, so they can't have learned too much."

"I think I know what it is," said Breeze. "We're trailing *something* behind us. A type of particle I don't recognize."

"The Planet Breaker!" said McGlashan. "It must have a signature."

"And they can detect it," said Duggan angrily.

"They haven't fired yet," said Chainer. "We're well within range."

"Get me some details about what's happening. How vulnerable are we?"

"There's a wide arc behind us, sir. If that's what they're following, they can't pin-point us."

"Nor can we lose them."

"I doubt they're going to let us go this time."

"Of course not," said Chainer. "What're the odds there's a mothership coming this way at Light-Z or whatever speed they can push it to?"

"I've got a plan," said Duggan through gritted teeth.

"Two waves of fifty missiles just went by us," said McGlashan. "They're close enough to launch and miss before I can open my mouth."

"Lieutenant Chainer, I want you to provide me with the most efficient course that takes us directly over each of the pyramids on the surface. Commander McGlashan, you're going to fire two nukes and thirty-six Lambdas at every pyramid. When we come across the weapon array, fire everything we've got. I want that emplacement reduced to a radiation-filled hole that won't cool down for a thousand years."

"Yes sir!"

"I've sent you details of the most efficient trajectory, sir," said Chainer. "If you have to deviate because of evasive manoeuvres, it should update automatically."

"Three more waves of fifty have passed by," said McGlashan. "One of them came within eighty metres."

"Crap," said Chainer. "Missed us by a whisker."

"They must be conserving ammunition for a long fight," said Breeze. They'd witnessed this same battleship fire many hundreds of missiles simultaneously in their previous encounter.

"First pyramid coming up, Commander. Prepare to fire."

"Nukes away and Lambdas close after. Twenty seconds to impact."

Duggan watched the missiles on his tactical screen. They flew unerringly towards the pyramid far below. Then, a cloud of smaller dots appeared from behind and tore across the intervening space. One-by-one the *Crimson*'s Lambdas and nuclear missiles were intercepted by the enemy battleship's anti-missile system. A handful of the Lambdas reached their target and detonated fruitlessly off the pyramid's energy shield. Both nuclear missiles were destroyed before they could explode.

"You'll need to get us closer, sir."

Duggan refused to let frustration take hold. "I'll bring us to ten thousand klicks. That should cut the travel time of our missiles sufficiently to prevent further interceptions."

"It'll need to be lower - much lower. Their interceptors travel far faster than the Lambdas."

"Very well. We'll launch from three thousand klicks."

This was much closer to the surface than Duggan wanted to be. The higher they stayed, the better the vantage they had. On top of that, he'd have to slow the *Crimson*'s speed. Tybalt's atmosphere was thin, but there was sufficient nitrogen and carbon dioxide to heat the alloys of the hull. The stealth modules were capable of disguising heat signatures, but Duggan didn't want to risk giving the enemy any advantage if he could avoid it.

Even at three thousand kilometres, the *Crimson* was travelling high enough and fast enough that they were upon the next target within a few seconds.

"Missiles away."

The Dreamer battleship launched its missile interceptors once more. This time they failed to destroy a single one of their targets.

"The pyramid's energy shield is down and the target destroyed," said McGlashan.

"Eight more to go," said Chainer. "Plus the big one, when we find it."

They came upon the main weapon array within a few seconds of destroying the first pyramid. At least they assumed it was what they were searching for. The *Crimson*'s sensors picked out a cluster of metallic objects on the ground. Chainer took less than a second to interpret the results of the scan.

"Four pyramids in a square, with a huge rotating turret in the centre."

"Blow the shit out of it," said Duggan.

"Six nukes and one hundred Lambdas away."

The travel time was a little over one second. It was more than long enough for the sixty-four Dreamer defence emplacements to track and destroy most of the inbound missiles in a spray of alloy slugs and airborne electronic scramblers.

"Only two Lambda strikes, sir. We have to launch the nukes first in order to disable the energy shield. Unfortunately, that means they get knocked out quickest."

"We'll leave the main site for the moment. If we can knock

out the remaining pyramids, the Planet Breaker will finish the job."

"What about the four pyramids around the turret?" asked Breeze.

"We'll take out the easier targets first and hope it weakens whatever defences they've got against the Planet Breaker enough that we can use it."

"It hasn't charged up yet," said McGlashan. "There's no way of knowing when it'll be ready and I'm afraid I didn't pay attention on the previous occasions we used it."

"None of us did," said Duggan. "It'll either be available when we need it, or it won't."

"Next target ahead, sir," said Chainer.

"The enemy battleship has commenced firing," said McGlashan. "Three waves of fifty followed by another three."

None of the inbound missiles hit the *Crimson*. There was no need to announce it aloud – the fact that they remained alive was enough.

"Nukes and Lambdas on their way...pyramid number two destroyed."

How long can we keep it going? thought Duggan. With surprise, he noticed how high the hull temperature had climbed. The distraction of the last couple of minutes had caused him to miss it. It jumped another five percent in the few seconds his eyes remained on the gauge, spoiling his hopes that it might stabilise long enough to complete the destruction of the remaining pyramids.

"They're still launching, sir. There's no sign of them letting up."

"We've ridden our luck for long enough. Hit them with the disruptor and launch both Shatterer tubes."

McGlashan gave a thumbs up sign. "Done and done."

"Their shields are down," said Breeze. "Engine output at zero."

The Shatterer missiles were incredibly fast. They burst out of the *Crimson's* front-mounted launch tubes and accelerated for several thousand kilometres. Then, they performed an impossibly tight turn in the air and shot back the way they'd come at a speed of four thousand kilometres per second. The two missiles flew to either side of the *Crimson*, before crashing into the enemy battleship. The combined velocities were enough to force the warheads deep into the spaceship's armour before they detonated with catastrophic force, peeling away the outer skin of armour and leaving two gaping holes, smouldering and angry.

"Where are they?"

"Gone, sir. Lost over the horizon."

"Their engines were coming back online," said Breeze. "The disruptor didn't last long."

"It did well enough. I should have used it sooner."

"It's done now, sir," said McGlashan. "We've got an opportunity to destroy a few more targets before the battleship finds us again."

"And find us it will," said Duggan, berating himself for being too timid. There'd been no need to delay using the disruptor. He asked himself if he feared his opponent, allowing it to cloud his judgement and make him act too defensively. *If I hold back, we have no hope.*

He permitted his anger to swell, released a small part of it into his conscious mind. His anger could not countenance defeat and it filled him with vigour. He turned the *Crimson* onto a new heading, in order to confuse the pursuing battleship. The next target was ahead and Duggan focused on getting them to it as quickly as possible.

CHAPTER THIRTY-FOUR

THERE WERE ONLY two pyramids remaining when the battleship found them again. It had waited high above the surface until the *Crimson* passed underneath. The enemy had evidently discovered a way that allowed them to track a cloaked vessel easily, yet without having enough precision to allow them to unleash the full force of their arsenal. Duggan didn't dwell on the reasons – he simply wanted to complete his task and see if he could destroy the planet in order to save the ten billion people who lived on Atlantis.

As soon as the battleship came close, Duggan ordered the disruptor and Shatterers to be fired again. The tactic wasn't nearly so effective on this occasion and the enemy got their shields back up before the inbound missiles could smash into them.

"It might be that they can adapt," said Breeze. "Each time the same disruptor is used against them, it becomes less effective."

"Do you know that for definite?" asked Duggan.

"No, sir. I'm just thinking out loud."

"We could do with the *Archimedes* right about now," said

Chainer. "Along with those Ghast warships to act as a meat shield."

"We're on our own for a while yet, Lieutenant," said Duggan, his eyes roving constantly over the screens around him. His tactical display showed an unending barrage of Dreamer missiles in the skies around them. He had the ship's AI run through the average distances by which the misses occurred. It was as he feared – the average had fallen significantly.

The fact wasn't lost on the others. "They're going to get us soon," said McGlashan. "I just registered one missile go by at fifty metres."

"We're hot, we're launching our own missiles and we're trailing particles from the Planet Breaker," said Breeze. "We must stick out like a sore thumb - it's a wonder we've lasted this long."

"What to do, what to do?" muttered Duggan under his breath.

"Pyramid number eight down," said McGlashan. "One more to go until we can take another shot at the main emplacement."

At that moment, disaster struck. There was a thumping roar far to the back of the *Crimson*. Waves of vibration coursed through the walls and floor. The noise of the engines changed, losing a fraction of the smoothness.

"Missile strike to the rear," said Breeze. "Now you can add positrons to everything else we're leaving behind."

"What's the damage? I need specifics, Lieutenant!"

"There's an armour breach and we've lost some of our engines, sir. The life support and stealth modules are undamaged."

"Three more missiles have come within twenty metres, sir," said McGlashan.

"Shit," said Duggan. The anger built and this time it was difficult to keep it under control. The battleship was faster than the

Crimson and could unleash four times the firepower. "But they didn't bother with the armour."

"What's that, sir?"

"How far behind is the enemy tracking us?"

"Less than one thousand klicks now."

"Commander McGlashan, get ready to launch everything we've got. I want the disruptor first, then everything else."

"The last pyramid isn't in range yet, sir."

"It's not the pyramid we're aiming for."

"Oh."

The timing was going to be crucial. In their haste, the enemy had allowed themselves to come too close, buoyed by the protection of their shield and the scent of victory over the much smaller *Crimson*.

"Get ready."

With that, Duggan wrenched hard on the control sticks. The gravity engines grumbled and the life support modules plundered the ship's power reserves in order to maintain the stability of the interior. The ESS *Crimson* decelerated suddenly. Caught unawares, the Dreamer battleship overtook within a second, barrelling past so close it was visible to the naked eye.

"Fire," said Duggan. At the same time, he increased their speed in order to match that of the enemy vessel.

"Disruptor fired. Four nukes away, with two Shatterers and a hundred and fifty Lambdas joining them."

"Their shields are gone and engines offline." said Breeze.

The dark skies of Tybalt erupted in light. There was too little oxygen for the nuclear warheads to produce anything more than a stunted explosion. They thumped against the battleship's armour, flooding it with toxic rays and utterly destroying the delicate equipment which generated the protective shield. Lambda and Shatterer missiles plunged into the warship, producing a bloom of white along its five-kilometre length. The warheads inflicted terrible damage, yet Duggan could see that it wouldn't be enough. He hadn't underestimated the strength of their armour, it was simply that the ship was so big.

Without pausing, Duggan put the *Crimson* into a roll, in order that the port-side clusters could launch. McGlashan didn't need his instruction and she fired immediately, sending a salvo of ninety-six missiles at the battleship. Whatever technology the Dreamers used to prevent missile targeting, it continued to function and the Lambdas were launched without guidance, relying on AI prediction and luck to find their intended destination.

"Their engines are coming back," said Breeze.

Duggan completed the roll, bringing the starboard clusters to bear again. "Fire more Lambdas, Commander. Use countermeasures immediately."

McGlashan fired the shock drones and they accelerated away from hundreds of launch tubes around the hull. The drones glittered and gleamed, sending bursts of static and a maelstrom of nonsense communications in order to confuse inbound missiles.

"Lambdas not ready, sir."

The Lambdas on the *Crimson* were equipped with the newest rapid-reload facility, which cut the firing interval to eight seconds. Even so, the crew were forced to endure the most agonising two second wait before McGlashan was able to complete the next launch.

"Done," she said.

"We're too close to the nuclear blasts," said Breeze. "The hull is absorbing a crap-load of radiation."

"I need to be sure we've taken the enemy down," said Duggan.

"They're not coming out of that, sir," said McGlashan.

The second and third wave of Lambdas had turned the battleship into a five-kilometre length of shattered metal. Nevertheless, it hadn't broken up in spite of its delicate appearance.

Struts and beams with unknown functions spun lazily away from the hull, while plasma fires continued to rage.

"Give them one last round," said Duggan, preparing to take the *Crimson* away.

"There they go," said McGlashan. "Another hundred to say goodbye."

The enemy battleship wasn't quite done with them. Somewhere within the remains of the ship, a command was given. Here and there, the few remaining operational missile tubes on the battleship launched their ammunition. The captain of the Dreamer vessel had disabled the missile guidance systems, in order to try and land a lucky hit on the stealth-clad *ESS Crimson*. The shock drones were useless against unguided projectiles and one of the Dreamer missiles exploded against the side of the *Crimson*, rocking the ship on its axis. Moments later, a series of Lambda blasts tore the last vestiges of the battleship into countless pieces.

Duggan grunted when he saw the damage warnings flood onto his screens. He pulled the *Crimson* high up and away from the defeated enemy vessel, rapidly escaping the sphere of intense gamma radiation.

"Give me the bad news," he said.

"The stealth modules have disengaged. That was a high-payload missile," said Breeze. "It burned out a chunk of our gravity drive."

"What's the shortfall before we can get the stealth modules online?"

"The AI is working on it. It predicts we might be able to achieve sixty percent of our maximum sub-light output in two hours, give or take. We'll have the cloak but we won't be going anywhere fast while it's activated."

"Any possibility we can scavenge some power from the fission drives?"

"In time, sir. Add several more hours to the total."

"There's more bad news," said McGlashan. One look at her face was enough to tell Duggan it really *was* bad.

"Tell me."

"The Planet Breaker is out of action, sir. Previously it was charging up, now I can't even access the command menu to check its status."

Duggan took a guess at the reason. "Radiation. The Dreamer stuff must be vulnerable to it."

Breeze rubbed his hands over his eyes. "I'll bet you've hit the nail on the head." He growled angrily. "We couldn't afford to lose it."

"No Lieutenant, we could not. The labs might be able to repair it, given time. However, for the moment we are denied the opportunity to use it for the purpose we intended. That does not mean we are about to abandon this mission when there is so much to do."

Breeze nodded at the words. "There's one more pyramid out there and a weapon array to disable."

Duggan smiled widely at his crew. "And on the bright side, our enemy fell for the oldest trick in the book, allowing us to snatch victory from the jaws of defeat."

"If any of them live, they'll not enjoy filing the report for that one," said Chainer.

The moment of levity passed. "Come on, people. Let's get on with business," said Duggan.

"How long until backup gets here?" asked McGlashan.

"Two hours or more," said Duggan. "Admiral Teron wasn't precise, so we'll have to wait and see."

"Should we wait?" asked McGlashan.

Duggan gave the matter serious thought. He was close to acquiescing when Chainer dropped a bombshell on them.

"When we arrived in this system I assigned a few spare cycles from the AI to the task of checking planetary alignments and rotations."

It was apparent from Chainer's voice that he was building up to something which none of them would be happy to hear.

"Until we found the position of the main array on Tybalt's surface, I lacked data to complete the task. It's been a little busy since then, but the report is complete."

"What does it show?"

"They'll have a clear shot at Atlantis in two hours thirty minutes, sir. After that, there's only another fifteen minutes until there'll be a straight, unimpeded line between the weapon and Sinnar."

Chainer's words took the decision out of Duggan's hands. There was no choice but to try and finish what they'd started and hope that backup would arrive in time to assist in the event that they failed.

CHAPTER THIRTY-FIVE

IN THE FEW moments it took Commander McGlashan to target and destroy the final pyramid, Duggan spoke to Admiral Teron to apprise him of the situation.

"Do you think you can take out the Dreamer weapon?" asked Teron.

"I'm unsure, sir. It's well-protected against missile attack. We've got plenty of ammunition, but not enough to sustain a two-hour bombardment in the hope that something gets through. When our ships arrive, we'll be able to swamp their countermeasures easily."

"I double-checked the *Archimedes'* flight logs. Their estimated arrival time is two hours and five minutes. It'll be more than just the *Archimedes*, of course."

"That gives them less than thirty minutes to get here and assist with the destruction of the emplacement, assuming we are unable to accomplish it ourselves. If they're late, Atlantis will cease to exist."

"You don't sound hopeful."

"I'll do what I can, sir."

"It'll have to be enough. I'll have a message sent to the *Archimedes* telling them to do an immediate lightspeed hop as close to the surface as they can get. They'll receive the coordinates of the target in the same message, as soon as they exit lightspeed. Admiral Franks commands the *Archimedes*, but she'll report to you for the remainder of the mission. It'll be easier that way."

"Yes, sir."

"Keep me informed."

With that, Teron was gone. It took a few minutes for Duggan to pilot the *Crimson* to a position high above the weapon emplacement. He looked at the sensor feed impassively as he tried to figure out the best approach.

"What if we fired Lambdas first, then nukes?" asked McGlashan. "One of the nuclear warheads might get close enough if we did that."

"Could we use the disruptor?" asked Chainer.

"The disruptor won't be much use," said Breeze. "There are four pyramids and a central turret. Assuming the pyramids are generating the energy shield, we can't use the disruptor often enough to disable them all simultaneously."

"We're reduced to throwing numbers at them and keeping our fingers crossed," said McGlashan.

"Let's give that a try," said Duggan. "I want the Lambdas first, to reduce the chance they'll intercept a nuke."

They gave it a go. Lambda missiles streaked towards the surface, followed by four of the *Crimson*'s dwindling supply of nuclear warheads. A handful of the Lambdas escaped the countermeasures and they detonated off the energy shield. All bar one of the nuclear missiles were intercepted. This final one exploded automatically when it reached a hundred kilometres above the surface. The blast itself was muted, but the radiation expanded in a huge sphere. Duggan watched on his tactical display as gamma rays beat down onto the surface.

"Something's happening," said Breeze, his eyes glued to the readouts in front of him.

"Did we get the shield generators?" asked Duggan.

Breeze swore. "Their power output stuttered for a second, but it's steadied. The nukes need to detonate closer to the shield."

"We need to go lower," said Duggan. "What about if we fired from a thousand klicks up? That would reduce their time to intercept our missiles."

"As long as we don't get caught in the blast ourselves."

"I'm taking us closer. Prepare to launch from a thousand klicks."

The method didn't go to plan. As soon as the *Crimson* came within twenty-five thousand kilometres, the Dreamer ground batteries opened up, firing thousands of uranium rounds against the spacecraft's hull. The slugs punched into the protective layers of armour, prompting Duggan to increase their height quickly. He imagined the spaceship groaning under the stresses of the attack and from the loads on its damaged engines.

"We're an easy target without the stealth modules," said McGlashan.

"What about if we perform a quick flyover at a low height and launch at the last moment?" said Breeze. "Their batteries won't see us coming over the horizon until it's too late."

"It's too risky," Duggan replied. "We might get our payload away, but they'll have an easy time shooting at us."

"Unless they're too busy firing at our missiles."

"We'll be caught up in our own nuclear blast," said Breeze.

"True."

"We'll be able to use the stealth units in slightly under two hours, not that the *Crimson* will travel fast with them active,"

Breeze added. "Then we can attack without the enemy being able to retaliate effectively."

"In that case, we'll wait for the time being. Once the stealth modules are available, we will be in a much stronger position."

"We don't have many options remaining to us until then," McGlashan said. "And what if we lack the firepower to overcome the array's countermeasures?"

"The *Archimedes* and *Maximilian* have the best AIs onboard, which means they'll arrive at the intended time, give or take a minute. There should be ample time for them to get to the target site," said Chainer. "I can't imagine the sixty-four cannons protecting the array will have much success against a hundred nukes and eight hundred Lambdas coming in at once."

Duggan didn't like inaction, especially when it was forced upon him. Nevertheless, he didn't hate it so much that he would do something reckless in order to avoid having to wait. "The timing will be tight, but we're going to hold back until our situation has improved," he said. "If there's any sign the reinforcements have been delayed we'll attempt a low-level flyover, with or without the stealth. We might have to sacrifice ourselves for the greater good, folks."

"Yeah, that's what they told me when I signed up for the Space Corps," said Breeze. "It was somewhere in the small print underneath the bit where it said I'd be a hero."

There was no more fuss than that. The crew were not desperate to rush to their own deaths, nor would they shy away from the risks. Duggan increased their altitude once again and kept them at a steady fifty thousand kilometres and slightly to one side of the weapon below. After a few minutes, he got it into his head that the Dreamers might be able to use the main turret to target nearby spacecraft, so he piloted the warship around the planet's curvature. It meant he was unable see if there were signs of activity from the array, but it was a price worth paying in the circumstances.

The greatest distraction during the wait was the series of countdown timers which Breeze sent to the bulkhead screen. The left-hand timer showed when the stealth modules would be ready to activate, the middle timer counted the minutes until the *Archimedes'* arrival, while the right-hand timer showed how long Atlantis had remaining until it was destroyed. In spite of his best efforts to only look at them infrequently, Duggan found his eyes drifting constantly to the numbers. He considered asking Breeze to take them down, before accepting the weakness was his and that the information was too valuable to hide.

Disaster struck when there was a single minute remaining on the stealth timer.

"Sir, the Dreamer mothership has exited lightspeed. They've come in right on top of the array," said Breeze.

There was no time for Duggan to appreciate how close they'd come to being killed. If he hadn't succumbed to his worries about the ground turret being able to shoot the *Crimson* out of the sky, the mothership would have destroyed them immediately.

"What are they doing?"

"I don't know, sir," said Breeze. "I only see the fission signature. They must be worried given how close they came in."

"They're hidden from me," said Chainer. "I don't recommend you have a peek over the horizon, though."

"Why does this always happen?" Duggan growled in frustration.

"The stealth modules are available for activation," said Breeze. "There should be just about enough juice remaining to keep us in the air and to travel at a walking pace."

There seemed like no point in waiting. "Activate them."

As soon as the stealth modules kicked in, the hum of the *Crimson's* engines became an intrusive roar. It was the sound of power being stretched to its very limit. Duggan reached for the control bars and attempted to rotate the spaceship. As he'd feared – there was close to zero response.

"Watch out for incoming," said Duggan. "We're not going anywhere fast."

"It should improve gradually, sir," Breeze suggested. "Though I wouldn't expect to be nimble any time soon."

Duggan increased their altitude and took them cautiously towards the Dreamer weapon site. It was a pitifully slow process to reach a position where the ship's sensors were able to gather a picture of what was happening.

"They're not moving," said Chainer. "They're completely still, directly over the emplacement."

"Are they aware we're here?"

"Almost certainly."

"They don't seem interested in coming closer," said McGlashan.

"I wonder if they've decided against taking risks," Duggan mused. "This place must be really important to them." He looked at McGlashan. "Can you access the Planet Breaker?" The question was asked in hope rather than expectation.

"I remain locked out. I've been checking it every few seconds and I'm certain it's completely out of action."

"It was worth asking."

"Yeah. Sorry."

Duggan didn't want to tempt fate any longer and he moved the *Crimson* away, until the mothership was no longer visible on the sensors. The depths of the bad news finally sank in. The Dreamers were going to sit it out until they'd destroyed both Atlantis and Sinnar. The *Archimedes* and the Ghasts would arrive soon. He didn't know what armaments the *Trivanor* and *Sandarvax* carried, but he doubted whether their Shatterers would be sufficient to worry the mothership. The Space Corps and Ghast navies were about to lose several of their most important warships and billions would die.

"Ladies and gentlemen, I think we've reached rock-bottom," he said.

"No we haven't, sir," Breeze replied. "There are two more fission signatures, consistent with the arrival of enemy cruisers."

CHAPTER THIRTY-SIX

THE ENEMY CRUISERS established themselves high above the weapon site and circled continuously. They were surely aware that there was a cloaked ship somewhere in the vicinity, but they showed no sign they wanted to look for it.

"They can't know we're as damaged as we are," said Duggan. "Otherwise I think they'd be less passive."

"There is no need for them to do anything," said McGlashan.

"I have Admiral Franks on the comms," said Chainer.

Duggan jumped to his feet. "They've arrived! Find them!"

"Captain Duggan, the *Archimedes* and *Maximilian* are at your disposal. The *Sandarvax* and *Trivanor* accompany us, but they have their own commanders."

"Things are not good, Admiral."

Duggan filled in the details. His mouth talked and his mind did its best to come up with a solution.

"The *Archimedes* is more than nine thousand metres long and the *Sandarvax* is eleven thousand metres long, Captain. From the reports of your previous encounter with the enemy, the prides of our respective navies will be blown into pieces even with our new defences against beam weaponry."

"The mothership carries two cannons, each of which could put a hole clean through either vessel. A head-on approach will result in failure."

"We must do something!"

"Bombard the planet. Launch nukes from far out in space. Ask the Ghasts to use their incendiary bombs. There is not long left. Also, be aware there are two enemy cruisers above the weapon site. I anticipate they will move to intercept."

Franks laughed, the sound mellifluous yet lacking in humour. "I've studied the details of their cruisers. They are technologically superior and will cause us problems, but we will destroy them. I have no doubt about that."

"Good, you will need to," said Duggan. "My comms man has located you an hour's sub-light distance away. Make preparations for a lightspeed hop. I warn you, Admiral. Do not come within sight of the mothership."

"Understood. What is your own status?"

"We're badly damaged and struggling to maintain stealth. We'll do what we can to disrupt them."

With that, Franks was gone. There was no unexpected delay and within two minutes, four warships emerged into view, a hundred thousand kilometres above the surface and on the blind side of the planet from the mothership.

Duggan had seen the *Sandarvax* once, without knowing what it was called. The memory and the reality were little different and the Ghast capital ship was as monstrously laden with weaponry as he remembered it, with sweeping curves, domes and the tell-tale signs of multiple Shatterer tubes. The Ghasts had kept the ship away from direct confrontation, apart from the single time they'd sent it against the *Archimedes* a couple of years previously.

"I'm glad they held it in reserve," said McGlashan, her eyes wide.

"They will have had their reasons and it won't have been sympathy for the Confederation," said Duggan.

The four warships didn't pause and they headed directly for the planet's surface at maximum speed. The *Sandarvax* was the quickest of the four and at fifty thousand kilometres, it launched its weapons.

"Atmosphere bombs," said McGlashan. "Dozens of them!"

"Here comes the first enemy cruiser!" shouted Chainer.

"The *Maximilian*'s powering up for something."

"Shatterers launched from both Ghast vessels. Six from the *Trivanor* and seventy-two from the *Sandarvax*!"

"Crap!" said Chainer. "How many?"

"We might as well fire our own two," said Duggan.

"Both forward Shatterers launched, sir."

"The Dreamer cruiser has shut down the *Trivanor* with its disruptor," said Breeze. "And the *Maximilian* has fired something in return. It's been fitted with a disruptor as well!"

Duggan felt useless as he watched events unfold on the sensor feeds and on his tactical display. Hundreds of missiles filled the air. The second enemy cruiser raced to engage. It tried to shut down the *Sandarvax*, succeeding only in knocking the Ghast engines offline for a couple of seconds.

Far below, the atmosphere bombs reached their detonation height. Duggan wondered how much effect they'd have, given the lack of oxygen on Tybalt. He was left in awestruck horror when the incendiaries exploded into a conflagration of unimaginable proportions, as though they carried a billion tonnes of accelerant. Within seconds of their detonation, the wave of flame had spread for thousands of kilometres in every direction, until it was lost from sight. The fires were not quickly extinguished and they continued to rage, far longer than Duggan believed was possible.

"The surface temperature is as high as fifteen hundred degrees in places!" said Chainer, his voice choking with shock.

"Is it going to be enough?" asked Duggan, hoping one of his crew would be able to tell him with certainty.

"I doubt it, sir," said Breeze. "I've seen how much power those pyramids can generate."

"There are several dozen nuclear blasts in the vicinity of the first enemy cruiser," said McGlashan. "The *Archimedes* has been hit several times by a particle beam as well as a dozen missiles or more."

"The *Trivanor* and *Sandarvax* have launched more Shatterers. The second cruiser has taken twin disruptor strikes," said Chainer, his voice rising an octave.

"First cruiser destroyed!" said McGlashan with excitement. "The second cruiser is back online and attempting to break away. Damn, it's fast!"

For once, the Dreamer warships found themselves comprehensively outgunned. The human and Ghast navies had the combined weaponry to counter most of the technological advantages their foes possessed, as well as their warships being overwhelming larger and therefore able to withstand a considerable amount of punishment.

"Second cruiser down!" shouted Chainer. "How do you like that, eh?"

"Good work, Admiral," said Duggan over the comms. "Who commands the *Sandarvax*? Pass on my regards."

"Subjos Gol-Tur is captain of their flagship. I believe you've met him."

"Once. What's your damage status?"

"We've taken several missile strikes. Their warheads have a far greater penetration than ours. We're operational for the moment. Reports from the *Maximilian* and the Ghast ships indicate they've suffered moderate damage only."

"This is where it's going to get nasty, Admiral. I think the enemy mothership is going to wait for us to act first. They have time on their side."

"There are fifteen minutes remaining," she said.

"Let's get to it. Attempt nuclear bombardment from a distance. Don't stay in the enemy's line of sight for longer than it takes to launch your missiles."

"Yes, Captain."

The four warships sped away, each taking a similar course to reach their destination. Duggan piloted the *Crimson* along the same path as the *Archimedes*. The spaceship felt slightly more responsive, but was still heavy and ponderous compared to what he was used to. By the time they had completed the partial orbit necessary to view the site of the Dreamer weapon, it was a nuclear wasteland for a thousand kilometres all around. The planet's surface was completely changed from how it had been and the rock had become molten in hundreds of places. Something caught Duggan's eye – a crater, far larger than the others. There was an object at the bottom, huge and metallic.

"The *Trivanor*," said Chainer. "It's full of holes."

"It didn't take long to knock them out of the sky," said McGlashan.

"Ten minutes until the enemy can fire towards Atlantis," said Breeze. He needn't have spoken – the countdown timers continued to tick in full view of everyone.

"Admiral Franks, please report," said Duggan. "Has your bombardment destroyed the target?"

"The target remains protected by its shield, Captain. We cannot get close enough to land a direct hit without risking instant destruction from the mothership."

"Have you tried?" he asked.

The response sounded as if it were spoken through gritted teeth. "Captain Duggan, we have an extensive collection of fifty-metre holes through our hull. The casualty reports have yet to come in. The *Trivanor* is out of action and the *Sandarvax* is as badly-damaged as we are. On top of that, they've hit us with an unknown weapon that is causing our engines to degrade. We will be forced to land in a short while."

"I understand the issues, Admiral. We can't allow them to fire that damned weapon!"

The sensor feed from the surface turned orange once more, hiding everything in a carpet of unnaturally hot fire.

"The Ghast incendiaries aren't any more effective than what we're doing," said Franks.

"We need to keep trying!"

"We will, Captain Duggan."

"They're too big and too powerful," said McGlashan when the comms feed was ended. She looked at Duggan sadly. "Perhaps we should consider a withdrawal before we lose everything."

"I can't do it, Commander. There's got to be a way."

At that moment, an idea came to him. At first, he dismissed it outright. It was something which, as far as he was aware, nobody had ever successfully accomplished. He didn't know if anyone had even attempted it. A voice whispered that he had no choice but to try. Gambling four lives to save billions was odds he couldn't refuse.

"Sir?" It was McGlashan. "What is it?"

"Are you ready to risk everything, Commander?"

"Always."

CHAPTER THIRTY-SEVEN

"LIEUTENANT CHAINER, I'm lifting us into a position where we can see the mothership. I need you to confirm its *exact* location, by which I mean the dead centre of their vessel."

"Okay, sir."

Duggan slowly took the *Crimson* above the horizon. At once, a particle beam flashed by within a few hundred metres, followed by a second and a third.

"Well? I don't want to stay here for long."

"It hasn't moved."

"At all?"

"No, sir. It hasn't moved more than a metre from the position it took up when it first got here."

Duggan took the *Crimson* lower towards the planet. Once they were out of the mothership's sight, the plasma beams stopped coming.

"Pass those coordinates to Lieutenant Breeze."

"Done." Chainer looked confused.

"After that, get on the comms and let Admiral Franks know that we're going to try and destroy the mothership. They must complete the job of destroying the emplacement. Don't spend time trying to answer any questions."

"I won't," said Chainer, his expression making it clear he would have dearly liked to know the answers himself.

"Lieutenant Breeze, deactivate the stealth modules."

"Sir?"

"Do it."

"Done."

"Ready the fission engines. Set a target for the coordinates you have received from Lieutenant Chainer."

Breeze opened his mouth to say something. After a moment, he simply accepted the order. "It'll be a couple of minutes until we can go. The *Crimson's* core is quicker than the *ES Lightning's*, but I still can't initiate lightspeed immediately after stealth."

Duggan nodded his understanding. "Commander McGlashan, please prepare to fire our conventional weapons."

She grinned. "Aye, sir!"

"Five minutes until the weapon array is in alignment to fire," said Chainer. He noticed a forgotten mug of coffee nearby. He reached out for it with a shaking hand and swigged off the contents in one go.

"Thirty seconds until lightspeed."

"The bigger they are, the harder they fall," said McGlashan.

"Ten seconds."

The *Crimson* spent so little time at lightspeed that their brains had no time to comprehend the dislocation. Duggan's eyes caught the change in the sensor feeds. Instead of fire-blackened rock, the *Crimson* was suddenly in the middle of a vast, unlit hangar. The sensors adjusted and they saw the distant walls. There were cruisers clamped in place, alongside a dozen or more of the Dreamer pyramids. Tiny rows of white dots lined part of one wall – viewing windows for the crew of this unimaginably vast machine of death.

"Fire," said Duggan. "Lieutenant Breeze, ready the fission engines. Take us back to the place we came from."

The exterior of the Dreamer mothership bristled with weaponry and countermeasures. Inside, there was nothing to prevent the carnage Duggan and his crew inflicted. Two hundred and eighty-eight Lambdas blasted from their tubes. They had no time to reach their maximum velocity before they exploded against the bulkheads of the enemy ship. There was no energy shield to stop them and they ripped vast holes through the interior.

"Commander McGlashan, fire the Lambdas and Shatterers when ready. Prepare the nukes."

"Thirty seconds until we're off," said Breeze, his mouth still open in shock. "One of those cruisers is powering up," he finished, almost as an afterthought.

"Not anymore," said McGlashan.

The next wave of Lambdas spilled out, with a hundred of them striking the enemy cruiser. It was ripped apart, utterly destroyed before its crew could think about a response.

"We're not doing enough damage," said Chainer. "This ship is too big."

He was right – the *Crimson* could launch a lot of missiles, but against the vastness of the mothership they were lost. The explosions inflicted terrible damage, yet it didn't look as if it would be enough. A third salvo followed the second, filling the mothership's interior with pure, brilliant plasma light.

"Ten seconds."

"Fire the nukes at one second," said Duggan.

There was time for a fourth launch of the rapid-reload Lambdas. As the countdown to lightspeed ended, Duggan saw McGlashan's hand move with agonising slowness across her console. *Don't miss this one, Lucy,* was the last thought he had before the *Crimson* flashed away into lightspeed, twisting reality in a way that allowed the warship to ignore anything so ephemeral as the alloy walls of the Dreamer mothership.

"Did you launch?" he asked.

She nodded silently.

"Did we get it?" His voice sounded panicked to his own ears.

"There're signs of a nuclear detonation across the lip of the planet's curve," said Chainer.

Duggan was desperate to have a look. The *Crimson* climbed steadily higher and nearer to the weapon site.

"More nuclear blasts," said Chainer. "That must be about twenty in one go."

"The countdown timer just hit zero," said McGlashan.

Petrified that his most daring plan had failed, Duggan willed the spaceship to go faster. When it reached a position from which the sensors could scan the target area, he slumped forwards, his head in his hands.

"I've got Admiral Franks for you, sir."

Duggan slowly raised his head. "Bring her through."

"Captain Duggan." There was relief in her voice. "You and your crew have destroyed the enemy mothership. The ground weapon's energy shield was destroyed by our nuclear warheads and the weapon itself by our Shatterers and Lambdas."

"It's over," he said. "For now."

"I will speak to Admiral Teron and let him know the good news, Captain. I'm sure he will be pleased at what you have accomplished." A rueful tone entered her voice. "I will also ask him to arrange a rescue party for us, since my technicians advise that the *Archimedes*' engines will fail within ten minutes. You must excuse me while I locate a suitable place for us to set down away from the highest concentrations of radiation."

In spite of the situation, there was something in Franks' tone that made Duggan chuckle. "Well fought, Admiral. I'm sure you'll enjoy the vacation."

"What are you going to do?"

"We're badly damaged, but we can fly. We'll wait until your rescuers arrive. There could be other enemy vessels headed this way."

"Thank you, Captain Duggan. In the meantime, I have a video feed from our sensors which might help you pass the time. It shows the final moments of the mothership."

"That would be appreciated."

The file arrived and the crew watched it over and over. The enemy ship had been huge, but eight high-yield nuclear explosions within its hold tore it apart as easily as if it had been made of paper. Duggan felt a number of emotions.

"You're not happy?" asked McGlashan as they sat together in the mess room.

"Relieved. Satisfied. If I knew that was the last Dreamer warship, then I might feel happiness."

"I know what you mean. We've earned some time to prepare."

"And some shore leave," he said with a smile.

"I hope so. We've earned it."

He put his arm around her and this time he did feel happy, if only for this fleeting moment.

———

The Survival Wars series continues in Book 5, Terminus Gate!

Follow Anthony James on Facebook at
facebook.com/anthonyjamesauthor

THE SURVIVAL WARS SERIES

Printed in Great Britain
by Amazon